Noah's Ark:
SURVIVORS

Harry Dayle

NOAH'S ARK:
SURVIVORS
Published by Shelfless Ltd.
Copyright © Harry Dayle 2013

ISBN 978-1492961611

First Edition (1.2) published 2013
Cover Design by HumbleNations.com

This is a work of fiction. Names, characters, businesses, places, events and incidents are either the products of the author's imagination or used in a fictitious manner. Any resemblance to actual persons, living or dead, or actual events is purely coincidental.

PROLOGUE

Darkness. Silence. Commander Grady Osborn squinted through the tiny window of the International Space Station, out across the vast emptiness of the universe. A black void, punctuated only by the tiny pinprick lights of distant stars and galaxies. They appeared brighter than usual, due to the total lack of illumination within the spacecraft. And yet, directly in front of the small portal, there was a hole. A giant black disc from which no light escaped. It was getting bigger.

"Whatever the hell that is, it's getting closer, damn it," Osborne said, breaking the silence. The science officer next to him glanced up from his computer screen. Of the three astronauts in residence, he was the only one wearing his NASA issued jumpsuit. The patch bearing his name had been modified by someone, although nobody was willing to claim responsibility for having inserted the extra letter in the surname, changing it from *Kingon* to *Klingon*.

"You don't know that. An absence of light can't get closer. It's just getting bigger," Kingon said.

"No, it's coming towards us. I can feel it."

And he could; at least, he believed he could. The hairs on the back of the commander's neck stood to attention. "Where did Hector go? I'll fix these lights myself if he can't get his sorry ass back here. And then there'll be hell to pay."

"He said something about radar and wanting to rig something up, try and bounce some radio waves off that hole of yours, see what comes back."

A clunk and a hiss behind the two men caused both to swing around. A hatch eased open and the darkness was sliced in two by the beam from a flashlight.

"Hector," Osborn shouted, "tell me what the hell this thing is!"

The third astronaut spun in midair, pushed the hatch closed, then pirouetted to face his senior officer.

"I can't be sure, but I'd say it was an asteroid."

"Bullshit!" Osborn rolled his eyes. "If there was an asteroid this close, somebody back home would have seen it and we'd know about it."

"Anyway, asteroids aren't—" Kingon began.

"Aren't generally black, I know," Hector finished for him. "But this thing is solid, fast, and headed right for us. I haven't run the full barrage of tests yet. If I had more time I could probably get a better idea of composition, density...maybe work out where it came from. But time is something we don't have. It's moving fast. Really fast. The deep space network must have spotted it, but they won't believe what the data is telling them, probably think it's a software bug. A beast that size, coming from nowhere? I wouldn't believe it myself, if I couldn't see it."

"How fast are we talking here?" Osborn asked, a note of concern creeping into his voice.

"My calculations aren't complete but, at a guess Commander, we have approximately one hour before that thing, whatever it is, smashes this tin can into a million little pieces."

It was said so matter-of-factly that for a moment, everyone was too stunned to speak.

"You're telling me that thing is an asteroid? That it's headed for this station?" Osborn managed.

"That is correct. Although given its apparent dimensions, it may better be classed a dwarf planet. It really is an order of magnitude bigger than anything we would ever see this close to home," Hector said enthusiastically. He sounded more impressed than worried.

"Sterling, can you reconfigure the stabilising thrusters to move us into a new orbit?" Osborn was trying to hide the panic in his eyes. Had to show leadership. Remain calm. Remember his training.

"A new orbit won't be enough to save us," Hector said before

Kingon could reply. "It really is a monster. We're talking four, maybe five hundred kilometres across at its widest point. Also, and this is mainly speculation, I think it's putting out a tail of dust that's maybe ten times bigger than that. Thick dust, really thick. We'll be pulverised. Or vaporised. Possibly melted. We can't get out of its way before it hits us."

"Dammit man, we're not going to sit here and wait for a freak asteroid to take us out of the sky; we're going to try and move this pile of junk. Now!" Osborn tried to claw his way through the air, grasping at the nothingness, willing himself towards the thruster control console.

"Grady!" Kingon shouted. He launched himself from his terminal, pushing off the wall with his feet. He floated in front of the commander, blocking his path. "If Hector is right, if that thing is as big as he says, then we can't get out of its way. We don't carry the fuel for that kind of manoeuvre. We have to contact mission control, right now! We have to tell them what's happening."

"I fear," Hector said, not looking at either man, "that telling Houston is not going to make much difference."

Kingon looked at the younger man. "What do you mean? It's our duty to inform mission control of anything that jeopardises this mission. I'd say getting liquidized by an oversized rock counts as jeopardy, wouldn't you?"

"He means …he means, we can't save them, don't you Hector?" Osborne's tone had changed. His voice was that of a man who knew he was beaten. "Because that thing's not just going to take us out, is it? It's headed for them. It's headed for Earth."

One

Jake shifted his weight from foot to foot. His position at the back of the theatre afforded him an excellent view of the assembled crowd, but not the comfort of a chair. Every seat in the house was taken. Every step of the aisles, between the blocks of seating, was also filled with people sitting, crouching, and some standing. The theatre was built to accommodate just over a thousand, yet somehow, between passengers and crew, more than twice that number of people had crammed themselves inside.

All of the doors were open. The main double swing doors at the back, and the emergency exits at the bottom. More heads and bodies squeezed in through them all, desperately trying to see the screen. The heat generated by so many human beings in one place was intense. The smell of sweat was inescapable, rising through Jake's nostrils, sticking in his throat.

Yet, despite the unprecedented number of people, the only sound in the vast auditorium came from the speaker system. The words of a reporter, whose face was being projected onto the giant display that lined the rear wall of the stage. A logo in the corner informed the assembled viewers that they were watching CNN. As if, Jake thought to himself, it really mattered who was reporting this. It wasn't as if history was going to recall the name of the station that managed to produce this broadcast. The final broadcast.

The image of the reporter was replaced with a video report. The banner across the bottom read simply, "The End?" Jake listened to the report as it echoed through the cavernous room.

"*The rumours had already begun to spread through social media networks, before the first confirmed sighting came from Australia. Footage captured on cellphone cameras and streamed live across the internet showed the sky darkening. As the asteroid approached, there panic in the streets. Then, the crack of a sonic boom as it passed overhead at incredible speed. It were as if an earthquake had struck. Windows were blown out, entire buildings destroyed, as the immense vibrations of the passing monster shook them to the ground."*

The report was showing hastily cut together video clips. It did indeed look like an earthquake, but it was as if the tape had been sped up. A deafening boom, dust and debris shooting into the air, and buildings apparently exploding or simply crumbling like sandcastles in the wind.

"And then came the dust. A minute after the asteroid passed, maybe two, the dust started to rain down. Thick, black, and molten. Even now, as the end approaches, we cannot, will not, show the images," the screen faded to black, but the sound continued. The screams. Gut wrenching, blood curdling, terrible screams.

"Anyone who made it out of the buildings alive was surely fatally burnt, or smothered by the dust cloud."

The screen faded again, this time to a computer generated graphic showing the Earth rotating serenely against a white backdrop. A black circle scanned across Australia, trailing a wide grey tail behind it.

"Data from NASA's satellites shows the asteroid as it began its orbit around our planet. Thirty three minutes to complete a circuit, the time increasing slightly with every pass as it spirals upwards, approaching the equator, cleansing the Earth of life with every turn."

The dot on the graphic wound around and upwards, as if painting the globe black. The grey tail was so wide that each circuit covered a band thousands of kilometres across. The clock on the graphic indicated that in a little over four hours, half of the world had been destroyed. Scorched from existence. Somebody in the stalls tried, and failed, to stifle a sob.

"Then, the riots began. As news spread, and as the asteroid approached Japan, amid widespread panic people took to the streets." More video montage, some from cellphone cameras, some from professional news crews. Every time the same. Panic. Screaming. An earth shattering crack as blackness streaked overhead, and then the pictures faded to black amid the howling and the anguished cries of people burning, suffocating, dying. Jake's stomach turned, his mind could hardly grasp the full horror of what he was witnessing. It felt unreal, like he was watching some kind of sick disaster movie. More people had begun to cry, someone close by him fainted, falling to a crumpled heap in a forest of legs. In front of him he heard a whispered prayer. But most remained silent, eyes glazed over, watching, listening, like Jake, unable or unwilling to believe.

As north Africa, the middle east, central China, and then the southern states of the USA were wiped one by one from the map, the graphic faded and the screen once again showed the reporter. Her eyes were red, her hand shaking slightly.

"And so, as the asteroid heads towards the northern states, it seems our time as guardians of the Earth is at an end. Maybe someone, somewhere, will see this broadcast and will survive. Maybe the human race will find a way to live on. All efforts to destroy the asteroid, or somehow change its course, have failed. In our final hour, our true insignificance is laid bare. We hold no special place in the universe, we are fragile, and now, we are finished." Her voice began to crack. "This is Emily Randolph, for CNN. May God help us. Mom, Dad, Russell, I love you…." The screen cut to black, and silence once again filled the theatre.

Two

Flynn bakeman was elated. He paced up and down the length of his cabin. It was one of the cheaper rooms on the ship, and his large muscular frame made it appear even smaller than it already was. A television screen in the corner of the room had just faded to black.

"This is it, Eileen! The end of times has come! So long I've waited. And I'll admit, once or twice I even had doubts. But the Lord told me to be patient, and He was right!"

Eileen was sitting on the bed, sobbing, head sunk low.

"What's wrong with you? This is a momentous day! We are to bear witness to the reckoning! Armageddon is approaching. It's happening in our lifetimes!"

"I don't want to die, Flynn. I wanted to see the kids married. I wanted to have grandchildren. I wanted to travel, see the world. I want to live!"

"Living? Living is nothing!" he shouted at his wife without looking at her. "Living is waiting. Soon the rapture will be upon us. Soon we will all depart this mortal world and meet our true destiny. We shall kneel before our maker, and become His servants. And you want to live?" He sounded incredulous.

"Flynn, I'm sorry. But I don't…I can't believe the same things you believe…" her sobs turned to wails. She was becoming hysterical.

"Sorry? You're 'sorry'?" He mimicked her high pitched voice as he said it, and lashed out, catching his wife's face with the back of his hand. A thin streak of blood wound its way down her right cheek.

"We must prepare our souls. This is no time to harbour regrets, or fear, or sorrow. You are weak, and you will suffer in eternal damnation. But not me. I will not be denied my true place at His side because of your weakness!"

He raised his hand, and struck her once more, harder than before. The blow knocked her flat. She was out cold.

THREE

Jake wiped the corners of his mouth with the back of his hand. A thin slimy layer of vomit clung to it. He stared out to sea. He'd always preferred the view from this position on the ship, gazing astern from the terrace on deck thirteen. Looking back, seeing where they had been, instead of the familiar view of where they were headed, the view he spent most days regarding from his position on the bridge. But the view today was different. The blue sky, so bright both day and night throughout the summer months up here near the pole, was blackening. All colour had been drained from the world. The huge icebergs, normally too dazzling to look at without sunglasses, appeared to shrink away, as if frightened by what was to come. Their sparkling sheen was gone; now they were just grey lumps floating in a black sea. The air was no longer crisp, the cold had lost its bite. The approaching molten dust cloud was already heating the atmosphere.

"Jake?"

The voice came from behind. He knew at once it was Lucya, not by her accent—she had almost entirely lost that—but from the confidence with which she spoke his name. If anyone could keep a level head in a crisis, it was Lucya. He didn't move, just continued staring out to sea. She leant on the railing beside him, taking in the same view.

"I knew you'd be here," she said. "I had to get away from there. It's chaos. Panic, total panic. Some people refuse to believe it, you know. They think it's some kind of sick joke, some kind of party trick to liven up the cruise."

Jake turned to look at her.

"How could anyone…?" his voice trailed off. "I mean, look at it! You can almost feel it coming. In less than an hour, we'll all be dead, Lucya."

Neither of them knew what to say, and for a while they both stared out at the ocean and the icebergs.

"I was going to quit," Jake said suddenly. "The ships. I was going to quit. I finally had it all figured out, finally worked out what I wanted to do with my life. No more responsibility, no more day after tedious day waiting to see land again. I was going to go to Africa."

"Africa? I thought you came onto the ships to travel the world? What's so special about Africa?"

"I came onto the ships because that's what my dad wanted. That, and because I didn't have a clue what else to do." He turned to look at the girl by his side, his face suddenly animated. "But I get it now, I know what I want to do. Humanitarian aid work, in Africa. I want to help people, people who need it, not rich tourists who just want help finding the casino or the bar. And I thought if I did that, maybe Jane…maybe she'd come round. Anyway, this was to be my last cruise. I was going to post my resignation letter as soon as we stopped at Edinburgh. Finally I had some direction, and now…now it doesn't matter anymore."

Behind them, a scream. They both turned to look. A woman was yelling manically at a man. He was climbing the railings, she was trying desperately to pull him back. Her efforts were in vain, and the man swung his legs over the handrail, turned to kiss the woman once, then leapt off. The splash as he hit the icy water below was drowned out by her hysterical cries.

"Doesn't she realise she's as dead as him?" Jake asked.

"People are jumping from all over the ship. I saw a dozen, maybe more, just coming up here from the theatre. I guess some would rather choose their own way out rather than lie down and take it." Lucya turned back to look at him. "Jake, we don't have much time. I figured, if we're going to die here, if this really is the end, then I can't go without telling you. I need you to know how I feel." She reached for his hand, but he pulled it away, turned back to look out to sea, avoiding her gaze.

"Lucya I…I'm married, you know that."

"You're separated. But what does that matter? I'm not asking you to marry me. I just want you to know how I feel about you. How I've always felt. We have a connection, you and me. Something deeper than attraction. There's something there. I only want to hear you say that you feel it too. Then I will be at peace. Then I will be ready to die."

She grabbed his shoulders, pulled him round to face her. They stared into each other's eyes, and all pretence was gone. Jake knew she was right, there was no use pretending, not now. He let her pull him closer to her. The corners of her mouth turned up into a smile. She leaned in, and then fell back with a gasp. From somewhere out at sea, behind the ship, came a deafening cracking sound, like the sky being ripped apart by an enormous bolt of lightning. The couple turned instinctively towards the noise. A giant black disc loomed on the horizon. It appeared to emerge from the sea, growing in size as it approached them, faster than either could believe possible. Behind it, the sky disappeared into a thick grey mist.

"Oh Jesus," Lucya said. "This is it, this is really it!" She crossed herself, and began to mutter a prayer in her own tongue, all the while watching the black monster swelling in the sky.

The ship had become silent. The cries of panic had stopped. Anyone out on deck had turned to watch the spectacle. They were joined by more, as those inside came out to see what had caused the noise. Some sank to their knees in prayer. Others closed their eyes and turned their heads towards the heavens. But most just stood and stared.

"It's going up," Jake said.

"What?" Lucya whispered.

"Look. Look at the distance between the asteroid and the ocean. It's getting bigger. The asteroid is going up. It's gaining height."

"Jake, I'm so sorry. This is the end. We are going to die here." She looked at him with huge black eyes, sad eyes.

"No, I don't think we are. It really is going up."

Other people had begun to murmur and whisper around them. As the rock grew nearer, it became clear that it was indeed increasing in altitude. There was no denying it. It was no longer headed right at them. It was headed skywards.

• • •

Half an hour had gone by since the asteroid had changed course and charged off into the heavens. It was now little more than a pin-prick in the distance. Hundreds of passengers and crew members had spilled out onto the decks to see for themselves. There was a palpable excitement in the air. Certain death had been averted, and although it seemed likely that the rest of the world had been destroyed, that families and loved ones back home were gone, that home itself was gone, the fact that they were alive, against all the odds, was enough right now.

Jake was one of the first to see the dust. To begin with it just appeared as a thickening of the haze already clouding the horizon. Before long though, clouds of grey were moving in towards the ship. The water around them began lapping and slapping against the hull as the wind picked up.

"Lucya, we need to get these people back inside, now!" Jake said. He pointed to the dust clouds, growing nearer by the minute.

The two of them turned and started calling to the people massed all around them.

"Get inside! Everyone back inside, now! The dust is coming, everyone needs to get in, quickly!"

But nobody listened. There was already too much noise from the assembled crowd to hear two voices in the wind.

"It's no good," Lucya said, holding her arms wide open. "We need to get back to the bridge, get on the PA. Come on!"

She pushed her way through the thick soup of bodies, trying desperately to make it back inside. Jake was right behind her, but they were quickly separated in the chaos as people pushed be-tween them. Jake made it to a door, took one look back at the ap-proaching dust, and dived for shelter. As the heavy door swung closed behind him it became instantly quieter, as if somebody had pressed a mute button somewhere.

He was in a corridor and it was entirely deserted. There wasn't enough time to get to the bridge before the dust cloud reached them, but Jake knew the ship well. It had been his home, on and off, for the best part of five years. He could find his way round in the dark, if necessary. After performing a quick route calculation in his head, he turned left and sprinted along the passage for a couple of hundred meters, turned one hundred and eighty degrees on his heel and down a wide flight of stairs. Then more running until he reached an unmarked door. He tried the handle. Locked. He swore to himself, turned to run back the way he had come, and ran straight into the shoulder of a skinny young man emerging sideways from another doorway.

"Hey! Watch where…" the man turned to look at him. "Oh, Jake. What's the rush? I heard Armageddon was cancelled."

"Martin! The dust…" he tried to catch his breath. "The dust is coming. We have to get people back inside or they'll burn. Lucya's gone to the bridge to use the PA but she'll never get there in time. I was going to use the emergency system in the hotel manager's office, but she's locked it."

"Sounds like Silvia. World's ending, better lock up. Come with me." Martin opened the door through which he had just come, and disappeared back through it, with Jake a step behind.

"Where does this go? I thought I knew this ship, but I never even noticed this door before," he said.

"Yeah, well, us engineering boys like to keep a few secrets. Here, quick way down. Let's go."

Martin promptly disappeared.

Jake looked round, his eyes adjusting to the dimmer light. He was in a tiny room, little more than a cupboard. There was no natural light, just a glow coming up through a hole in the floor. Also protruding through the hole was a metal ladder. Jake peered down to see the chief engineer sliding down it at high speed.

"Come on!" Martin called up. "Not scared, are you?"

Jake didn't have time to be scared. He wrapped his hands around the tubular sides of the ladder, put his feet either side, released his grip slightly, and felt himself plunge into the depths of the cruise ship. The descent was exhilarating, and terrifying. It lasted only about fifteen seconds, and he arrived with a considerable thud, his knees buckling under the heavy landing. He found himself standing in front of an open door, and he instantly recognised what lay on the other side; the engine room. Martin had already gone in. Jake followed.

"Here, use this." The engineer was pointing at a box on the wall. It was labelled "Emergency Address System".

Jake flipped up a protective plastic cover, paused for a second to compose himself, and then pressed down the button marked "Talk".

Four

THE VOICE BOOMED out throughout the ship. It rang out in the theatre, now empty. It echoed through the casino, heard by only a few souls who had come in to collapse on the comfortable chairs. It reverberated through every deck, inside and out.

"This is First Officer Jake Noah. This is an emergency. I repeat, this is an emergency! The dust cloud that follows the asteroid is headed for this ship. All passengers and crew must get inside now. The cloud is molten rock and will burn anyone and anything it touches. I repeat, everyone must take shelter inside the ship now. Please proceed in an orderly fashion to the nearest exit and get back inside the ship."

He let go of the button, thought for a moment, then added: "Deck thirteen may not be safe from the dust. Try and get to the lower decks for protection."

Outside there was a stunned silence. Heads and eyes turned to scan the sea. Somebody somewhere screamed. It was as if a touch paper had been ignited, the scream quickly spread, and with it, panic. There was a stampede as hundreds of people tried to pile through small, single doorways. Some fell, and were trampled upon without a second thought. Many made it inside, but just as many weren't quick enough. The dust cloud had already arrived.

At first it looked like snow. Dark grey flakes, floating lazily in the air. It was pretty, in a way. Pretty, but deadly.

Maisie Warwick was the furthest from a door, and so the first passenger to feel the force of the asteroid's poisonous payload. The recently divorced mother of two had come on the cruise to celebrate her newfound freedom. Years of physical and verbal abuse from her ex-husband were at an end. This trip marked her new beginning, a new life. She looked at the scrum of people pushing, kicking, and fighting their way to the door and knew she would never make it. Turning to look at the first flakes of dust as they glided gently towards her on the breeze, she smiled. A flake landed on her forehead, burning through the skin instantly. As it cooled, it embedded itself into the bone of her skull. She didn't have a chance to scream, as more flakes dusted her, burning holes through her clothes, and through her flesh. She was dead within seconds, a pile of charred flesh and bone on the wooden deck.

Then the full force of the cloud hit the ship.

• • •

Deep in the engine room, Jake and Martin were oblivious to the carnage being wreaked on the outer decks. They were spared the smell of burning bodies. They were saved from hearing the terrible screams.

On the bridge, Lucya wasn't so lucky. She had made it back just as Jake had finished putting out his emergency call. The place was nearly deserted. The ship had dropped anchor as the news of the asteroid broke. A skeleton crew were supposed to be present at all times, no matter what; company regulations were very clear about that. Such rules were of little concern now though, and every last crew member had abandoned their post, in search of a television screen to see the horrific events unfold. The theatre, the casino, the crew bar, anywhere with a live feed and some space.

Lucya walked onto the bridge just as the dust cloud hit. It came from the rear. The prevailing wind had, until then, been in the opposite direction. Had that not been the case, Lucya would have been killed instantly as the bridge windows blew in. As it was, only those windows that wrapped around the deck to provide rearward visibility were hit. Small in number they may have been, but they still sprayed an impressive amount of glass across the room as they exploded with the force of the wind and dust. Lucya instinctively threw herself to the floor. Searing heat roared into the room. It lasted ten, maybe twenty seconds, and it stopped as abruptly as it had arrived.

When she was sure it had passed over, she got to her feet and made her way to the front of the bridge. Looking out over the decks below, she saw destruction and devastation. Most of the lifeboats were on fire, and smaller fires were burning on most levels. The pristine white paintwork of the Spirit of Arcadia, the flagship of Pelagios Line, was blackened and charred, making her look more like a navy vessel than a luxury cruise liner. Bodies littered the decks. Some were on fire, some were still moving, but barely. She couldn't bear to look, there was nothing to be done to save them. Instead she took a deep breath, and assessed what needed to be done most urgently. The burning lifeboats represented the greatest hazard. The smaller deck fires were blowing themselves out, but the lifeboat fires could spread. She ran over to a control desk and quickly located the release button. Hesitating for only a second, she hit it with the full force of the palm of her hand.

Nothing happened. It was only then that she realised that the usual blinking lights of the console and the whirring and chattering noises of the radar were absent. The bridge was devoid not just of crew, but of its own mechanical and electrical life. Everything lay still. Motionless, and silent.

• • •

The Spirit of Arcadia was equipped with three gigantic diesel engines. Two were used for propulsion, and lay idle. With the anchor down there was no point wasting fuel keeping the motors ticking over. The other, smaller engine drove the electrical generator that kept the ship's systems running. A life support machine for the three thousand people aboard. Something was clearly very wrong with this engine, though. Within a few seconds of the dust cloud hitting, it started to emit an earsplitting whine. To begin with, it sounded like a washing machine gearing up to run a spin cycle. The noise quickly increased in intensity though, and then it began to vibrate.

"What the hell?" Jake looked around anxiously.

"Sounds like the exhaust is blocked. We have to shut this thing down, now!" Martin said, sprinting to the other side of the room.

He fiddled with chunky black plastic knobs, twisted graduated rotary dials, then stepped back and scratched his head.

"Problem?" Jake walked over to join him.

"I don't understand, it's not responding to the manual controls."

The noise continued to grow louder, the men having to shout to make themselves heard. It was becoming intolerable, to the point that they wouldn't be able to remain in the engine room much longer without risking permanent hearing damage. Jake spotted a glass cabinet on the wall. Inside were safely helmets, goggles, and ear protectors. He took out two sets of the bright red headgear and passed one to the mechanic. Martin gave him a sideways look that suggested health and safety was for other people, but as the sound ratcheted up another notch he grabbed the protectors and snapped them over his head. He tried a few more combinations of buttons, shrugged his shoulders, and walked back towards the huge motor. The vibrations had become so intense, the huge power plant was now visibly shaking.

Martin held out his forefinger and traced a line in the air. Jake watched, following his eye line until it alighted on a copper pipe, painted white. The pipe entered the underbelly of the engine, and Martin was tracing it backwards. It ran up the side of a supporting metal post, along the low ceiling, and then along the wall. Just before it disappeared through a bulkhead it made a U shaped detour, at the bottom of which was a bright red lever. A small padlock prevented the lever from being operated. A glass box next to the lever contained a key. Martin walked over to the box, picked up the tiny hammer attached to it with a chain, and smashed the glass. He removed the key, unlocked the padlock, threaded the loop of metal out of the catch, and pulled the lever closed. At first nothing happened. Then, slowly, the whining noise started to drop in pitch. The vibrations of the engine reduced, becoming more of a rattle, before finally abating altogether. The beast of a motor was dying.

"Emergency fuel cut-off," Martin said, cocking his thumb at the lever.

"Aren't you supposed to know where that is without having to look?" Jake asked.

"Sorry officer," Martin emphasised the second word a bit too much for Jake's liking. "We would have covered it when we took delivery of this ship. Never had cause to use it since then, so yeah, I probably should know where it is, but I can't remember everything I did five years ago."

"You think the dust cloud blocked the exhaust?"

"Could be, that would explain the noise. If enough dust blew down the funnel it could have caused this."

"There's an easy way to unblock it, right?" Jake feared he already knew the answer.

"Oh yeah, sure. Someone has to climb down the funnel and clear out the gunk. You volunteering?"

"Engineering isn't my strong point, as well you know. I think I'll leave it to a professional," Jake said.

"Well, whoever does it, they're going to have to do it soon. Without that motor turning, this ship's got no power, and that means no heat, light, fresh water, or sanitation."

"Aren't there batteries or something?"

"For emergency systems only. We can bring the bridge online if we need to. The emergency PA system too, as well as some emergency lighting in some areas."

"Ok, get the PA working, but leave everything else off for now. We don't know how long we're going to be stuck without power, so we should conserve what we can." Jake turned to leave.

"So you're in charge now, huh?" Martin called after him.

Jake turned and looked at him.

"Captain Ibsen is in charge, I'm just trying to offer my advice," he said.

"Your advice is noted, First Officer Noah," Martin said, before turning back to his console and fiddling with more buttons.

FIVE

THE DUST CLOUD had completely vanished. The sky remained grey, the sun partially blocked by more dust higher in the atmosphere. In the half light, Lucya made her way to the exterior of deck ten. Most of the lifeboats were tethered on this deck, and they were still burning furiously. One fire had already spread and the wooden surface of the deck itself was burning. A number of people, Lucya couldn't see if they were passengers or crew, were already tackling that blaze with fire extinguishers. She sprinted to the first lifeboat, found the manual release handle, and tried to crank it. The instant she touched it she felt the skin on her hand melt. She pulled her hand away instinctively, leaving skin on the hot metal, charred and blackened. She screamed in pain, looked round for some way of easing the burning, but saw only more flames, hot metal, and burning bodies. Swallowing hard, she turned back to the crank. She pulled off her jacket, wrapped it around the handle, and pulled it round towards her. To her relief, the lifeboat gave a jolt and started to descend towards the sea. It took all of her effort, but after several minutes winding, the small craft hit the water with a hiss and a fizz. One last tug on the handle and the steel cables were released. The lifeboat floated free, away from the Spirit of Arcadia.

"One down," Lucya said to herself, "fifteen more to go".

• • •

Jake returned to the bridge, taking the more conventional route via the stairs. This place was home to him, it was where he spent most of his working day as first officer. He'd always thought it a soulless place. He was no stranger to ships and boats, having a captain for a father. But this bridge had none of the character or the romance of older vessels. There was no great wooden wheel, no impressive high perched captain's chair, no beautiful polished brass instruments. This bridge looked more like a cross between a call centre and the control room of a power station. It was all clean lines and sleek grey control panels with embedded screens. Two rows of four consoles dominated the space. They filled almost the full forty metre width of the room. The ship was largely automated, so the consoles weren't designed to be manned by more than a handful of people. The absence of human presence only heightened the lifelessness of the place.

One concession to traditional seafaring ways was the map table, towards the rear. A huge brushed steel surface, under which a set of drawers held charts of the world's seas. It was never used, of course, at least not for its intended function. GPS ruled the waves now. But every ship had to carry a set of maps as a backup. The map table of the Spirit of Arcadia was sometimes commandeered for the odd game of ping-pong on dull days, and this morning a game of Monopoly had been in progress upon it. Now the board was on the floor, lying among the thousands of tiny pieces of shattered glass from the rear windows, and a dusting of the grey ash that had caused the damage. Standing at the front of the bridge, surveying the carnage below, was Staff Captain Johnny Hollen, the second in command. He turned to see who had entered behind him.

"Jake. Good work on that announcement."

"Thanks. Where is everyone? I thought the crew would come back here. Where's Lucya? She was headed for the bridge last time I saw her," Jake looked anxious.

"Place was deserted when I got here, a few minutes ago. Have you seen anyone else? I think we should gather the senior crew members together."

"Apart from Lucya, only Chief Engineer Oakley down in the engine room. He had to kill the generator, we're without power for I don't know how long."

"Yeah, I noticed. Any suggestions on how we find the rest of the senior officers? No power, no comms."

"The emergency PA system should be working, Oakley said it runs off a battery backup."

Hollen walked over to a console, picked up a handset that looked more like it belonged on a telephone. He flicked a button, and spoke quietly.

"All senior officers are to report to the bridge immediately. I repeat, all senior officers to the bridge."

"That's it?" Jake looked surprised. "You're not going to try and calm the passengers down, tell them what's happening?"

"What is happening, Jake? Do you know? Because I have no frigging idea. This morning I was winning at Monopoly. Half an hour ago, the world was ending. Then we get sandblasted or something, and now…" he stared outside. "Now I don't know what happens next. So what do you suggest I say to the passengers?"

Jake didn't have an answer.

Six

Flynn bakeman stepped outside into Palm Plaza. The park was located in the centre of the ship, a vast open space planted with trees and lush vegetation. Balconied cabins towered above on each side. Shops and restaurants opened out onto the plaza over two levels. Normally, the place was buzzing, packed with people walking through, or sunbathing on the patches of grass, or spilling out from the cafes, drinking brightly coloured cocktails while enjoying live music being played under the palm trees. For this arctic cruise, huge gas heaters had been installed too. The cruise company were apparently oblivious to the irony of burning thousands of extra tons of fossil fuels so that passengers could enjoy outdoor activities in the warm whilst on a trip to see ice caps that were melting because of global warming.

Today, though, the park was, like the rest of the ship, grey and burnt out. The palm trees were smouldering, the rest of the plants and flowers lost under a thin layer of grey ash. Some of the shop windows had blown in, and many of the balconies had shattered, scattering shards of glass throughout the former greenery.

To Flynn, the grey, desolate scene before him mirrored the despair he felt within. He was alive. He had, against all the odds, somehow survived. Judgement day had come, and his life had been spared. He couldn't understand. He had always been a faithful servant of the Lord. He prayed every day. He was a true soldier of the faith. And yet, when the end came, he had not been taken.

He walked to the middle of the plaza, and looked up at the grey, ashen sky.

"Why?" he cried at the top of his voice. "Why have you done this to me? What must I do to make this right?" His words sounded weak and pathetic in the vastness of the open space. He sank to his knees, and with balled fists, began pounding the floor, roaring incomprehensibly. Clouds of dust puffed into the air with every impact. When he had exhausted himself, he remained on the ground, curled over, his head on his knees.

And then, he smiled.

God had spoken to him. He knew now why his wife had won this cruise holiday in a radio phone-in competition. He understood why he had been taken away from his home, and certain death. More importantly, he knew exactly what he was supposed to do now.

Seven

Lucya was torn. She had managed to lower five burning lifeboats to sea, but there were three more to go on this side of the ship, and another eight on the other side. She was drained of energy, her burnt hand was in agony, and now the staff captain had called all senior crew to the bridge. As chief radio officer, responsible for communications and navigation, she certainly counted as senior crew, but Lucya decided the lifeboats were more important. Emergency flares in one of those she had already released, had exploded as it drifted away from the Spirit of Arcadia. They had turned the already raging fire into a true inferno. If the same thing happened to a lifeboat still on board, they would have a serious problem on their hands.

She put her jacket around the release handle of the next boat, and heaved with all her might. It refused to budge. She gave a scream, took a few steps back, and gave it a kick with the heel of her sturdy black boot. Nothing. Taking a closer look it became obvious why; the steel cable wrapped around the drum of the winch had started to fuse to itself with the heat of the fire.

"Young lady, maybe this would help?" a voice from behind her called.

She looked around and found a tall thin gentleman smiling at her. He was much older than her, in his seventies, she thought. Thinning white hair, and dressed casually. Passenger, not crew. He held out a pair of heavy duty bolt cutters, and raised an eyebrow.

"We really should get a move on. I believe the flares in some of these could go off with quite a bang."

He spoke with a refined accent, London or thereabouts. Lucya had worked on ships long enough and met enough people to have become quite good at placing accents. She gave a half smile, grabbed the bolt cutters, and in one smooth movement, snipped through the cable that connected the lifeboat to the winch. The bows of the small craft fell away, but with the stern cable still attached it couldn't entirely free itself, and swung dangerously close to the hull of the cruiser.

"I did say 'we'," the man said. He walked to where the second cable fed down through a shackle before connecting to the winch, and with a second pair of bolt cutters, set it free, sending it crashing into the ocean below. The man wandered off casually in the direction of the next boat.

"Wait, who are you, anyway?" Lucya shouted after him. She sprinted to catch up.

"Tom Sanderson," the man said without looking at her.

"What are you doing, walking around this ship with bolt cutters, Tom Sanderson?"

"I'm cutting free burning lifeboats, before they endanger the ship and those people on board who have survived events up to this point." He still didn't look at her; instead, he positioned his bolt cutters on the cable of the next lifeboat. "Shall we try and better co-ordinate this one?"

Lucya placed her own cutters on the second cable.

"After three," Tom said. "1…2….3".

The two of them snipped at the same moment, sending the burning lifeboat smashing into the dark and icy water. Tom had already set off towards the next one without waiting to watch the descent.

"What I meant," Lucya was out of breath from all the physical exertion, "is where did you get them?"

"If that's what you meant then that's what you should have asked, don't you think?"

Lucya stopped in her tracks.

"Listen," she said. I'm a senior officer and I need to get back to the bridge. Think you can manage the rest on your own?" She handed her bolt cutters to Tom. He couldn't help but notice the state of her hand as he took hold of them.

"You want to get that looked at," he said, then turned and set off towards the next burning lifeboat.

Eight

Jake was getting worried, there was still no sign of Lucya. Chief Engineer Martin Oakley had made his way to the bridge. Hotel Director Silvia Brook, responsible for passenger facilities, was also present. The only other crew member who had turned up so far was the head of security, Max Mooting. There was no sign of Captain Ibsen.

"Looks like this is the best we can hope for," Hollen said. "We should probably get started."

As he spoke, the bridge door opened slowly. Jake felt a surge of hope, but it wasn't Lucya who entered, it was Grau Lister, the chief medical officer.

"Grau, what happened?" Hollen asked.

Lister limped in, aided by a crutch. His left leg dragged uselessly behind him.

"Ash," he said. "Hot ash. Burned right through the muscle. I was lucky, I think it also took out the nerves, I can't feel a thing."

Silvia rushed over and tried to support him, but he brushed her away.

"No, no, it's nothing, don't fuss. I've seen much worse," he said. And he had.

The assembled crew arranged themselves around the map table. Jake found a chair for Lister. The table was high and the medical man could only just see over it from his perch.

"So, what on Earth do we do now?" Hollen asked, looking around the table. "I can't work out if we're the lucky ones or not. We survived, but for what? I mean, where do we go?"

"We don't go anywhere!" Silvia piped up. "Why is that your first question? We need to get this ship secure, assess damage, and most importantly make sure the people aboard are all safe. Those still alive, anyway."

"With respect, Silvia, and I know the wellbeing of passengers is your job, we can't stay here, we'll freeze. Visiting the Arctic Circle is all well and good when you have a nice heated ship to retreat into, but with our generator out, we don't have that luxury." Hollen gestured towards Oakley, who nodded in agreement. "Starting the main engine will provide us with heat and power, and we can head for warmer waters. That doesn't stop you getting the people aboard organised en route."

"Staff Captain," when Lister spoke, all at the table automatically turned to look at him. He was the oldest person present, and his clipped German accent gave him an air of authority. "You speak of warmer waters. Just how warm are you thinking?"

Hollen raised an eyebrow in response to the question.

"I ask," Lister continued, "because we have witnessed first-hand the devastating ash tail that followed that extra-terrestrial rock. We were lucky, we caught only the end of it as it disappeared into the sky. Further south though, we don't know what that ash has done to the sea. In more significant quantities it could have cooled, lumped together, formed lava rocks. Do you want to sail into these unknown dangers?"

"Rocks sink. I don't see the problem?"

"Lava rocks are light, full of air pockets. They may float," Lister said.

"If they are light enough to float then they are no danger to this ship."

"And if the ash has formed into a carpet of molten rock, floating on the surface of the ocean?" Lister wasn't giving up his position.

"Grau's right, we don't know what's out there." Jake was surprised to hear himself speak up. "Martin, how much fuel are we carrying?"

"About three thousand tonnes, give or take. We're good for nine days cruising, ten at a push."

"Once that fuel is gone, we have no electricity. No heat, no light, no fresh water if we can't operate the desalination plant. No sanitation. What could still be out there that's worth risking all that on?" Jake rubbed his eyes, the gravity of the situation sinking in.

"Or to put it another way," Hollen said, "we stay here for what, a month? Running just the generator. And then what? In a month we have no heat, light, water, and certainly by then no food, and no prospect of finding any elsewhere, because we can't start the engines!"

Martin pulled a face.

"Problem?" Hollen asked him.

"Maybe. Probably. Not sure yet. It's just, well we may not be able to start the engines yet anyway."

Hollen remained silent and waited for the engineer to explain further.

"We had to cut the generator because the exhaust is blocked with ash in the funnel. There's a good chance the exhaust for the main engines will be blocked in the same way. I found one of my guys when I was on my way up here, I've sent him to gather together a small crew and go and assess the damage, and start repairs if they can."

"Listen, personally I don't care whether we stay here or move, I think we're dead either way," Max interjected. All eyes turned to the security chief, who had until now remained silent. "But whatever happens, we need to talk to the passengers and we need to do it fast. If we don't show some leadership, let them know we're still here running this ship, we're going to have riots on our hands before long."

"We've already had riots breaking out, everyone thought the world was about to end," Hollen said.

"No, Max is right, things are already starting to get heated out there," a voice said from the doorway.

"Lucya!" Jake felt a wave of relief wash over him. As she joined the others at the table, he caught sight of her hand. "What happened? Are you ok?"

"It's fine, a bit painful, but I'll live."

"Two of my nurses are getting medical back into working order. It is not easy, without electricity, but we have a lot of wounded to treat. I suggest you get yourself down there as soon as we are done here." Lister nodded at the radio officer.

"There are others who need help more than me," Lucya said.

"This is true, but we need you more than we need some others. Get yourself a patch on that, it won't take long."

"Have you seen the captain, Lucya?" Hollen asked?

"No."

"Make an announcement, Johnny, let the passengers know we're in control. We can't wait around for Isben to turn up and do it. We don't even know if he's still alive." Max looked serious.

"Okay," Hollen banged both his palms on the table, brought the focus back to himself. "Jake, you and I need to get out there and try and find the captain. You take decks six to thirteen, I'll check his quarters and the lower decks. I can't call for him over the PA, it won't look good to the passengers that we've lost him. Lucya, get your hand sorted and then come back here, get on the radios and see if you can find out what's happening out there. We don't know what damage that asteroid did between the satellite feed going off and now. The situation might not be as bad as we think. Martin, you can get power to the comms console, right?"

Martin nodded.

"Great. Do it, then help Jake look for the captain. Grau, you need to get back to medical and do what you can for the wounded. Max, we've still got fires burning on the main pool deck, probably up on deck thirteen too, that ash burnt right through the roof. Get some of the crew together if you can, organise putting those fires out and getting this ship safe. If you can't find crew, use passengers. Some of them are already out there doing the job. Silvia, you and your team are our public face. You need to reassure the passengers that we know what we're doing here. Brief as many of your people as you can, tell them everything is under control, and get that message out as far and as fast as possible. The longer we can keep everyone calm the better. We'll all meet back here in an hour, hopefully with the captain, and we'll take it from there." Hollen looked around at his tiny crew. "Well, come on then, get to it!"

Lucya helped Grau up from his chair, placed his arm around

her shoulder, and supported him as he hobbled off. Everyone else headed for the door. Once they'd gone, Hollen returned to his position at the front of the bridge, picked up a telephone handset, flicked a button to activate the emergency PA, and closed his eyes.

NINE

EILEEN BAKEMAN WAS curled up in the middle of the bed when her husband came back into the cabin. She had taken a handful of headache tablets and cried herself to sleep. She had missed the end of the world.

Flynn rocked her gently by the shoulder, whispering in her ear. "Eileen, wake up Eileen. Something wonderful has happened."

She made a whimpering sound; her eyes squinted open and she looked around, disoriented. When she saw Flynn she instinctively pulled away. He put his arm around her to reassure her.

"We're alive, my love. You were right! It wasn't our time to die."

"What do you mean, alive?" Slowly, memories of her last hour awake trickled back. "Flynn? The asteroid!" She sat bolt upright, looked at him, then flung her arms around him, hugging him tight, sobbing once again.

"Shh. It's okay, Eileen. The asteroid couldn't kill us. I don't know why, but it was never going to destroy this ship." He disengaged his wife's arms, put his hands on her shoulders and pushed her away to arms' length, looked at her, beaming. "That's why you won this cruise, so I could be here for this. Because He has one last job I must do. He chose me, of all his soldiers, for the most important mission of them all."

A crackle came from a speaker mounted in the ceiling, then a voice spoke. Hesitant at first, but gaining in confidence.

"Can I have your attention please. This is Staff Captain Hollen." A pause, the sound of a deep breath being drawn. "We have witnessed a terrible event. We all have many questions, not least of which is just how much damage the asteroid has done, and the fate of our loved ones at home. We are working to find answers, but right now our priority is the safety of everyone on board the Spirit of Arcadia. My crew are hard at work securing the ship. I ask that all passengers and crew remain calm at this most difficult time. Please return to your cabins, where you will be safe. If your cabin has been damaged, make your way to the casino instead. For the time being, I must ask that all outdoor decks remain closed until we have been able to fully assess the damage caused by the ash. If you are injured, you should make your way to the medical centre on deck five. Your patience will be necessary, our medical facilities, whilst excellent, are not designed for an emergency of this scale. If there are any doctors or nurses among the passengers, your assistance in treating the wounded would be very much appreciated. Once again, I urge everyone on board to remain calm. Your crew have the situation under control."

Flynn and Eileen stared at each other.

"You hear that, Eileen? You hear how he spoke? 'Under control'? Nobody says they have a situation 'under control' unless they are afraid of losing control. This is where it starts, right here. But I need to be smart!" He looked serious now. "Only fools rush in. I will take my time. I will not fail Him. When the time is right, I will complete his work!"

Ten

Jake wasn't convinced that Hollen's message had been very effective. Everywhere he went, people were stopping him to ask him questions. In some of the bigger areas of the ship that he visited, he was virtually mobbed by crowds of passengers and crew members alike.

"Did the world end?"

"Are we the only people left alive?"

"Is it true the ship is sinking?"

"Why aren't we moving? When are we going home?"

This last question was the most common, and the most difficult to answer. All he could do was repeat the party line: "Everything is under control. We are in the process of securing the ship and assessing the damage. The captain will update us all, in due course."

He did his best to try and calm people, send them to their cabins, but it was clear he was never going to win this battle. In desperation he headed back down to his cabin to change out of his uniform. He had already searched two decks for the captain and there was no sign of him. A detour via his own cabin down on deck three would slow down the search briefly, but once no longer recognisable as a senior officer, he knew he would be able to pick up the pace. And anyway, he supposed, the chances were good that Johnny would find Ibsen in his quarters and that this search was pointless.

Taking a crew only staircase, hidden behind an unmarked door, he reached deck three in no time. Jake had worked on other cruise ships before coming aboard the Spirit of Arcadia, some of them considerably larger. Normally the senior officer cabins were on the upper decks, one of the privileges of rank. But the Pelagios

Line, who owned and operated the Arcadia, were not known for awarding perks or spending money on staff unnecessarily. The upper decks represented an important revenue stream, they weren't to be wasted on pandering to the crew. So Jake, like all the other crew members, was based down here in the bowels of the ship. His cabin was barely big enough to house the double bed, small desk and chair, single armchair, wardrobe, television, and shower room that it was equipped with. Indeed, getting around between these items of furniture more often than not involved turning sideways and walking like a crab.

He changed quickly, jettisoning his navy blue jacket and swapping his previously white shirt, now turned grey by the ash, for a plain black t-shirt. With arms bare he noticed that the temperature had already begun to drop now that the heating system was off. He rummaged through a shelf of clothes in the wardrobe and found a grey sweatshirt, which he pulled on as he stepped back outside into the corridor. That was the moment he heard the first gunshot.

ELEVEN

LUCYA AND GRAU knew before they arrived that there was going to be trouble in the medical centre. The corridor leading down there had been pressed into service as an overflow waiting room.

"Oi, where do you think you're going? Get in line you bloody queue jumpers!" A young bearded man was shouting at them. He had his arm around a small woman who had terrible burns to her face. She was weeping softly onto his chest. Several people turned to look, some began mumbling in agreement.

"Sir, I understand you are impatient to be seen, but I am the chief medical officer abroad this ship. It would be very much in your interests to let me and my colleague through quickly, so that we can start processing the wounded."

"Oh yeah, granddad? And I'm the bleedin' captain! Get to the back of the line and wait your turn!" Another man joined in, moving to block their passage.

Lucya unhooked Grau's arm from her shoulder, steadied him, and strode up to the angry passenger. Unencumbered by the wounded medical man, the stripes on her uniform were now plain to see. She wasn't a tall woman, around five feet four in flat shoes, but when she spoke it was with a ferocity so unexpected it stunned all present to silence.

"Now you listen to me, sir," she stabbed her index finger towards his nose, emphasising every word. "This is not a military ship so we don't have a brig where we can hold troublemakers. But personally, I've always been in favour of capital punishment as a way of maintaining order at sea. Doctor Lister asked you to let us through. I suggest you oblige immediately, or you are going to be in even more serious need of medical attention than you are now. Got it?"

The man swallowed hard. Someone further down the line whooped, and a couple of people giggled, nervously. He stepped back in line, said nothing. Grau smiled, and hobbled on towards medical.

Lucya was of the opinion that "medical centre" was a somewhat grand name for what really amounted to a couple of small rooms stuck, in the bow of the ship. With the number of passengers piled into the corridor outside, it had never seemed so inadequate. Two nurses were trying to maintain order and treat people at the same time. Normally the first room was used as a reception and waiting area. A door at the back led to the main treatment room. Given the size of the task at hand though, both rooms were being used to tend to the injured.

"I'll take care of your hand and then you'd better get on," Grau said, surveying the chaotic scene.

"This is ridiculous. You can't cope with this many people in this space!"

"No, I know. I'm going to commandeer the gym, but that's my problem to organise, not yours. Come on, we need to patch you up."

"And who is going to patch you up?"

"I'm an old man, I'm used to working at reduced capacity," Grau said with a grin. He leaned his crutch against a cabinet, opened a cupboard and pulled out a large plastic box. With a quick rummage inside he produced a sterile patch.

"This will take away the burning sensation and protect the remaining skin. It also contains a mild anaesthetic which will help with the pain," he said, sticking the self-adhesive patch on Lucya's hand. "It will be good for twelve hours, then it needs to be changed, so come back and see me then."

"In the gym," Lucya said, smiling.

"Yes, in the gym. I hope you will bring with you good news from your radios."

"I hope so too, Grau, I really do."

She left quickly, intending to return to the bridge as instructed, but at the stairs she hesitated. Her hand had been dealt with quickly, perhaps she had time to change out of her clothes? They were covered in smelly ash, and had begun to melt in places, no doubt from the heat of the burning lifeboats. She took a snap decision, and headed down towards deck three.

TWELVE

THE SOUND HAD come from further down the corridor. A couple of cabins away, at most. Jake's heart leaped into his mouth. He had heard a gunshot only once before. He was just a child at the time, visiting a store with his father late one night. It was in their home town of Portsmouth, a wealthy area with a low crime rate, and an even lower rate of violent crime. On that particular night the store was having its takings collected by the security company. A pair of masked gunmen had burst through the doors just as the security van driver emerged from the cashier's office. They didn't even threaten him in order to take the cash, they just shot him once, in the neck. His bullet and stab proof vest and his helmet offered no protection, and he was killed almost instantly. Jake witnessed the whole thing. The gunman had even winked at him, through his balaclava, on his way out. He'd had to provide a statement to the police. He'd also needed a year of counselling from a specially trained child psychologist.

The sound of the gunshot brought the memory flooding back. Sweating, he paced silently along the passage. He could hear his heart pounding in his ears. There was no question of trying to locate the source of the sound. Better to get back to the bridge and find Max Mooting, tell him to get down here pronto. He was passing the door to Johnny Hollen's cabin, and stopped. Was that a groaning sound coming from within? He hesitated. There was nobody else out here in the passage. If someone had been in that cabin with a gun, they were still in there. He turned to walk away, when the cabin door flew open. A tall thick set man with horn rimmed glasses stepped out. In his right hand he held a semi-automatic pistol. In his left hand, a whistle.

"Hello Jake," the man said. His voice was flat, devoid of emotion.

"Captain Ibsen, we've been looking for you. Are you alright? I heard a gun." Jake said, staring at the gun in his captain's hand. A hand, he realised with horror, that was being raised into the air. A gun, he saw, that was now pointed directly at him. He tried to speak, managed only one word: "Why?"

The captain took a step towards him. "This is my duty, First Officer. We were supposed to die, like everyone else. We all saw it on the final broadcast, the fate of the world. Death. Now it is up to me to see that fate is met on my ship."

"You're going to try and kill everyone on board?"

"Not an easy task, I grant you. But I suspect that if I eliminate the senior crew, the general panic caused will give me a helping hand in terminating more lives." Jake tried to back away. "Captain, where is Staff Officer Hollen? What have you done, Captain Ibsen?"

"I told you, I am eliminating the crew. I am going in order of rank, more or less, so you're next."

He took a step towards Jake, curling his finger around the trigger. Jake felt his trouser leg become warm and moist. He hung his head, resigned to his fate. Then, slowly, a smile crawled its way across his lips. He raised his head again and looked the captain in the eye. The expression clearly unsettled Ibsen.

"Something amuses you?"

"Three things, actually," Jake said. "The first thing is, aren't you being a bit dramatic about all this? I mean, if you are going to kill me, just kill me, right? The second thing, well I've just realised that I'm not afraid of dying. I nearly died twice today, already. A bloody great asteroid missed me, and then I avoided a molten ash cloud. I must be the luckiest man alive, or I really should be dead already. Either way, if you kill me now, I've already won an extra hour or two of life that I should never have had."

"The third?" Ibsen asked.

"The third?" Jake queried.

"You said three things amused you. What is the third?"

"Oh! Oh yes, the third," he paused for effect. "The third thing is, you should probably watch your back if you're going to go around pointing guns at people."

Ibsen swung round. He completed the move just quickly enough to see Lucya swing a bottle of Dom Pérignon at his head. It connected with crack that rang out through the corridor. Ibsen's arms dropped to his sides, his grip on the gun which clattered to the floor lost, along with the whistle. The captain followed, landing with a thud.

"Thanks," Jake said, wiping his brow with the sleeve of his sweatshirt.

"My pleasure," Lucya said.

"Johnny!" Jake ran into the staff officer's cabin.

He found his superior, half lying, half sitting against the wardrobe. The quarters were bigger than Jake's, not exactly spacious, but there was enough room to circulate freely. Jake froze, staring at Hollen. Blood soaked the carpet around him, and more continued to trickle from the bullet wound to his chest.

"Shit," Lucya said from his side. "Is he still alive?"

"I…I don't know. How do we tell?"

Lucya dropped to her knees, put her fingers against Johnny's neck, feeling for a pulse.

"Nothing. I can't feel anything. I think he's dead, Jake."

She pulled her hand away, stood slowly and backed away from the body. The two of them remained there, in stunned silence, not sure what they should say or do.

Finally Lucya spoke.

"We should get Max down here. I'll go and find him. You need to tie Ibsen up before he comes round. Johnny must have a belt or a tie or something you can use." Jake said nothing, he was still staring at his colleague, processing what had happened.

"Jake," Lucya placed a hand on his shoulder. "I'm going to go and find Max. Tie him up, okay?"

"Yeah. Um, yeah, sure, you're right. I'll tie him up."

Lucya left the cabin and Jake began to search for something he could use to secure the captain.

Johnny appeared to have very few clothes in his cabinet. The first drawer was full of magazines, mostly about building ecological houses, and green energy generation. The second drawer was full of knick-knacks that he must have picked up from various ports of call. Cheap souvenirs, tat made for tourists. The third drawer held some clothes, and bundles and bundles of letters. Johnny wasn't married, and had never mentioned a girlfriend, or boyfriend for that matter, so Jake wondered with whom all the correspondence took place. He realised just how little he knew about his immediate superior. They had never really been friends, though they had got on well enough, he thought. Yet looking through these possessions was like rifling through the drawers of a complete stranger.

A click behind him caused Jake to snap out of his train of thought. He looked around expecting to see Max or Lucya. Instead, for the second time he found himself looking at the wrong end of a gun.

"You're girlfriend isn't here to save you now, sonny." Ibsen said. He was having trouble standing up straight, clearly still somewhat concussed.

"I still don't understand why you think we must die, Captain?" Jake blurted out the first thing that came to mind, playing for time. He stood slowly as he spoke.

Ibsen grabbed the open door to steady himself.

"Because it is God's will, Jake. You can see that, can't you? God meant for everyone to die today. Punishment for our sins against this planet, no doubt. But by a freak of nature, we survived."

"Maybe it was God's will we survived?" Jake took a step towards his captain.

Ibsen fired the gun.

THIRTEEN

LUCYA RACED THROUGH the labyrinth that was deck three. She charged straight past the express elevator that would, under normal circumstances, have carried her to the bridge. But the ship was without power, so in the dim glow of the emergency lights she carried on to the stairs and started to climb.

Seven decks later, she arrived at the bridge out of breath. There was a group of passengers outside, banging on the door, shouting angrily.

"You can't hide in there all day. We demand to know what's going on," a large woman dressed entirely in red called out in a high pitched voice.

"You ask us to go to our cabins, but how are we supposed to do that when there's no light in half the ship?" another passenger bellowed. He held his hands cupped around his mouth as a makeshift megaphone.

Lucya could hear more angry people approaching. This was, she decided, not the best place to hang around for long. She couldn't imagine Max was on the bridge. Given his nature he wouldn't have stayed in there listening to the angry mob, he would be out there confronting them. She headed back to the stairs, went down a deck, and outside to where she had last seen fires burning.

The air outside had cleared considerably since she had been on her mission to free the burning lifeboats. Most of the fires were out, and the ash in the atmosphere had drifted away on the breeze. It was cold again, the arctic chill bit at her cheeks.

She found Max organising a group of older men, fighting one of the remaining fires. A storage locker filled with deck furniture was burning furiously. The men were armed only with tiny red fire extinguishers that they must have found somewhere inside, in a bar perhaps. Max was showing them how to aim at the base of the flames for maximum effect.

"Max. Max!" Lucya called at the top of her voice. The hiss of the extinguishers discharging in bursts made it difficult to be heard. She sprinted over and pulled him round to face her.

"What's the panic?" Max asked, clearly surprised to see her.

"Johnny's dead."

Fourteen

At the precise instant Captain Ibsen pulled the trigger, Jake lunged towards him. A tenth of a second's hesitation and he would surely be dead. Instead, he knocked Ibsen through the open door and the two of them crashed to the floor of the corridor. The gun clattered to the ground and skidded away from the men.

Jake had never been in a fight in his life. He had no absolutely no idea what he was going to do; his plan had extended no further than avoiding being shot. Now he'd achieved that, he had lost momentum, and therefore the advantage. Ibsen was stunned, but his considerable size and weight gave him the upper hand. He rolled over so that he was astride Jake, and dealt him a heavy right hook to the cheek. Jake saw it coming, and though he wasn't able to avoid it entirely, the fact he had begun to move his head away meant the blow lost some of its force. Even so, as the captain's knuckles connected with his face, he felt a flash of pain like he had never experienced, and his vision lost its focus. Instinctively, he lashed out with both hands curled into fists. Ibsen grabbed the left hand, but the right caught him in the gut, winding him. Jake tried to wriggle free, but the big man was not so easily beaten. Ibsen pinned his left hand to the ground, and wrapped his right around the younger man's throat. For Jake the world came back into sharp focus, then started to fade as the supply of oxygen to his brain was cut off. He wriggled and squirmed, but to no avail. He could feel the life begin to drain out of him, and once again found the sense of calm he had felt the first time the gun had been pointed at him that day.

The gun. Where was the gun? His head began to swirl. He saw Lucya standing over him. Why wasn't she helping? Lucya turned into Jane, his estranged wife. She was holding a baby, his baby. He reached out to touch the infant, which is when he realised he still had a free hand. Gathering all his will, he refocussed his eyes. Ibsen's face was deep red with the effort of pinning him down and strangling him. With a monumental effort, Jake thrust his free hand forward, stabbing his fingers into the captain's eyes. Ibsen roared with pain and flew backwards, releasing his grip as his hands flew up to his face. Jake pulled his own hand away and rolled onto his side, choking, gasping for breath. Ibsen was on his knees. One hand covered his eyes, blood streamed down his face. The other thrashed around wildly, trying to find its target. Jake tried to roll onto his front, to crawl away, but as he did so a hand found his ankle and closed around it in a grip that nearly crushed his bones. He felt himself being dragged backwards, and pawed helplessly at the smooth surface of the linoleum floor, desperately trying to escape the claw-like grip. When a second hand grabbed his other ankle, he knew the game was up. He had no strength left, nothing with which to fight back. The image of Jane flashed before his eyes once again. Her lips were moving, she was saying something, speaking almost silently.

"The gun, Jake. Get the gun," she mouthed.

He looked around desperately, but there was no sign of the gun. Ibsen was reeling him in, and there was nothing he could do. Then he spotted it. A shadow on the dark floor. A tiny glint of light reflected from the shiny surface as his head was dragged past it. Not the gun, but a shard of glass from the smashed champagne bottle. His right hand shot out and he grabbed it, just as Ibsen got a hand on his waist and yanked him towards him. Jake was still face down, and Ibsen was put a knee in his back, pinning him to the floor. He could feel him lean over him, the hairs on the back of his neck stood on end as he felt those hands approach once more. With one final effort, he gripped the glass and thrust it behind him as far as his hand would go. Ibsen was a big target, and his proximity meant Jake couldn't miss. He felt the glass meet resistance, and pushed it as hard as he could with a grunt. The sharp edge of the shard cut into Jake's hand. Ibsen gasped. Jake felt hot blood spurt out around the glass. He had no idea if it was his own or the captain's.

"No! What have you done? What…what…" Ibsen rasped, then gurgled. He keeled over onto his side. As he did so Jake felt the glass slide out of his hand, cutting it even more deeply. Freed from the weight of the captain, he attempted once more to roll himself over. But he was spent; he had no energy left. With blood pouring from his hand, he passed out.

• • •

When he came round, Jake found himself lying in his own bed, back in his cabin. For a brief, blissful moment, he thought perhaps that recent events had all been a bad dream. The sight of Max, Lucya, and Grau crowded round the end of the bed quickly put paid to that idea.

"Welcome back," Lucya said softly, smiling.

"No, don't try and get up, not yet. You need some more rest." Grau was the only one of the three seated.

"What happened? Where's the captain? Did you find him? He's gone crazy, he wants to kill us all. We have to stop him, he's got a gun!" Jake lifted his head as he tried to sit up, felt dizzy and immediately fell back onto the pillow.

"Slow down there, fella," Max came round the side of the bed. "The captain's not going to be doing any killing, you saw to that."

"I slowed him down? You got to him in time to tie him up?"

"Jake," Lucya glanced uneasily at Grau. "The captain is dead. There was a fight, do you remember?"

"Of course I remember! Sorry, I'm sorry, I didn't mean to snap. What I mean is, I haven't lost my memory, I know what happened. But how can he be dead?"

"You stabbed him, with a piece of glass."

Jake pulled his hand out from under the bed cover and looked at it, remembering how the bottle had cut it open, remembering the blood. His palm was neatly and comprehensively bandaged.

"I'm thinking of specialising in hand wounds, you two are certainly keeping me busy," Grau said, looking from Jake to Lucya.

"Listen, you did what you had to do, son." Max tried to reassure him. "Given the state we found you in, it was pretty clear that you had to defend yourself. That piece of bottle went straight into Ibsen's heart. He would have been dead within minutes. The cut was deep, nobody could have saved him."

"He said that we were supposed to die, that it was God's will. He was mad, I've never seen anyone like that before."

"I must share some responsibility for what has happened here," Grau said, a grave look on his face. "I couldn't say anything before, because of patient confidentiality." The others looked at him expectantly. "Captain Ibsen has been seeing me regularly with a stress related condition. I was of the opinion that it did not affect his capacity to run this ship. Clearly, I was wrong."

"This isn't your fault, Doctor Lister," Lucya said. "Today has hardly been normal circumstances, it's been enough to send anyone over the edge."

"That is possible, and I appreciate your kind words. Even so, at sea we are meant to expect the unexpected, to deal with unplanned and dangerous events. I should have made a recommendation to the company that the captain be given leave, to rest."

"Look, this is not yours or anyone else's fault Doctor," Max said. "We can debate this all we like, it doesn't change what happened here. We have more pressing things to discuss, like what we do now. Jake, you understand you're in charge now, right?"

The thought had not occurred to him, and Max's words hit him with almost as much force as the captain's punch to the face. His head began to spin. He, Jake Noah, had just killed a man. He was responsible for taking a human life. And now he was responsible for safeguarding three thousand more human lives, aboard this ship. Possibly the last three thousand human lives on the planet. If the rest of the world had been destroyed as the broadcast had suggested, he was in charge of the rest of the human race. With that thought, he passed out again.

• • •

"Nothing. No response to my distress calls. No radio chatter. Nothing on the shortwave. I can't even pick up any navigation beacons," Lucya said, setting down her headset on the dull grey communications console.

"We mustn't give up hope," Silvia said. She and Lucya were the only two people on the bridge. They had used the fire escape staircase that went directly from the bridge all the way to the roof of deck thirteen in order to enter without being seen by the angry mob camped outside the main door.

"You're right," Lucya said. "Just because nobody is transmitting, it doesn't mean there isn't anyone around to transmit. For all we know, that asteroid may just have knocked out the electrics. We still don't really know what happened to the northern states and other countries."

"But what do I tell passengers? It's not just out there that things are getting difficult. There are groups massing all over the ship. Whatever we decide to do, we need to announce it."

"That's down to Jake, now. We have to wait for him. In the meantime, we stick to what Johnny told us to do, his orders still stand."

There was a clanging noise, and a hole appeared in the ceiling. A pair of feed dangled through it, found the ladder, and grew into legs, and eventually into Max.

"It's getting worse out there. I need to disperse the crowd, but I'm outnumbered. I need a weapon," he said, walking to an innocuous looking locker at the back of the room.

He took a key out of his pocket and went to insert it into the lock, but found another key already in there. Cautiously, he pulled the door open. Inside were eight rifles, neatly stacked upright. He pulled open a drawer under the rifles. Neatly packaged in a foam inlay were four automatic pistols. There was a conspicuous space where a fifth pistol clearly should have been.

"Well that explains where the captain got his gun from," Max said to nobody in particular.

Lucya walked over, saw the contents of the cupboard, and whistled.

"What are these doing on board? This is a cruise ship, not a navy transport!"

"Anti-piracy measures," Max said. "We've been carrying weapons for the last year, in case we were attacked by pirates."

"How come nobody told us? What good are weapons if nobody knows they're here?"

"Captain knew. And I knew. Johnny knew, too. We each have a key to this cabinet. The company wanted to keep it quiet, figured it might make folks worry if they knew we were prepared in case of attack. The guns were put here at the same time a bridge recording system was installed. It records video and audio of everything that happens up here. Can't see the point of it myself, they've never been able to prosecute these pirates, having video evidence isn't going to change that."

"I would have felt a lot safer knowing we had those handy," Lucya said. She pulled out a rifle, held it up and looked down the sights.

"I always forget you were in the Russian Navy," Silvia said, taking a step back involuntarily. "I hate guns, I hope you're not expecting me to carry one, Max?"

Max pulled the gun from Lucya's hand.

"I'm not expecting anyone to carry one. The intention is to keep the peace. Situation outside calls for a little extra persuasion, so I'm just going to borrow this for a bit."

He closed the lock, turned and removed the key, slipping it in his pocket. He strode over to the main door, unlocked it, and swung it open quickly, taking those outside by surprise.

"Ladies and gentlemen, would you please return to your cabins or the public areas of the ship." He made a show of placing the strap of the rifle over his shoulder.

"We've been here for over an hour, we want some answers," a man called out.

"Yeah, got that right, man!" another man chimed in.

"Where's the captain? We want to speak to the captain," said the woman in red, apparently the ring-leader.

"The captain will be talking to the whole ship when he is good and ready," Max said. "Right now, he's busy. As I'm sure you can imagine, he has a lot on his plate. The safety of all passengers on board is his priority, it is the priority of every crew member. Now, please kindly get back to your cabins, or I will have to treat this little gathering as a specific threat to the crew."

There was a lot of mumbling, but the impressive firearm strapped to Max's shoulder was enough to persuade the rabble that they were better off complying. They shuffled off, muttering amongst themselves.

Max closed and locked the door. "We need Jake. He's had a couple of hours to rest, we can't wait any longer. We need some decisions, and to get word out about what we're doing."

"I'll go and wake him," Lucya said, jumping from her chair a bit too enthusiastically. "There's not much I can do here, anyway. I've set up a couple of radio scanners to sweep the main channels. If they pick up any signals they'll lock onto them and you'll hear it."

"Silvia, can you go and fetch Martin?" Max said. "We need his input too."

"Sure. What about Doctor Lister? Anyone else?"

"No, the doctor is busy enough looking after the wounded. They need him more down there than we do up here."

Max opened the door again, checked that the passageway outside was clear. The two women slipped outside and headed for the stairs. Max remained on guard outside the bridge.

FIFTEEN

"DID YOU SEE him? Did you see the captain?" Flynn asked.

"No. I got a good look inside when the guy with the gun came out. There were two women in there, I didn't see anyone else." Eileen looked pleased with herself. She had carried out her husband's instructions perfectly He would be pleased with her, and that meant life would be a bit easier. For the time being, at least.

"Something's going down, Eileen. For the captain to leave the bridge at a time like this, something ain't right, I tell you. Only reason he wouldn't be there is if he was out touring the ship, and we ain't heard of no tour going on. So that means either he's injured or he's dead. This is it, Eileen, this is my chance already. I didn't think it would happen this quickly, but God must believe I'm ready. I need to get me to the bridge. I'll be ready. The people need a leader, and I'm going to show them a better way to live."

Sixteen

Jake had drifted in and out of consciousness several times over the last couple of hours. He saw visions of his wife, but every time she appeared she would be blasted to atoms by a giant asteroid. When he slept, he dreamt of a burning planet, a molten ball, floating alone in space. After a particularly upsetting dream, in which the world exploded, he realised he wasn't going to get much more sleep. Easing himself out of bed, he wobbled to his feet, stepped into the bathroom and caught sight of himself in the mirror. The light from the small porthole was not bright, but he could see that the side of his face had turned blue, and that his hair was matted with blood

He tried the shower, unsure of whether or not the flow of water relied on electric pumps. Miraculously a jet of water spurted out. It was freezing cold, but Jake didn't care. Using only his good hand, he wriggled out of his clothes and stepped under the icy flow. The chilled liquid on his skin jolted him awake, and brought with it a new clarity. As he watched the grime of the ash and the blood of his captain wash off his body and mix with the clear water, turning it a muddy brown, he resigned himself to his fate. He was in charge now, effectively the captain of this ship. The job he had never wanted. The responsibility he had always feared. He had nearly been killed three times. He should have died; the passengers deserved better. He was no leader, he had no idea what to do. If he hadn't survived, Lucya would probably be in charge, as the next most senior officer on board. Or maybe Max. There was a man who people would respect, look up to. If Max told you to do something, you would do it without question. He inspired confidence.

He would make a great captain. He would know how to lead these people to safety.

Could he pass up his duty? Appoint Max captain? Or even Lucya? Did he have the authority? He hadn't even begun his staff captain training, he didn't know what he could or couldn't do. He'd never wanted to go as far as first officer, but he'd gone along with the program, taking courses, exams, moving up the ranks, keeping his family happy whilst all the time wondering what he really should do with his life. He'd made it this far by accident, not by design. And now he'd just been fast tracked to the top, in the worst possible circumstances.

The jet of water slowed to a trickle, and eventually stopped altogether. Jake stepped out of the shower and dried himself on a fluffy white towel, embroidered with a tiny image of the ship, and the name Spirit of Arcadia. He didn't think he could appoint another in his place. He was going to have to try and give this a shot.

"Don't think about the end of the world stuff," he said to himself aloud. "Think of this as a temporary assignment. A training exercise, You're just acting captain, until we reach a safe port. That's the objective here. Reach a safe port." A little voice in the back of his mind tried to tell him that there were no safe ports, that the asteroid had destroyed them, that they were alone at sea, destined to slowly starve to death. It tried, but Jake chose to ignore it. He couldn't think like that. If he accepted that as their fate, they were already dead.

There was a gentle knock at the door.

"Jake? Are you awake? It's me, Lucya."

"Give me a moment," he called back.

He opened his wardrobe and picked out the first clean clothes that came to hand. A pair of jeans, another t-shirt, and a navy blue sweater. He dressed as quickly as he could with the limited use of his hands.

"Come in," he said as soon as he was decent.

The door opened and Lucya walked in. She looked exhausted. Her long black hair was dishevelled, her clothes partially melted, and her face bore patches of ash like badly applied makeup.

"Hey you, you're looking much better." She looked around the room. "I thought I heard you talking to someone?"

"Talking to myself," Jake said, and blushed a little.

"Hmm, you know what they say about that! So erm, we need you up on the bridge. You know, to need to decide what happens next?" She let the words out carefully, as if they were going to turn around and bite her in the face.

"It's okay, Lucya, I know what I have to do." He was sitting on the edge of the bed, fumbling with the laces on his shoes. His bandaged hand prevented him from gripping them. "Shit, sorry, oh hell, could you…would you mind…?" he looked up helplessly.

"Yeah! Of course!" Lucya dropped to her knees and proceeded to tie the laces neatly, her own smaller patch less of an impediment to free movement.

"I can't even put my own shoes on, how am I going to run this ship, Lucya?" Jake felt panic well up inside him. He wanted to cry. He wanted to bury himself in his bed and never come out. He fought back the tears, keeping his head bowed low; he didn't want her to see.

"Hey! Hey, hey, it's going to be okay you know? You're going to do fine. No, you're going to do great! Everyone respects you, and nobody thinks it's going to be easy. We're all around to help you, you haven't got to do this on your own." She put an arm around him, pulled him close to her. Her hair smelt of fire and smoke. As it touched his face, something stirred within him. He immediately felt a pang of guilt. He pulled away from her, got to his feet. Sniffed. Tried to pull himself together.

"I'm sorry," he said. "Just tired. Thank you. It means a lot to know you have confidence in me."

Lucya stood as well. She smiled, understood this was hard for him. "Come on," she said. "Let's get back upstairs and get to work."

• • •

Acting Captain Jake Noah, and Chief Radio Officer Lucya Levin left the cabin and set off down the passageway towards the stairs.

"Where did the captain go?" Jake looked around. There was no sign of the body, and the broken glass and blood had been cleared away.

"Max took care of it. He cleaned up, didn't want anyone stumbling across it and asking questions."

"What about Johnny?"

"He and Grau took both the bodies down below. They've set up a makeshift morgue in one of the store rooms, one of those ones that are always cold because they're below the water line and the heating never seems to work properly."

"How did they get them down there without being seen?"

"I don't think they worried about it, Jake. There are hundreds of people dead. The captain and Johnny were just another couple of anonymous bodies, wrapped in sheets and carried down below."

They walked in silence, reached the stairs, and began to climb.

Seventeen

Max greeted them at the door and let them inside before he closed and locked it behind them. Silvia had already returned with Martin, who nodded once at Jake. Everyone assembled around the map table. Jake felt all eyes were on him.

"Right, so, erm…"

"Jake, we're your friends, we have every confidence in you," Silvia said kindly.

"Yes, yes of course, thank you Silvia. Okay, first things first, what is the state of the ship, Martin?"

"I've got a couple of guys in the funnel, they're clearing out the ash. It's a slow job, they're having to scoop it out with their bare hands, we don't have the equipment to get in there and do it any quicker, our machines are just too big to get into that sort of space."

Silvia perked up. "Would a couple of vacuum cleaners from housekeeping help?" Her face fell again. "Oh, but there's no electricity."

"No, you're right, that's not a bad idea Silvia. We have a few portable generators knocking around in the engine room, we could run them off those. What sort of size are we talking about? It's a pretty tiny space."

"They're about…so big," Silvia indicated the dimensions with her hands.

"Perfect! They can get those down there, that will really save some time."

"Okay, so with the cleaners, how long before we can get the generator working?" Jake asked.

"Maybe four hours? But it would make sense to clean out the exhaust for the main engine at the same time. If we start the main generator the guys are going to have to work around the hot exhaust from that, it will make the job ten times harder."

"So how long to clean them both?"

"Well," Martin pondered the question, drumming his fingers on the steel table top. "At a push we could do it in six hours, seven tops."

"Alright, push as hard as you can, we have to get power back, as a priority. Once we do, how long can we keep the generator going?"

"If we don't start the main engines, and depending on which services we keep running, we're okay for at least ten days."

"Right, services." Jake paused and thought. "We need light, the passengers are really unhappy about that."

Silvia and Max nodded in agreement.

"We're going to need heat too," Lucya said. "I'm not the only one who noticed how cold it's getting on board, right?"

"Yes, heat. But the minimum, Keep the temperature at sixteen degrees, at the most. We'll tell people to wear more clothes if they're cold."

"Fifteen," Max interjected. "Fifteen degrees. That's more than enough."

"Okay, fifteen. But no hot water. I just took a cold shower and I feel better for it. Hot water is a luxury we can do without."

"Water is a whole other question," Martin said. He was met with questioning looks from around the table. "Desalination? You all know we get our water from the sea, don't you?"

It was clear that this was news to everyone except Jake.

"I thought it came out of the tanks?" Silvia asked. "We fill up tanks at every port, don't we?"

"Sure, but that's really a backup supply. We use it when docked because water in the ports tends to be full of diesel and other crap," Martin explained. "As soon as we're a couple of miles out, we switch to water from the desalination plant. The tanks would never be enough to supply a ship this size."

"And the plant runs off electricity from the generator," Jake added.

"Right. And so does waste water treatment. So we have to ask ourselves, how much water do we really need?" Martin looked around the table.

"There has to be basic sanitation," Silvia said. "People need to wash, to flush toilets, or we could end up spreading germs and disease."

"Silvia, you do understand we could be stranded for who knows how long?" Max didn't look impressed. "Toilets I'll grant you, but come on, back in the army you were lucky if you got a cold shower every couple of weeks on some tours. I say we switch off water to all the showers in the cabins, just leave one block running in the gym. If people have to queue, they won't bother."

"I wish we could," Martin said. "But there's no way to do that apart from visiting every cabin individually and cutting the supply, one by one. It would take days."

"Okay, so we introduce a ration system," Jake said. "Martin, I assume you can shut off the water to the whole ship from the desalination plant?"

"Of course."

"So we let people know that the water will be on for one hour in the morning. Outside those hours they'll have to make do."

"The passengers aren't going to like this. They're not going to like it one little bit," Lucya said, rubbing her neck.

"If we tell them it's that or we switch the lights and heat off, they'll understand," Max said.

Everyone nodded, the matter seemed settled. Jake opened one of the draws under the table and moved around the contents until he found what he was looking for. He extracted a large blue crayon-like pencil. They were designed for plotting courses on laminated maps, but he had other ideas in mind. He started writing directly on the shiny table surface: "Water" Underneath, he wrote "Rationed, 09:00 – 10:00"

"Okay," he said. "Anything else on water, while we're at it?"

"What about the pools?" Silvia asked. "Five swimming pools and a few hot tubs, there's a lot of water in those. Can we use any of it?"

"The pools drain through the waste water plant," Martin said. "We could disconnect them and reconnect them to the fresh water tanks, drain them into those. That buys us a bit of extra fuel as we can use that water instead of the desalinated stuff."

"Speaking of waste water," Jake was stroking his chin, deep in thought, "you said that it gets treated by another machine?"

"Yes. Water from showers, sinks, the kitchens and bars, all that stuff gets filtered then goes overboard. Anything from the toilets goes through a shredder then dumped at sea. It's the shredder that needs the power, that and the pumps. I know what you're thinking, but it's not a good idea."

"Why not?" Jake asked. "Can't we bypass the shredder and dump everything as it is? Nobody is going to complain!"

"Because within twenty four hours this ship is going to be floating in a lake of its own shit," Martin said. "And sucking that same shit up into the desalination plant to use as fresh water."

Silvia screwed up her face. "Won't the sea carry it away, on the currents?" she asked

"I doubt the currents up here are strong enough to have much of an effect," Lucya said. "We could move to a better location, we'd need a few hours sailing time. Are you willing to burn that much fuel, Captain?"

All eyes turned to Jake, waiting for his response, but he remained silent. He looked around the table, not seeming to understand why nobody had answered.

"Captain Noah?" Max said.

"Oh, right, that's me. Sorry, this captain thing is going to take some getting used to. Lucya, work out a course to take us somewhere where the water problem won't be an issue, but make sure we're headed towards land. If we're going to burn fuel, we should at the very least get closer to land. We all know we can't survive at sea indefinitely, even with rationing. Our objective has to be to try and find land, and land that hasn't been destroyed by the asteroid."

Once again everyone nodded their agreement.

"What else is in limited supply?" Jake looked around at the others. "We don't know how long we'll be stuck at sea, what can we not live without, and how much of it have we got? Food has to be the next priority, after water and fuel."

"We're well stocked, but of course supplies are finite," Silvia leapt in, glad to be back in her comfort zone. "I suggest we close all the restaurants and bars immediately. Anything non perishable should be preserved. The freezers are going to need power, they have to be a priority, no?"

"Agreed. We can't afford to let any food spoil. Martin, can we keep a supply to the freezers and still cut other non-essential services?"

"Yes, they're run on a separate supply. They draw a lot of power, but sure, we can keep them running."

Jake was scribbling more notes on the surface of the table. He had added two more headings and drawn vertical lines between them, creating columns for water, fuel, and food. As tasks we assigned, he noted them in the relevant column along with the initials of the person responsible.

"I know it's a big job, Silvia, but can you organise some of your people to take an inventory of all the food we have available? Then get the head chef to get a team together and figure out a menu that can feed everyone on board three meals a day for at least the next five days, and still have five days food in reserve?"

Silvia whistled through her teeth. "It's not going to be easy. Five days? With as much again in reserve?"

"I'm not talking fine dining here. We need basic meals, the minimum required to provide everyone with enough calories to live on. Chef will love it, a new challenge."

"Try and work it so that the frozen stuff gets eaten first. Any freezers we can empty, we can switch off," Martin said.

"Alright, we're getting there. This will buy us some time that we can use to work out a longer term plan. I'll make an announcement, let everyone know what's happening. Is there anything else we need to deal with urgently?"

"There is one other matter," Max said. "We need to deal with the dead. There are a lot of bodies down below, people who got caught up in that dust cloud. Grau's got them in some kind of chiller, but they're going to go off pretty quick."

"Your suggestion?" Jake feared he already knew the answer.

"Those bodies should go over the side. It ain't gonna be popular, I'll grant you, but for the safety of everyone else, it has to be done."

Jake sighed. "No, you're right. It has to be done. But it should be done with dignity. I'll announce a service, we'll get the minister to say a few words, assuming he's survived."

Max rolled his eyes.

"They're still people, Max," Jake said. "Many of them will have relatives who have survived. We can't just dump them over the side like a sack of spoiled potatoes. They get a proper sea burial, even if the service takes a whole day. And nobody is obliged to attend," he added quickly. "Max, I need you to do what you do best. Get out and about around the ship, get a feel for the mood. Things are going to be hard going for the next few days, I expect not everyone is going to accept that. We need to be ready for problems before they arise."

"You want me doing community policing?"

"You could call it that, why not. Call it intelligence work, if it makes you feel better. You're head of security and, the way I see it, maintaining the peace is one of the most important things we can do if we are to survive this. But put that weapon back in the locker please, we're not at war, and I don't think we need to worry about pirates. Walking around with that on your shoulder is just going to alienate us from the passengers. Martin, can you find whoever is in charge of maintenance and get them to organise a crew to go over this ship top to bottom and check for serious damage? Someone needs to fix the windows in here before we freeze to death, and no doubt the bridge isn't the hardest hit area. Anything that can be fixed without using power, should be fixed, within reason. Windows, the deck thirteen roof, that kind of thing. Get the place weathertight."

"Okay, shouldn't be a problem," Martin said.

"Great, then I think that's all, for now," Jake felt relief that this was almost over. "Let's arrange to meet back here at," he checked his watch, "twenty two hundred. That gives us six hours. I want everyone to try get some sleep before then, too, it could be a long night. Any problems, I want to know. Are the internal comms working?"

Martin nodded. "Yeah. I mean, I'll get them back online from the battery."

"Okay then, let's get to it. And by the way, I want all of you in uniform. Until we know otherwise, we are all still employees of Pelagios Line, and we need to show that the crew are still running the show."

Max, Silvia and Martin filed out of the door, leaving Lucya and Jake stood at the table. Neither said a word until the door was closed.

"You did really well, Jake, you're going to be fine at this, really."

"I'm winging it. Martin can tell, he's going along with it for now, but he won't take orders from me forever."

"What is it with you two anyway?" Lucya tilted her head, looked at Jake with huge wide eyes.

"Surely you don't need to ask that?" He felt suddenly very uncomfortable.

"Yes, I do. You two used to be such good friends."

"Oh, hey, I'm taking up your table. You need to get to the maps to plot your course."

"Don't change the subject! And I don't need the maps, I'll just use the navigation computer."

"I don't think any of the computers have power yet. Looks like you're going to have to work the old fashioned way. What do you think, can you remember how?" He grinned at her.

"Cheeky. You are a cheeky man. I will show you just what I can do with a map. But first I am going to get washed and changed before Martin switches off the water. I might even have a little rest, Captain's orders you know." With that, she rounded the table, and slipped through the door.

Jake stared at his scrawled notes across the steel surface. He opened a draw and took out a pad of paper and a pen. He began to plan out just what he was going to say to everyone on board.

Eighteen

"Ladies and gentlemen can I have your attention, please. Your attention, please. This is acting Captain Jake Noah. Earlier today, Staff Captain Hollen addressed this ship and promised that we would update you with news of how the asteroid we witnessed has affected the rest of the world. Surely everyone aboard has someone back home they are desperate to hear from. The news I bring is not what you will want to hear, but I am not going to lie to you. So far, we have not been able to make contact with anyone back on land. It is important we do not draw any hasty conclusions from this fact. It is possible, likely even, that the asteroid damaged radio equipment, or even that the dust and ash cloud which trailed it is casing interference. The only way we can know for sure if there are other survivors, on land, is to go and see. We are, however, limited by our fuel supply. The same fuel that drives this ship also drives all the services, including power and light. Tempting though it may be, we cannot just sail off and start our search, we must plan ahead carefully, to make the most of our resources.

"Although this ship is large, it does carry only a finite quantity of fuel and food. If we wish to survive much further into the future, we must be smart about how we consume both. For this reason, effective immediately, we are introducing a rationing system ship-wide…"

Jake proceeded to announce all that had been discussed, the food and water rationing, the limited use of electricity and heating. He announced that a service for the dead would be held on the deck four rear terrace the following morning, anyone who wished to attend was welcome.

"These measures, I know, will not be easy, but I hope you all understand that they are necessary. They apply to everyone aboard, crew and passengers alike. It goes without saying that all normal services on board are suspended. All crew members are relieved of their regular duties. We are, to all intents and purposes, in a kind of hibernation. I recommend everyone tries to get some rest. Those who are injured and have not yet been treated should attend the medical centre, which has now been relocated to the gym. If your injuries are not serious, please do give consideration to others who may need attention more urgently than yourself."

Jake felt he was beginning to ramble. He knew he needed to wrap it up.

"I know you may have many questions and concerns, and we will address these as best we can, in due course. For now, I ask for your patience as we adapt to our enforced circumstances. Urgent problems can be addressed to uniformed senior crew members, who will do their best to help. Thank you."

He breathed a sigh of relief. He knew that the announcement was lacking in authority and conviction, not to mention structure and coherence, but he was just happy to have got it over with. The questions would come, of that he had no doubt. For now, though, he wanted to take his own advice and get some more rest. He settled down in the captain's chair, closed his eyes, and was asleep within seconds.

• • •

He was awoken by the sound of Lucya working on her maps behind him. Checking his watch he saw, to his horror, that he had been asleep for more than four hours.

"Hey, sleepy!" Lucya called over.

"Why didn't you wake me?"

"You needed the rest."

"We all need rest."

"Yeah, don't worry. I got my head down for a few hours, too. I've only just come back."

Jake got to his feed, stretched, yawned, and took a look outside. The sky head cleared even more, there was even a hint of sunshine.

Looking at the flat calm water, at the mass of ice in the distance, once again starting to shine in the light like the dawn of a new day, it seemed impossible to believe what had happened only hours earlier. The serenity of the scene gave him hope. If this place, this inhospitable arctic desert, could look so placid and beautiful after the onslaught it had suffered, then there was a real chance that other parts of the world had survived too. He desperately wanted to give the order to fire up the main engines, to pull up the anchor and to sail south to look for survivors, for civilisation, for land. But he knew that was impossible. He had one throw of the dice, and the lives of everyone on the ship depended on getting it right.

He wandered over to the map table to find Lucya deep in concentration. There were two huge nautical charts laid out, as well as a long plastic rule, coloured pencils, and a circular slide rule.

"Having trouble?" he asked.

"It's been a while since I did these kind of calculations by hand. Don't laugh, and don't say I told you so. I'll get it, I just need to refresh my memory."

"I have total confidence in you. Listen, I think I'm going to head out and try and get around the ship a bit, see how the others are getting on. There are nearly a thousand crew members I haven't spoken to, apart from over the PA. I should at least try and talk to more of the department heads, let them know what's occurring."

"A few people have already asked me why you're acting captain, they want to know what's happened to Ibsen and Hollen."

"What have you said?" Jake felt a pang of concern.

"I said you'd brief everyone in due course," Lucya pulled a face, like a naughty child expecting to be told off. "I was right though, wasn't I? That's what you're going to be doing now, as you go round the ship?"

"Yeah, yeah, you were right. But what do I say? How do I tell people Ibsen killed Hollen and I killed Ibsen?"

"You don't. You simply say that they both died following the ash cloud. Hundreds died, nobody is going to question it."

"But Hollen spoke to the ship after the ash cloud had passed, so that won't work. I suppose," he stared into the middle distance, his mind turning over possibilities, "if I just say that he didn't survive his injuries following the ash cloud, then technically that's the truth."

"Right, and if people assume that his injuries were caused by the ash, that's not really your fault, is it?" Lucya smiled.

"I'll see you back here in a few hours for the senior officers' meeting," Jake said.

"You sound like a captain already."

Nineteen

His first port of call was the kitchen. He wanted to catch up with Claude Dupont, the head chef. There was one huge kitchen, on deck seven. It serviced the three restaurants and four cafes on board, as well as the crew canteen, and provided snacks for the bars. Normally the place was a hive of activity, with Claude shrieking out orders to the hordes of cooks who scurried about. It was a very different scene today, though. No columns of steam rising from hotplates, no bubbling pots, or clanging pans or hissing griddles. Claude was seated at a stainless steel bench. Behind him, a couple of people wearing white and blue cooks uniforms were busy loading food into a giant freezer.

"Hi, Claude," Jake smiled jovially.

The chef looked up at him with a sour expression. He was a tiny man, bespectacled, and slightly balding. Jake had always thought he looked more like he belonged in a magic shop, or a very niche second hand book store, not a kitchen. Despite his diminutive stature, he was a formidable character. He had a reputation for whacking errant cooks on the back of the legs with a ladle, although to be fair, nobody could attest to ever having seen this happen. Nobody wanted to find out if it was true though, so when Claude told anyone to do anything, they would eagerly cry "Yes chef!" without question, no matter how odd or unreasonable the order.

"Well, well, a visit from the captain himself. Sorry, the acting captain," Claude corrected himself, loading the words with sarcasm. "I did not think I was worthy."

"How are you getting on with the inventory?"

Claude ignored the question entirely. "I hear there is a new club, a group of elite staff who meet on the bridge. A bridge club, you might say," he laughed at his own joke, but it was a hollow, false laugh. "Mr Noah and his band of cronies, planning out the future, creating their empire while the rest of us wait for our orders to be handed down from on high."

"Claude, if you are upset at not being at our meeting, then I can only apologise. Our immediate priority was to stabilise the ship. Now our concern is the wellbeing of everyone on board. If there are any elite staff, then you are certainly one of them. Feeding three thousand people with limited resources and power is a challenge unlike any other, and I honestly cannot think of anyone better qualified to take it on than you."

"You are laying on the compliment a bit thick, Monsieur Noah. I am not stupid, do you think I am stupid?"

"Far from it, and I mean what I say. In fact, now that emergency repairs are underway, you are the first person I have come to see. I came straight from the bridge to find out how you were progressing, and to ask you to join us at the next bridge meeting in," Jake looked at his watch, "just over two hours. If you cannot make it then I will understand."

"No, no you are right. It is true that without sustenance, without nourriture, all your efforts will be in vain. I will come to your meeting, and I will report my progress to you at that time."

"Great, that's good. Well, I will see you later, on the bridge, then."

"A tout a l'heure, Captain."

Claude returned to his notes. It was clear that Jake's audience was at an end. He left the kitchen relieved. It looked like he'd won Claude over, but there were so many others still to see.

• • •

The next person Jake wanted to visit was the head of housekeeping. New Yorker Tania Bloom had held that post for as long as Jake had been on the ship. Like so many from her home town, she was a straight talker. Likeable, and friendly once you got to know her, she presented a tough exterior to the outside world. Her shoulder pads were legendary, as were her heels.

Jake wasn't sure where he would find her. He tried her office on deck seven, but it was locked and his knocks failed to elicit any response. He made his way down to her cabin on deck three, but it was the same story. Thinking that perhaps he should see if the medics had seen her, he headed back up a level to the gym. It was quieter than he expected, a few people he didn't recognise, presumably passengers, were seated on the side of the room waiting to be seen. One nurse was on duty, Jake recognised her as Kiera; he knew she had briefly dated Martin. Grau was with a patient, securing bandages to her arm. As soon as he was done he waved Jake over to join him on the far side of the gym.

"How is your hand, Captain?" he asked quietly, but his voice still echoed around the impressively voluminous space.

"Fine, fine. But never mind that, how are you doing down here?"

"I think we've dealt with the most urgent cases. We lost three this evening, they're down below, along with those who were DOA. It looks like it was smoke inhalation from the dust cloud. Mostly it has been burns, though. Burns, and quite a lot of cuts and bruises from broken glass. Many windows blew in."

"Have you had any rest, Grau?"

"I'm about to go and get some sleep now. Kiera and David have got everything covered here, now it has calmed down."

"That's good. Listen, do you know Tania Bloom, and have you seen her down here? She's not in her office or cabin?"

"Yes, I know Tania, but I haven't seen her. Let me check the log in case one of the others has." Grau opened a thick notebook and ran his finger down a list of handwritten names. "These are the people we've seen since we have been here. We didn't get to log everyone we saw before moving to the gym, it was just too chaotic. No, it doesn't look like she has been down here."

"Okay, thanks Grau. I have other people to see, hopefully I'll run into her on my way around."

"There is another possibility, of course. I know we don't want to think of it, but it wasn't just passengers that were caught in that cloud, there were crew out there too."

"You think she could be dead? Do you have a list, of the…deceased?"

"Yes, and she's not on it. But she could be one of the unknowns."

"The unknowns?"

"You know, the John Does, or the John Smiths, whatever you call them. Unidentified. Our list only carries the names of those positively identified by their families who brought them to us. At least a third of the bodies down there, we don't know who they are yet."

Jake suddenly felt sick at the thought. He hadn't considered the question of the dead any further than just holding a service and then disposing of them respectfully.

"Don't panic," Grau said, clearly sensing that Jake didn't know what to do. "People are already coming to us when they can't find family or friends. We have got names for at least a dozen bodies that way. But a lot of the crew members won't be missed by anyone for some time. And there are many couples who died together, they may not have anyone else on board who will miss them. We need the passenger and crew manifest and then we must go through and find out who is alive and who is dead. We may not be able to match all the names to bodies, but at least we will know. We cannot bury these people at sea until we know who they are, or at least have made every effort to find out."

"No, you're right, of course. It's a morbid affair, but yes, it has to be done. It won't be easy to organise. Unless…" he pulled up a chair and sat down opposite the doctor, lost in thought. "I kind of had this idea that we should find out more about who we have on board, who these people are. If we are…if the rest of the world has…if there's nobody else out there, then this is it. This ship could represent the last community of people. If there are no towns left, nowhere to settle, then we will have to build a new home. We cannot live on a ship indefinitely, and even if we are stuck at sea for weeks or even months, we will have huge challenges to overcome. We will need to produce food and energy. Every person here will need to pull their weight, to do their bit. And that means we need to know who these people are and what they can do."

"You are thinking of a census?" Grau was nodding slowly.

"Yes, a census. But we don't have to call it that, because we don't want to cause people to panic. It's probably easier for them not to think too far ahead. Right now, we've survived, and that fact alone is enough. When reality really sinks in, that's when our problems will begin. If people think there is no future, no hope, then who knows what they will do? So we don't want to encourage them to think about the future, not yet."

"So we dress up our census as part of a crew and passenger roster. Interesting idea. But you think people will give you personal details without question?"

"It depends how we ask for those details," Jake said, thinking hard. "Rather than just checking names off the passenger list and saying 'by the way, what do you do for a living?' we must reframe the whole exercise. We tell people that the passenger list was destroyed by fire. We say that we need to know who is on board so that we can calculate the food rations, that kind of thing. So we say we're recreating the passenger manifest."

"Yes, this could work, it gives us a reason to talk to everyone on board. A true census. We would have to insist everyone returned to their cabins for the duration of the exercise, to be sure that they got counted."

"Right. And we issue them with a piece of paper to say that they have been processed, that their name is on the list. Make it that they must present the paper to get their meal ration. So it's in their interest to make sure they are counted. We'll send out a team to take the census. We'll ask the minimum questions we can while still gathering useful information. Name, date of birth, country of residence, profession."

"You'll need many people to do go knocking door to door, this needs to be done quickly."

"If I can find Tania, I can mobilise her team. The housekeeping folk know the ship inside out, they spend their days going round every cabin on board. They will be perfect, and it will give them an important role to fulfil."

Jake stood up and walked over to the wall, where a telephone was mounted. He picked it up and dialled a three digit number.

"Hey, Lucya, it's Jake. I need you to put out a ship-wide call for Tania Bloom and Barry Nickelson to contact the bridge. If and when they do, can you send them both down to Barry's office. I need to talk to them. Thanks." He hung up and returned to his seat.

"Barry Nickelson?" Grau asked.

"Entertainment manager."

"Oh, that Barry. I've heard about his parties. Not so much my, how do you say, cup of tea?"

"Barry's okay. His team is one of the biggest on board, I really need to brief him on what's happening."

TWENTY

MAX MOOTING WAS not happy. He had always been loyal to Ibsen and Hollen, and now suddenly he had to answer to some young upstart. It was true, he thought to himself as he roamed the ship, that young Noah was coping pretty well, considering he had been thrown in the deep end. He just wasn't convinced that he truly had the new captain's ear. Young men always seemed to have something to prove, to show the world that they could go it alone. They were so often too proud to ask for help, or accept it when offered. He'd lost more than one soldier that way, men who with a bit more experience and training would have been fine officers. Sent to war too soon and too young, their naivety and ego were their downfall. Would Jake suffer the same fate? He wasn't ready to be captain, hadn't had the formal training, and much more importantly, didn't have the hours at sea. If Jake screwed up, then they were all in trouble.

What worried Max even more was that he could tell he wasn't the only one who had concerns about the leadership on board. Everywhere he went he heard whispers, gossip, chit chat. He had ignored the captain's request and was not wearing uniform. He viewed that order as meant for the others. It wasn't realistic to expect him to blend in and gauge the mood if he stood out as some kind of policeman, or even a crewman. So the security uniform had been ditched in his cabin, and he was now clad in black jeans, black shirt, and a black leather jacket. In his civvies, he went where passengers congregated. Most of the bars were busy, despite being closed. Groups of people packed around tables, discussing whether or not the world really had ended. He noted with mild interest how like-minded people somehow seemed to congregate. One bar had a particularly high concentration of conspiracy theorists. He sat with them a while, as they talked at length about how the final broadcast had been a hoax, CGI effects and green screen work. They'd convinced themselves that this was part of the cruise experience, that they would soon sail into harbour where their families and loved ones would greet them with cries of "surprise!"

A cafe off Palm Plaza appeared to be the favoured spot for the doom mongers. Generally a bit older than the conspiracy theorists—more middle aged—they were chewing over the depressing details of how exactly everyone was going to die through starvation. That was, if there wasn't an outbreak of some disease first, possibly even an alien space-disease, dispersed by the tail of the asteroid.

The happiest groups had been the older folk, the pensioners. Maybe it was because they had, for the most part, already lived long fulfilling lives that they seemed more carefree. Their main cause of concern was the "young people" and what a shame it was that their lives were going to be cut short. The largest group looked like they were enjoying themselves so much that Max wasn't sure at first if they understood what was happening.

"Oh yes dear, the world has ended. But what can you do?" said one purple haired old lady when he asked her if she knew why they weren't moving, why there were no lights, and why the cafe in which they were sitting was shut. "It's terrible, of course, some of my friends have lost their entire families back home. But I say if we've been granted a few days more, then let's enjoy them! Would you like to join in our card game? We're playing canasta."

Max said that yes, why not, he would play some cards to pass the time of day.

The real concern came later when he wandered into the cinema. It was so dark he tripped over the first row of seats, causing the voices he had heard from outside to stop talking abruptly. When his eyes eventually adjusted to the dark he saw that a group of about twenty people, almost all young men, were seated at the back. Nobody spoke another word until he left. Now the question was how to find out what was going on. It was possible there was an entirely innocent reason for the men to be huddled in a dark room to hold their conversation. Possible, but highly unlikely. Max had a nose for trouble, and this didn't smell good at all.

His first thought was to try and listen from the projection room, which was accessible without going through the cinema's auditorium. That was locked, but Max had a master key that allowed him access to most areas of the ship. He entered quietly, taking care not to fall over any equipment, this time. He'd never been in there before, and had expected to find a huge projector, maybe some reels of film. Being a modern ship, though, the cinema was fitted with state of the art digital projectors. The projection room was really just a control room with a table, a couple of computers, and some servers sat in a rack in the corner. He tip toed to the front where there was a small window that overlooked the auditorium and its impressively wide screen. The window was triple glazed. The whole room had been fully soundproofed. Cursing under his breath, he left the room and found a place where he could sit discreetly, watching the door of the cinema, without drawing attention to himself. He hated stakeouts, but knew what had to be done.

• • •

"So you understand why it has to be done like this, right?" Flynn said.

"I don't know, I still think my way could work."

"Melvin, you're smart, think about what would happen. If you want this to work, you've got one shot at it. By all means start tough, but be realistic about what we can achieve so soon. Rome wasn't built in a day. We must take our time, do this properly or not at all."

"Flynn's right, you should listen to him," a thin man with huge hair added.

"Thank you, Clayton," Flynn said.

"I guess…I need some time to think about this," Melvin said. He stood up and paced around in the aisle between the seats, kicking at the floor.

The other men in the cinema whispered among themselves.

"Sure, take some time, but not too long or we'll miss our best chance. It's getting late. If we leave it too long, there will only be a night watch on the bridge. When we show our hand, it has to be with the captain present." Flynn looked the mobile phone in his hand and smiled. No signal, no surprise. There was no regular service this far north even before the asteroid, only that provided by the ship itself, and the power cut had killed that. He wasn't hoping to make any calls though, he was looking at the picture he'd snapped earlier. The picture that was going to move his plan to the next phase.

In the dim light of the screen, Melvin's lanky frame cast a long shadow over the seats on the other side of the aisle. It made him look even taller than he already was.

"Okay, we'll do it your way," Melvin said.

Flynn smiled to himself. This was going to work out just fine.

Twenty-One

Barry nickelson had an office down on deck two, at the back of the casino. Jake's only dealings with the man had been in the crew bar. The sailing crew, responsible for the operation of the ship itself, and the hotel staff, who looked after passengers and passenger facilities, had little interaction. The crew bar was the one place where these two worlds collided. Barry, being very much a people person, saw it as his personal mission to get all staff on board together as often as possible. This involved organising themed party nights in the crew bar. There was dancing, singing, and plenty of drinking. The parties had been responsible for several romances, and more one night stands than anyone would care to count. Barry, believing in a hands-on management style, somehow managed to do a bit of DJing, as well as serving drinks. It was with little hope of an answer than Jake tapped on his office door.

"Yes?" a voice called from the other side.

Jake pushed it open and walked in. The room was sparsely furnished with a small desk, a chair either side, and a filing cabinet in the corner. It was not what Jake expected. Barry must have sensed that as he watched him look around.

"Jake, my man. How's it going? Huh, not very impressive, is it? If I'd known I'd be receiving the acting captain, I would have decorated!"

"It's fine, yeah, fine." Jake smiled, offered his hand, which seemed to confuse Barry.

"Oh, yeah, okay dude!" He shook the hand vigorously. "So, end of the world. What about that then? And even more amazing, you're the captain now! What happened to Ibsen?"

Jake winced at the mention of the name. "He…he didn't survive. Neither did Johnny Hollen. So you're stuck with me, for now."

"Huh! Get that, that's a shame. I liked Johnny, he was a top man. Ibsen's no great loss though. Sit down dude, sit down. So, what's up? What are we doing?"

The two men took a chair each.

"You have one of the biggest teams on this ship, Barry. Between the bar staff, the casino, the theatre performers and the sports trainers, that's a lot of people you're responsible for. And the thing is, right now, they're all out of work. This ship is on hold, while we figure out what to do. Your team, and the passengers, once everyone starts getting over the shock of what's happened, it's going to be tough to keep everyone happy. There are going to be people with different views on what we should do, and keeping order is going to be more and more important."

"What are we going to do?" Barry's mask slipped, just a bit. His voice betrayed how hard he was fighting to keep it together.

"Until we know otherwise, we assume that the world didn't end just because that broadcast stopped. For all we know, there could be dozens of northern countries, territories and states that survived. But we have to be realistic too. We can't go sailing off, visiting every continent, looking for a safe haven. We all saw what that asteroid could do, it left entire countries flattened. We don't have the fuel to search indefinitely. Anyway, what I'm trying to say is that morale seems to be high right now, because we survived, against the odds. But that feeling is going to fade, and reality is going to bite. I need your team to do what they do best. I need them to entertain, to make people feel good about themselves, to keep them happy. And most of all they need to show that Pelagios Line is still in control. It's not exactly situation normal, but neither is it a lost cause. If we make a show of the fact we are confident and in control, it will help to maintain the peace."

"I don't know, Jake, we got hit hard. A lot of people dead. You can't expect my guys to pick themselves up, dust themselves down, and carry on like nothing happened."

"No, and I'm not saying they should. This isn't about being in denial about what happened. It's about staying positive, saying 'yes, the situation is bad, but we're not going to lay down and die'. It's what my dad would call 'wartime spirit'. This is a critical time. If everything just stops, the passengers will rebel. If we show them that we're not beaten, that we're tackling this thing head on, then they're more likely to follow our lead."

Neither man spoke. Barry's seemed to be weighing up Jake's suggestion. Finally he came to a decision.

"I guess it's worth a try. What's the worst that can happen, right?"

"Right. I think. Can you brief your team?"

"Yes, but I think it would be better coming from you, dude."

Jake had no intention of speaking to more people than he had to. All he really wanted to do was get back to the bridge and delegate everything via the telephone. On the other hand, shouldn't he practice what he was preaching? Lead by example?

"I'd love to, but I can't, not straight away. I have too much to do as it is. Besides, I don't have your charisma, Barry. Nobody can motivate a group like you can."

"You're such a creep. But I understand. I'll get on it."

"Thanks, Barry. Now, two more things. Firstly, can you join me in the temporary morgue in the morning? There are a number of unknowns down there, some of them will be crew. I need help identifying them. Let's say oh-seven hundred hours?"

Barry pulled a face.

"You know nearly everyone who works on this ship. If there was anyone else, I would ask," Jake pleaded.

"Okay. But I might have a few drinks first, to help me get through it."

"All food and drink is rationed."

"Not my personal supply, and I'm not telling where it's hidden!"

"Fair enough. But I'll find out later. Now, one other thing, have you seen Tania Bloom anywhere?"

"Tania? No, not for days. But if I do, I'll ask her to go see you."

Jake got up to leave, and as he did so there was a jolt, a noise like a huge washing machine spinning up, and a vibration. With a flicker, the lights in the office came on."

• • •

The screen popped to life and Lucya let out a sigh of relief. In front of her were a disarray of pages, scribbled notes, folded navigational charts, and a couple of reference books. Finding the nearest and most northerly permanently inhabited settlement had been easy. Calculating the course taking into account currents, the shifting ice, and the maximum fuel efficiency had taken some doing. She was reasonably happy with her results, but seeing a computer resurrect itself filled her with joy. She grabbed the topmost page of scribbles, and the biggest chart, and put them down next to the navigation terminal. There was still a bit of time left before Jake and the others were due back, and she wanted to make absolutely sure her calculations were correct.

No sooner had her fingers alighted on the keyboard, than there was a bang at the door.

"Who is it?" she called without looking up.

"We want to see the captain," came the response.

"Who's 'we'?"

"We represent those who have not been given a voice."

Lucya stopped what she was doing, stood up slowly, and walked very quietly to the door. It was locked, but there was an extra security bar that was supposed to be used in case of piracy attacks or terrorism. As gently as she could, she slid the bar into place.

Three more bangs.

"We demand to speak with the captain, now. We aren't going anywhere until that happens."

"The captain isn't here."

"Bullshit."

"If he were here, he would probably be telling you to leave. Most likely in stronger terms than that. You're wasting your time. He's not here."

"Then we'll wait."

"Shit," Lucya muttered to herself. "Shit, shit, shit. Where are you when I need you, Max?"

She briefly considered calling for Jake over the PA, but dismissed the idea quickly. Those outside would hear the call and would be waiting for him. She didn't know what they had in mind when they got to see the captain, but from their tone she was sure it wouldn't be good.

She looked around the bridge, making sure that she was safe. The broken windows had been covered up with high strength plastic sheeting by a team from engineering. The hatch for the fire escape was bolted shut from the inside. There was no possibility of using it, it couldn't be locked from the outside, and leaving it open would compromise the bridge. Nobody could get in. The only problem was that she couldn't get out. She picked up the telephone and started calling round the heads of departments.

• • •

As he was already down on deck two, Jake figured he should make the effort to go down one more flight of stairs and congratulate Martin on getting the generator going again. He walked into the engine room to see a group of three engineers, high-fiving each other.

"Captain on deck!" one of them shouted upon spotting him.

"Yes, yes, you can dispense with all that. So, the generator's going? That's excellent news, well done."

"It was harder than we thought, that ash had fused together in the confined space, and when it cooled it went rock hard. We had to chisel some of it out, and even now there's some still in there, but we made good time," a short tubby man in greasy overalls said, beaming. Jake thought that he couldn't possibly have got into the funnel himself, but didn't say anything.

"Make sure Martin lets you guys get some rest soon, you've earned it."

"Taking over down here too, are you?" Martin appeared from behind a mass of pipes.

"No, of course not, Martin. Just saying what a great job you and your team have done. What about the engine, is she ready to start?"

"I'd like to run some diagnostics before we do that," Martin said. "She's probably fine, but we need to check the cooling intake. She'll need the preheaters on too, with the generator out for so long, she'll be cold. When we start her up it will have to be done gently. I hope you're not expecting a fast getaway."

"Far from it. Take all the time you need, as long as we can move tomorrow morning."

Martin nodded, and disappeared back the way he had come.

"So," Jake said looking around, "I don't suppose any of you chaps have seen Tania Bloom around have you?"

Three heads shook in unison.

Twenty-Two

Max slipped back down the corridor. He'd followed the men without being seen, heard their demand at the door to the bridge. He knew he shouldn't have listened to Jake, should have kept the rifle handy. He wondered if he could pull the same trick as earlier and use the bridge fire escape to go and get it back. The trouble was that pesky Russian girl was in there. She went all doe eyed every time the captain was around, probably wouldn't stand for him using a gun when lover boy had asked him not to. No, the captain wanted things sorted out by peaceful means, so the captain could sort them out himself. He just had to find him.

• • •

"He was here, but that was a while ago, I haven't seen him since."

"Okay, thanks, Martin."

Lucya sank into her chair. She'd called everyone she could think of, and every time she'd either just missed him, or he hadn't been there at all.

Three bangs at the door.

"We're still here. If you've been lying to us and the captain is in there, there's going to be trouble."

"I am trying to locate the captain!" Lucya was losing patience with these people. "If you are not happy about that, then perhaps you should return to your cabins and have a lie down!"

• • •

Max called on various areas of the ship and was met with the same responses Lucya had encountered.

"You've just missed him."

"Haven't seen him."

"Wouldn't know what he looked like if I had seen him!"

He decided all he could do was wait until twenty two hundred hours, when everyone was due to reconvene on the bridge. If he waited further up the corridor, he had a chance of intercepting Jake before he got there, and could at least warn him there may be trouble ahead. In the meantime, he fancied a cigarette. Now the power was back on he couldn't risk smoking inside, the detectors would probably start blaring out their horrible high pitched squawk. He pushed open a door and stepped out onto the deck thirteen stern terrace.

"Well now, isn't that just grand," he said. "I spend half an hour looking all over for you, and here you are, taking it easy outside."

"Hey, Max. what's up? I was taking five minutes quiet time before going down to the bridge."

"Right. About that. You're not going to get much quiet time on the bridge, there's a horde of angry passengers waiting for you."

"What? Who let them in?"

"No, no, not on the bridge. But they're in the corridor, waiting to ambush you when you arrive. I followed them up from a little meeting they held in the cinema. I can't be sure, but I'd say mutiny is on the cards."

Jake laughed. Max didn't look impressed.

"Mutiny? Really? Have you been watching too many films, Max?"

"This isn't a laughing matter. We knew this was a possibility, and now it's happening."

"Well then we'd better go and see what they want," Jake said, and strode off towards the door.

Twenty-Three

"Gentlemen," jake said as he approached the group camped out in front of the bridge entrance. "Oh, and lady, excuse me."

There were twelve of them in all, eleven men and a woman. All were in their late twenties or early thirties. Only one was standing, and he appeared to be the ringleader, because the others all looked to him for a response when Jake spoke.

"I am Melvin Sherwood, and I am the representative for the unrepresented, the voice of the unheard, spokesperson for the silent majority."

"I think that means he's in charge of this rabble," Max said loudly.

"A pleasure to meet you, Mr Sherwood. I'm Jake Noah, captain of the ship." Jake offered a hand, but it was ignored.

"What happened to Captain Ibsen?"

"Shall we discuss this inside?" he indicated the door.

"Jake, I don't think that's a good idea," Max said. "Shall I disperse this crowd so we can get on with business?"

"Nonsense. Sorry, Mr Sherwood, this is Max Mooting, he's head of security."

Max raised his eyes to the ceiling. So much for keeping a discreet eye on goings on. Sherwood didn't quite know what to say, the wind had been taken out of his sails. He'd come expecting confrontation, prepared for a fight, and was met with a young captain acting very reasonably. But it was early days, he thought. The captain hadn't heard their demands yet.

"Lucya, could you open the door, please," Jake called.

There was a clunk, the noise of sliding metal, the click of a lock, and the door swung open.

"Please, let's go inside."

The group scrambled to their feet and rushed onto the bridge. Sherwood joined them, followed by Jake and Max, who closed the door behind them, but left it unbolted.

"I'm afraid we don't have seating for everyone," Jake said looking around at the sparsely furnished control room. "We're not used to having such large groups up here. So, if you don't mind standing? Now, how can I help? What's this all about?"

Once again the assembled passengers looked to Melvin as their spokesperson. He glanced around at the expectant group, and began his barely rehearsed pitch.

"In the last twelve hours this ship has not moved. We have been told that food and water are to be rationed with immediate effect. We have spent most of the day without power or light, and no effort has been made to inform us why."

"That's not true!" Lucya interjected.

Jake held up a hand. "Lucya, please, let him continue."

"We all saw the television report of the asteroid, we all have friends and families, back home. We need to go back, to see what has happened to them. We cannot sit here and wait to die. Passengers outnumber staff by two to one, yet these decisions have been made without the involvement of any passengers. The minority are deciding for the majority. This cannot continue. We are here to take over control of the ship. I will assume the role of captain, and your staff will answer to me."

"I see," Jake said. "You understand, of course, that our priority since the asteroid passed over has been to save lives by making the ship safe, and by preserving our resources? You are quite right, passengers' views should be taken into consideration going forward," Jake winced as he heard himself use the phrase, he had always hated management speak. "Am I to assume you have been elected to the position of spokesperson by a majority of passengers?"

"You're not listening to me, Mr Noah. This isn't about taking our views into consideration. This is about redistributing authority. We're taking over. You're done here. This ship is going home."

Max took a step towards Sherwood, but Jake glared at him to back off.

"Mr Sherwood, this ship is the property of Pelagios Line until evidence says otherwise. Myself and my crew are employees of Pelagios Line, and are responsible for the safety of the Spirit of Arcadia and her passengers, our customers. Who knows, perhaps the world has ended and there is no more Pelagios Line, or shareholders, or indeed anyone else, but until someone can prove that to me, nothing has changed. I'm willing to listen to the views of passengers through a properly elected spokesperson, which it seems, as you ignored my question, you are not. Now, if that is all, I have a lot to discuss with my crew, so if you'd like to return to the public areas of the ship?"

"We thought you might react this way," Sherwood said, a nasty grin spreading across his face. "So we came prepared. We aren't taking no for an answer." He turned to look at the woman in the group, nodded to her. She fished a mobile phone from her pocket, passed it to Melvin. He pushed a button, slid a finger across the screen, held it out for Jake to see.

"No!" Jake said. "Where is she? What have you done with Tania?"

• • •

Tania Bloom opened her eyes and looked around as best she could. Her hands and feet were bound, her knees were pressed against her chest and more binding held them in place. A woman's scarf had been folded and tied in a gag over her mouth. Not that anyone would hear her scream if she tried. Not up here in one of the luxury suites; they were soundproofed.

She was shut in a wardrobe. Not many people would have been able to recognise the precise wardrobe if they were in the same position, but Tania knew every cabin and every suite on board like the back of her hand. She was a hands-on kind of manager, and regularly inspected the work of her housekeeping team. Her spot-checks were legendary. She had the ability to find dust in places no human should ever have to look. Even now, bound and gagged in the bottom of a cupboard, she couldn't help but notice a cobweb between the back wall and the hanging rail.

• • •

"I said, what have you done with Tania?" Jake repeated.

"She's safe. Well, as safe as you can be when you're tied up. She's with the passengers now. It's an equitable swap. We've taken one of your senior staff, you get to take a passenger. That would be me. Like I said, I'm taking charge."

"You're doing no such thing, son," Max said. In two giant paces he was behind Sherwood, clamping the young man's hands in his own.

"Tell your ogre to unhand me."

"Tell us where Tania is," Jake said.

"This is very simple," said Sherwood. "My people are holding Mrs Bloom. They are under strict instructions that if they don't get confirmation I'm in charge by ten thirty, they are to kill her. Then they will abduct another of your crew members, and we'll start again. Now, unhand me."

"You animal!" Lucya spat the words in his face. "You piece of shit!"

Three of the rebel passengers surrounded her, restraining her hands. She kicked and screamed until they forced her to the ground.

"She can't be far, we'll search the entire ship if we have to, but we'll find her." Jake's mind was racing while he spoke.

"Really? You've got about forty five minutes to do it. Of course, you would have had longer, but you kept us waiting out there. That's less than five minutes per deck. Think you can find her in time?"

"Max, let him go."

"What? You're not going to listen to this jumped up little idiot are you?"

"Tania's life could be at stake."

"You think he's going to let her go? Come on, think about it.

You give him what he wants, he can't let her go, he knows what we'll do to him afterwards," he glared at Sherwood as he spoke.

"Your ogre isn't as stupid as he looks," Sherwood said. "We have no intention of letting her go. Like I said, an equitable exchange. She becomes a passenger, I become crew. Well, captain. Unless you refuse, in which case she becomes polar bear food. Did the polar bears survive, do you think?"

"I can't relinquish control of this vessel. Maybe we can come to some sort of compromise."

"Oh for goodness sake, have you gone insane?" Max propped himself up against a console, his forehead in his hand.

Melvin said nothing. He was thinking hard. So far everything was happening exactly like Flynn had said it would. Now he had to decide. He wanted to hold out, to force their hand, to take charge of the ship. But Flynn had been adamant; they would never let him take control, he'd said, it was out of the question. They would take the risk of losing Tania and lock down the ship, they would have emergency procedures for that. He had to play the long game, to get a foot in the door. That was the true purpose of the mission. But he couldn't be seen to give in too easily.

"The passengers have a right to be heard," Sherwood said coolly.

"And I agree with you," Jake said. "But this isn't the way to go about it. There is a chain of command, procedure to follow. I cannot hand over control to a passenger. But I could appoint a passenger representative to join the senior officers when we are making any important decisions."

"Not just for meetings. There should be a passenger representative on the bridge at all times. Overseeing the operation of the ship, with the power to veto any decision."

"Okay, we could have a passenger here all the time, but no power of veto. There are international rules and regulations that must be respected. The captain has the final say," Sherwood was shaking his head, Jake continued regardless, "but the passenger representative will have an equal voice among the senior crew."

"We can quit saying passenger representative, that will be me.

And when I am not on the bridge, it will be one of my deputies." He looked at his fellow passengers, three of whom were still restraining Lucya.

"You haven't been elected. There are nearly two thousand passengers on this ship. How many have given their support for this?" Jake raised an eyebrow.

"We don't have time to ask them all. But I have many supporters."

"Alright. You get a seat on the bridge. But we're going to be holding a census tomorrow. We can ask the passengers to vote for a representative at the same time."

Melvin hadn't anticipated this, and he wasn't sure how to react. He certainly couldn't take the risk of any kind of election, not yet. He needed to prove himself first. He decided to stay on the attack, it had worked quite well so far.

"Yes, there should be an election," he said. "But it will be for captain of the ship. We set sail tomorrow, we return to port to find out what has happened. If, as the television suggests, the asteroid has destroyed everything, then Pelagios Line is no longer the owner of this ship, and the rules no longer apply, right?"

"That would be the case, yes," Jake agreed.

"So I will be the representative until we know what has happened. And then, we will hold an election to see who will be the captain. These are my terms. You now have about forty minutes, but it shouldn't take that long to decide."

Jake considered the proposition. It seemed fair. The passengers did deserve a say in what happened. And if, as he was sure would be the case, they turned out to be the only survivors of the asteroid, then an election would be the perfect opportunity to stand down, He hadn't asked to be captain, didn't want to be captain, and certainly didn't want to be leader of the last human settlement on earth.

"Then we have an agreement," Jake said. "But I need to see evidence that Tania is untied and being treated properly."

Max banged his head against the console. "This is a really bad idea," he groaned.

"Now please release my radio officer, and tell me how we get your message to those holding Tania."

Melvin nodded to his supporters on the floor, who helped Lucya to her feet then stepped back in with the others behind their leader.

"There must be an announcement from the captain that we will set sail tomorrow morning."

"I can't promise that, I don't know if the engine will be ready by then."

"You'd better hope it will be, because if you don't put out that call in the next thirty five minutes, chomp chomp."

Jake sighed, walked over to a console, picked up a handset, and flipped up a button marked PA.

• • •

The wardrobe door opened and light streamed in, blinding Tania. Two pairs of hands grabbed her and pulled her roughly from the confines of her prison and onto the cabin floor.

"Congratulations," a voice above her said. "You just got promoted to passenger."

TWENTY-FOUR

"I DON'T UNDERSTAND, Flynn, how is this good news? Not only are you not in charge, you're not even the guy on the bridge?"

"You stupid woman, haven't you listened to anything I've said?"

"Yes! I thought you were sending those boys to take over, to organise some kind of mutiny," Eileen backed away from her husband, his red face a sure sign she was making him angry.

"But they were never going to be put in charge. This is my foot in the door. Now we have a spy on the bridge, someone who can judge the lay of the land. Someone who can plant the seeds of doubt in the crew. While we work on the passengers, Melvin will work the crew. Softly softly, Eileen."

"But if the captain is deposed—"

"When, Eileen. When the captain is deposed," Flynn cut in.

"Sorry, Flynn. When the captain is deposed, won't Melvin take over?"

"Melvin has a more important role to play than he knows. But trust me when I say that he will never run this ship."

Twenty-Five

There was a knock at the door to the bridge. Max opened it, letting Martin and Grau in.

"Did we miss something?" Martin asked. "Who were that lot we passed on their way out?"

"Nobody important," Max grunted.

Melvin cleared his throat, loudly. "I wouldn't say that. Sorry, we haven't been introduced. I'm Melvin Sherwood, representative of the passengers."

Grau cast a glance in Jake's direction, then reached out to shake the new man's hand.

"Grau Lister, doctor. Chief medical officer. Pleased to meet you."

Melvin shook his hand limply, then looked at Martin.

"Oakley, Martin. Chief engineer."

The two men shook hands briefly. Lucya watched the scene, tutted loudly, and walked off to her communications console.

"So, shall we?" Jake said. He led the group over to the map table, now cleared of charts. "Lucya, can you join us?"

"Just checking the radios, be there in thirty seconds."

There was another knock at the door. Max sighed and went to open it.

"How many more are we expecting?" he called back over his shoulder.

"Two. Silvia, of course, and Claude Dupont," Jake said.

"Oh Jesus, why the hell did you invite him?" Martin looked aghast.

"If we don't want to die of starvation or malnutrition, we need to keep Claude on side. And anyway, he's not so bad. If anyone can keep that kitchen in order and enforce strict rationing, Claude can."

"He's French, how do we know he won't go on strike?" Lucya asked, pulling a face.

"By including him in these meetings. Hi, Claude, thanks for coming. Hi, Silvia"

They joined the group at the table.

"Claude, I think you know everyone except Melvin Sherwood, he's here to represent the passengers on board."

"Who cares what the passengers think about anything? Will you be inviting some penguins up 'ere too? Perhaps the polar bears would like representation?"

"Claude, you know how important it is to listen to everyone's view. Liberté, égalité, all that?"

"Hmmph," Claude gave a shrug. He looked around, found a stool, and sat down.

"Silvia Brook, hotel director," Silvia said offering a hand to Melvin. He shook it while looking down his nose at her.

"How's the leg, Grau?" Jake looked sympathetically at the doctor.

"Much improved, yes, thank you. Kiera patched it up for me, and some painkillers and a little rest have helped."

Lucya stood up from her post, shook her head, and wandered over to the map table. Jake looked at her and raised an eyebrow enquiringly.

"No, nothing. Static on all channels. All the satellite feeds are dead, nothing on the shortwave. I still can't even find any working navigation beacons. It's like the world outside just disappeared."

"Would you say," Melvin piped up, "that it is therefore likely that Pelagios Line has bitten the dust and that this ship is no longer the property of anyone or any organisation?"

"Now now, let's not jump to any conclusions," Jake said, trying to keep the peace.

"Actually, Mr Sherwood, no I wouldn't say that," Lucya fixed him with a stern look. "There could be many reasons for radio silence, including loss of power."

"Okay, we discussed all this last time," Jake wanted to move things forward. "We'll go round the table quickly. Martin, good job on getting the generator going. When do you think we can start the engine?"

"The guys are running their final checks now, but they're going to have to stop for some rest before long. Cleaning out that funnel took it out of them. We can probably start winding her up slowly around nine hundred hours."

"Right, that means we can start moving in the morning, as I promised in the last PA call." He looked pointedly at Melvin as he spoke.

"Grau, things calmed down in medical?"

"Yes, for sure. There is just the problem of the unknowns we talked about."

"Right. Barry and I will join you down in the temporary morgue in the morning, to try and identify any crew. Melvin, I need you to come too, you'll need to photograph all of the deceased for our records."

"I'm not your lackey!" Melvin looked shocked.

"No, you're the passenger representative. You need to pull your weight just like every other department head here. I would have asked the head of housekeeping to perform the task, but she is unfortunately not available, for the time being."

Melvin snarled, but said nothing. Lucya smiled, and studied the nails of her left hand.

"Max, anything I need to know about?"

"There was, but the problem has reached a conclusion," Max was staring at Melvin.

"So, Lucya, where are we headed tomorrow?"

"I've plotted a course for Longyearbyen in Svalbard. It's the most northerly permanent settlement that we can reach with the least fuel. Technically speaking, Barentsburg is nearer, and we'll have to almost go past it, but it's difficult to access, we can't dock there."

"Svalbard? What use is that? We need to head for Portsmouth, or New York, and see what's happened to the civilised world!" Melvin said.

"We couldn't reach either without taking on more fuel," Lucya said flatly. "And as we don't know if there is anywhere left where we can get fuel, it would not be prudent to set off on such a pointless voyage. If we go to Longyearbyen, we can assess the state of the place, and possibly find fuel there."

"Whoa, I thought we were just repositioning, not actually going anywhere?" Martin said.

"We were. But now we're not. Plans have changed," Jake replied. He knew that was coming.

"So you take over the ship, then let the passengers run the show? Bloody marvellous, I've heard it all now." Martin walked away from the table and slumped into the chair at Lucya's radio console.

Jake ignored him, looked back to Lucya to continue.

"Longyearbyen has diesel reserves that they use for their own vehicles, mostly snowmobiles. If, and it is a big if, the town and its fuel are still there, then we can consider exploring further."

"How much fuel, if it's still there?" Jake asked.

"Next to nothing by the standards of what this ship consumes. But there's an airport, three kilometres from the town. This is Martin's area, but I'm hoping we could use aircraft fuel, as well as the diesel?"

Martin looked up, he couldn't help but be interested in the technical aspect of the plan.

"Kerosene burns hotter than diesel," he said. "We'd need to put in some kind of additive, or make some adjustments to the engines." He rubbed his chin absent-mindedly. "But if we mixed it with the diesel we're already carrying, it could work. The more diesel we could find though, the less chance of damaging the engines."

"This sounds excellent, good work Lucya. How long will it take us to get there?" Jake asked.

"Going slow for better efficiency, it will be about fifteen hours sailing time, but it could be more. I tried to factor in currents, but they are really a guess. The harbour is tiny, but it can take us—just.

It will be some tricky manoeuvring. Normally they would supply a pilot, but…well…you know."

Jake nodded. He understood perfectly. "Claude, how's the menu going?"

"It is not easy, this job that you 'ave given me. But, I rise to the challenge. With a small breakfast, a modest lunch and dinner, we can feed everyone for twenty two days. Provided we can keep the freezers running for another week."

"Great work, Claude. People will already be hungry, we haven't served food all day," Jake said. Everyone around the table agreed heartily. "I'll put out a call announcing breakfast service will start at six hundred hours. You can organise some breakfasts for then?"

"My boys will work through the night."

"I'll also announce the passenger manifest. We need to organise it quickly, issue people with meal vouchers at the same time."

This drew some blank expressions around the table, so Jake filled in all present on his plans for a census, disguised as a passenger manifest, and the reasons why. Melvin protested at the whole idea, calling it a "deception of the highest order", but was summarily overruled by all present, much to Lucya's delight.

"So returning to the meal arrangements, you will divide the passengers between the restaurants, of course?" Claude said. "We should have a list in each restaurant, cross their names off when they have eaten, so they do not take more than their fair share."

"Yes, yes you're right. Another good reason to get the census and manifest done quickly," Jake agreed. "Silvia, can you join me on the bridge for breakfast? I'll need your team to go door to door."

"Of course, I'll be there for six."

"Great, so I think we have covered everything then. I will make those calls, then take first watch on the bridge. It's now twenty two thirty. Lucya, you can replace me at oh-two thirty, in the meantime, get some sleep. All of you try and get some sleep, tomorrow is going to be a very long day."

The group slowly disbanded. Martin and Claude both ignored Jake's call for sleep and went back to work. Lucya, Silvia and Grau headed for their cabins and some much needed rest. Melvin went to find his cronies to nominate someone to take his place on the bridge for the night shift.

Max remained on the bridge, something on his mind. Jake took to the PA to announce that food service would resume with breakfast, and that a census would take place the next day.

"Max, are you not going to catch forty winks?"

"I'm concerned about the security situation on this ship. I didn't want to talk openly in front of the others, particularly Sherwood."

"What's on your mind?"

"Given all that has happened today, people have been remarkably calm. Probably a mixture of shock and grief. But that's not going to last. Sherwood is just the tip of the iceberg, a taster of what is to come. If we hit land tomorrow and…and everything is gone, then reality is going to set in. There could be mass panic. Probably more suicides, although that's no bad thing."

"I'm sorry?" Jake said. "How can suicide not be a bad thing?"

"From a security point of view, it means fewer people to keep in line. Every jumper is one less person to keep an eye on."

Jake sighed. "I'm really glad I don't live in your head, Max. So what are you saying? That we're going to be dealing with kidnappings and mutinies on a regular basis?"

"Yes, that's more or less it. I get your softly softly approach, we're the good guys and all that. But it's not going to work if we discover the worst. The dynamic will change. As long as there's hope, then the passengers are passengers—customers. We're here to protect and serve them. They paid to be here, we are in their employ. When that changes, we will become the enemy, repressors, prison guards."

"I meant what I said to Melvin, you know. If that happens, if home is gone and we are all that's left, then there should absolutely be an election. Every passenger will have the chance to stand, to take charge. People can't argue with a democratic process."

"Jesus. Do you even watch the news, Jake?"

"Well an elected captain will have a certain amount of authority. Obviously you can't please everyone."

"We're getting away from the point here."

"Which is?"

"Which is that before the shit hits the fan, we must beef up our security effort. Amazing as I am, there is a limit to what I can do with a team of one. I'm the head of security, and I have one guy."

"Ah. So this is a recruitment campaign? You want staff?"

"I need a team of people. People who are loyal to the company, to me. To you," he added quickly.

"Anyone in mind?"

"Some of the sailors are ex-military boys, Navy, know how to handle themselves, and can handle a weapon."

"Ex-military, Max. Ex. We're not creating a new army here, I don't intend to see gun toting sailors prowling the decks. You're worried about people panicking, that's a great way to start a panic. No guns."

"Not now, maybe. But I need people who can cope if things turn ugly."

"How many?"

"At least twelve. There should be a security presence on every deck. Twelve new guys plus Reeve, and I could cover each deck."

"Okay, why not. You make some good points. And it will keep the sailors busy and out of trouble."

"Good. I'll get on it then."

"That's all?"

"Yes, that was all. Good night then, captain."

"Good night, Max. Remember, not an army," he called after him. But Max was already halfway out of the door.

Jake was alone once again. He settled into the captain's chair and looked out to sea.

Twenty-Six

THE NIGHT PASSED by uneventfully. Melvin returned after about half an hour and informed Jake that his replacement would arrive by oh-two thirty. Jake smiled to himself when he heard that. He didn't know if Melvin was trying to avoid a shift on the bridge alone with Lucya, or if he wanted to be around while Jake was in charge. Either way, he couldn't help but be amused.

The replacement turned up as promised. It was the only woman from the group of passengers that had been on the bridge earlier, an American by the name of Stacey Martel. She was a larger lady, in her late twenties, Jake guessed, and dressed for all the world as if she were on a Caribbean cruise rather than one visiting the Arctic. Her pink flowery top, bright green shorts and orange flip-flops certainly brightened up the bridge. Stacey made no real effort to talk to Jake, who had to wait around for an extra quarter of an hour, as Lucya was late. He didn't mind, he'd already had some sleep during the day, she needed rest more than him.

Lucya and Stacey didn't exchange a word the entire time they were alone. Lucya spent most of her watch scanning the radio waves for signs of life, but nothing had changed, she heard only static. The passenger representative simply sat and stared into space, presumably only there to make sure no decisions were being made without Melvin's input. Within an hour she had fallen asleep, and didn't wake again until Jake returned to the bridge just before oh-six hundred hours.

"Morning, Lucya. Oh, sorry, Stacey, did I wake you?"

"Morning, Captain," Lucya said. "Did you get some sleep?"

"Yes, thank you. All quiet? Anything to report?

"Radios remain dead. Nothing to report, ship-wise. No calls,

I've not heard from the others. I imagine everyone has been catching up on some rest."

"Let's hope so, they're going to need it."

Stacey pulled herself to her feet and stretched, still silent. She watched as Jake wandered over to the console, picked up the telephone and dialled a short number.

"Good morning, Claude, I hope you haven't been up the whole night? Good. Are we set for a breakfast service? Thank you, Claude, you are amazing, I knew I could count on you. I'll send someone down to collect something for the bridge if that's okay? Thanks, I'll catch up with you later." He replaced the handset. "Lucya, would you mind bringing up four breakfasts?"

"Sure, no problem. I could do with stretching my legs."

As Lucya left, Melvin returned.

"Stacey, situation report?" he said.

"Nothing to report. It was a quiet night. The captain has ordered breakfast for us."

"Oh, sorry Stacey, not for you. I've ordered for the bridge crew. You'll need to get to one of the restaurants if you want to eat."

She glared at him, looked to Melvin, but he simply nodded. She rolled her eyes and left the two of them alone. Jake picked up the PA and spoke quietly into it.

"Good morning, ladies and gentlemen, this is Captain Jake Noah. The restaurants are now serving breakfast. Service will continue for one hour. There will be lunch and dinner services later today. We are hoping to set sail sometime this morning, and the crew will keep you up to date with our progress. Thank you for your patience and cooperation at this difficult time." He set down the receiver, picked up the telephone, and dialled another number. "Morning, Martin, didn't wake you I hope? Okay, sorry, only joking. How is the engine situation looking? Excellent, that's really excellent news. I'll wait to hear from you then."

"I take it that means we will be able to move today?" Melvin asked.

"Yes, it sounds like it. Martin's team worked through the night and they are going to start the engines in an hour or so. Another hour of running tests and we should be good to move off."

There was a knock at the door. Jake opened it to Silvia, and spotted Lucya not far behind, carrying a tray of food.

"Morning Silvia."

"Good morning, Captain."

"I suggest we take breakfast while working out the details of this passenger manifest business."

"I don't care what we do, as long as we eat while we're doing it," Lucya said. "I feel like I haven't eaten in a week."

Lucya set down the tray on the table, and the four of them dug in to meagre rations of cereal, bread and jam, and orange juice.

"Claude's using up the fresh milk with the cereal. He's using it in all of today's meals so he can switch off one of the big refrigerators," Lucya said.

Jake opened a drawer and pulled out some Spirit of Arcadia headed writing paper and a couple of pens. He handed one to Silvia and kept one for himself.

"So, the manifest," he said.

"I thought it was a census?"

"It is, but we're going to stick with calling it a manifest. I just think it's less confrontational and controversial that way."

"Have you got something to hide from the passengers?" Melvin asked.

"Not at all. I just think that if we call it a census then people are going to automatically think that we're planning for the worst. That this is it, life stuck on this ship for who knows how long."

"But that's the case. You are planning for that. That's the whole point of the census, as I understand it. Lying about what you are doing isn't the right way to go about this. If you want cooperation from people, you'd better start being honest with them. I say we call it a census."

"Silvia? What do you think?" Jake was trying to ignore Lucya's grimaces.

"I think Mr Sherwood has a point. Just because we are seen to be preparing for the worst, doesn't mean we expect it."

"Right, I see. I'm outnumbered then."

"Er, no you're not," Lucya chipped in. "I say we call it a manifest. And what about the others? Don't they get a say?"

"We haven't got time," Jake said. "We need to get this done. Okay, we'll call it what it is. The advantage is that we can ask more questions. So, a list of the questions. Bearing in mind this needs to be done quickly, we mustn't get carried away. Obviously we need full name, date of birth, and occupation."

"Date of birth?" Melvin looked skeptical. "Intrusive, isn't it?"

"If we have to put people to work, then knowing their age is important. We can't be assigning heavy lifting jobs to pensioners. We may also need to think about education for the children. Speaking of which, nationality and country of residence should be noted too."

Melvin nodded.

"Useful skills," Silvia said. "We may as well come out and say it. If there are people on board with useful skills, we need to know. We could dress it up as hobbies or interests, but nobody ever tells the truth about those, they make stuff up that makes them sound interesting or intelligent."

"Alright, that's enough to be going on with. So how do we deal with this, I mean, logistically?" Jake scratched his head, the thought of trying to canvass nearly three thousand people in a day was a lot to cope with so early, and on such a light breakfast.

"We send people to their cabins between lunch and dinner services," Lucya said. "Passengers and crew. The only people with good reason to be out of their cabin should be people like the engineers, some of the sailors, obviously the bridge staff. And then we do all the decks simultaneously. Get it over with quickly."

"I'm assuming the housekeeping team will be the best for the job? They go to every cabin every day anyway," Jake addressed the question at Silvia, and couldn't help but think back to the photograph of Tania, tied up and gagged. Melvin had assured him that she was now being treated properly, but he still couldn't help wondering if that was true.

"Yes, they're all twiddling their thumbs now. But for them it will be more or less like a regular day, pop into each cabin, but ask questions instead of clean. They should easily get the job done in the afternoon."

"Keeping passengers locked up all afternoon is a bit much," Melvin looked agitated. "Why not let them out once they've done their questionnaire?"

"Because having people wandering around the ship mid-census will cause confusion," Jake said. "And those who get processed last are not going to be happy about waiting the longest while others are free to go wherever."

"Why even put them in their cabins? Why not issue questionnaires during a meal service, have people hand them back when they're done?"

"Because I don't want families inventing children they don't have, in order to get extra meal rations. No, every person who goes on the list must be seen, in person, by a crew member."

"You have a lot of faith in your crew Mr Noah," Melvin snarled. "How do you know they won't invent passengers to claim extra meals for themselves?"

"I don't, I have to trust them. But I would point out they are already trusted to clean your cabin every day without stealing your belongings."

"That's different, the rules have changed. This is about life or death now."

"Forgive me," Silvia cut in. "If I'm not mistaken, the passenger manifest didn't actually get destroyed, did it? That was just going to be a cover story, before we agreed not to dress this census up as something else."

"That's right. But we still need to update it so we know who survived. Right now we don't know how many are on the ship, and how many jumped," Jake didn't know why he felt he was on the defensive, Silvia was on his side.

"I understand. But if we have a passenger list, then the crew doing the census can't invent new passengers, can they? Because we have the means to find out."

"In that case, neither can the passengers," Melvin said. "So why don't we just hand out questionnaires like I suggested?"

"Because," Silvia said, "the housekeeping team can issue meal passes on the spot. They visit a cabin, do the questions, issue the pass, job done. If we leave questionnaires in the restaurant, someone has to process them afterwards, then find the passengers to hand out the passes. It really is easier this way. Speaking of the passes, Jake, how do we do those?"

"We've got working computers and printers, right?"

"Yes."

"So we print up numbered passes on headed paper. Issue them to your team, they hand them out to passengers and note the numbers on the completed questionnaires. Then we make up lists for each restaurant, to divide the passengers and crew between them. When a passenger claims a meal, they show their pass, and their number is checked against the list."

"Claude won't like it, it's a lot of extra work for his people, but yes, it sounds like it should work. I think we'll have to have two sittings for each meal, we can't fit everyone in in one go."

"Why the emphasis on passengers?" Melvin asked. "What about crew, they're subject to rations too, right?"

"Of course," Jake said. Melvin was annoying him. "Crew eat in the crew cafe."

The four of them worked out a few final details about how crew members doing the census would themselves be canvassed, as well as other staff who wouldn't be able to return to their cabins. When they were happy that the plan was good, Silvia left to start work on printing up questionnaires and meal passes, and to organise her team. Jake put out another PA call informing everyone aboard that there was to be a census. He emphasised that it was mainly to help plan the food rationing. Everyone was to be in their cabin by fourteen thirty, and once the operation was complete, which was expected to be before the evening meal service at twenty hundred hours, an announcement would be made.

Twenty-Seven

Seven o'clock rolled around quickly. Jake had been trying not to think of what lay ahead, but there was no putting it off now.

"Melvin, ready?"

Melvin looked up, wearing a confused expression.

"Morgue," Jake said. "It's time to go and photograph the dead and identify those we can."

Melvin said nothing, but followed Jake to the door. Lucya came over to join them, her face a picture of sympathy. She rested her hand on Jake's arm.

"Will you be okay?" she asked.

"I have to be."

"It will be over quickly, and then we'll be getting ready to sail."

"I'm not sure which I'm looking forward to the least," Jake said. He turned and left, Melvin a few steps behind.

The temporary morgue had been set up on deck one, below the water line. It was a large storage area that could be configured for a variety of uses. It most often served for holding extra food, but that was something it would never do again, not now that it had accommodated human corpses.

Jake and Melvin found Grau and Barry, waiting for them outside. Jake introduced Melvin to the entertainment manager, and then nobody quite knew what to say. There was an awkward, protracted silence, in which each waited for another to lead off. In the end Jake realised that as captain, he was probably meant to take charge.

"Well, shall we?" he moved to open the heavy steel door.

"Jake," Grau put a hand on the door to stop him. "Are you ready for this? It's not an easy thing to do, you know."

"I know, let's just get it over and done with."

"Before we go in, you should probably put these on." Grau fished around in the large pocket of his white coat and produced four sterile masks of the sort used in medical procedures. "They won't do much, but they're better than nothing."

The four men covered their faces with the masks in silence. Jake pushed open the door and they stepped inside.

He hadn't really known what to expect, he just knew it would be cold, and possibly a bit creepy. The fact he was wearing a mask alerted him to the idea it might smell, but he wasn't prepared for the overwhelming odour of death. It wasn't so much the smell of rotting flesh; the low temperature was keeping the bodies in reasonable condition. It was the burning smell that took him by surprise. Corpses that smelt like steaks, overdone on the barbecue.

"Jesus," Melvin managed to say. Nobody else spoke.

There were more than two hundred bodies, neatly lined up in four rows on the floor. Each one was draped in a white bed sheet. The room was lit by fluorescent tubes, and even though the place was supposed to be sealed, flies buzzed around the lights and the covered corpses.

Barry noticed that some of the sheets had sticky notes stuck to them with tape. He walked over to the nearest and read the note.

"Beverly Stracken, Ohio. P. ID by Barry Stracken, husband."

"P?" Barry asked.

"Passenger," Grau replied. "All the information on the stickies is also recorded in a log book. We've got about eighty bodies still unidentified, but we've done much better than we thought. A lot of passengers have come forward to say they've not seen friends they made in the first days of the cruise. And a lot of the staff have been down here too, looking for friends and colleagues."

"Those you've identified, you've photographed them, just in case? You know, any mistakes, or people lying about who they are?"

"Yes, all done."

"So we have to photograph the others, and hope Barry and myself might be able to identify some."

"Yes, but I warn you that it will be difficult," Grau didn't seem to know how to phrase what he was about to say, he was clearly struggling with the words. "Of those who remain nameless, many are too…damaged…by the ash. Their faces are no longer…intact."

"I see," Jake said, and wished he didn't have to.

"Do we split up, take a row each?" Barry asked.

"No, you and I both need to see every unidentified corpse, we have a better chance of recognising them, that way. Melvin, you can take the pictures," Jake said.

Grau handed a camera to Sherwood and showed him briefly how to operate it. The four men walked over to the first unlabelled sheet.

"Ready?" Grau asked.

The three others nodded. Grau crouched down and slowly pulled back the cover. Melvin immediately vomited, just managing to turn away from the charred and blackened head quickly enough to avoid defacing it any further with the contents of his stomach.

"Shit, sorry," he said, sniffing, and wiping his mouth with the back of the mask he had pulled off just in time.

"Don't worry," Grau said, "we will clean that up later."

Melvin took a deep breath, held it in, lined up the camera and pressed the shutter. Barry and Jake looked at each other, shaking their heads.

"Sorry, Grau," Jake said. "No idea."

The doctor replaced the sheet, and the group moved on to the next body in silence.

At the third body, Barry gasped. The face was twisted and contorted, burnt in an expression of pain.

"I know this one. Her name is Sarah. Sarah Grennan."

He knelt down next to her, a tear running down his cheek.

"She worked in the theatre. She was a stage hand, but wanted to be on stage, acting. She had talent, but we didn't have any positions for her to fill. This was her first cruise. I was sure we'd get her performing before long. She was 18. So young, so full of promise, and hope."

"I'm sorry, Barry, truly I am," Jake said. He noted the name on a pad of sticky notes that Grau had given him, labelled it "C" for crew, and recorded the fact Barry had identified her. Melvin snapped a photo, Grau carefully replaced the sheet, and Jake attached the note.

It took them over an hour to work their way up and down the four long rows. Jake recognised several seamen, as well as one of Lucya's deputy navigators. Barry proved the most useful, identifying eighteen of his staff. Six worked in the theatre, backstage. Eight worked in the bars and shops, and the rest were from the casino. With every positive identification, Barry wept, silently.

After they had looked at the last unmarked corpse, Grau marched them back to the door. Jake noticed that he avoided passing in front of the last two bodies in the final row. He had no doubt that they were Ibsen and Hollen.

"Thank you, gentlemen, I know that wasn't easy," Grau said once they were back outside. "I'd recommend going outside, for some fresh air, before doing anything else. The smell of death… well, it can hang around, stick in your nose."

Jake was thinking. "There are too many. We can't hold a memorial service for all of them at once. It will take too long, and logistically, we can't bring up over two hundred bodies on deck."

"Do the bodies have to be present? Can't we just hold a service for the dead? All those who perished back home and here on the ship? We could do that in the theatre," Barry said.

"We still have to dispose of the bodies," Grau looked worried. "Keeping them in there for much longer will present a health risk. You saw the flies."

"We'll have to send them overboard from the tender platform," Jake said.

Melvin grimaced, but said nothing.

"It's only one deck up, it will be more manageable. We'll hold a service, tell the survivors that the deceased will receive a burial at sea, but we wont give any more information than that. Nobody needs to know the details. Grau, can you organise moving the bodies?"

"I can try, but there are only three of us in medical, and we are stretched as it is."

"I can find you some men to help," Barry chipped in. "Some of the bigger guys are used to heaving beer barrels and the like."

"Bodies aren't beer barrels. Are you sure they'll be okay with this?" Jake wasn't convinced.

"Don't worry, dude, I won't ask just anyone. I've got a few people in mind, they'll be discreet. I'll send them down to you, doc?"

Grau nodded.

"I'll make the announcement then. Memorial service in the theatre in an hour," Jake said. "See you guys later."

Jake and Melvin headed back to the bridge as Barry wandered off somewhat in a daze. Grau returned to the cold store to clear up the mess on the floor.

Twenty-Eight

The theatre was busy, but nowhere near as packed as it had been the previous day. A service to remember the dead wasn't as big a draw as watching the apocalypse, streamed live via satellite. The atmosphere was decidedly different too. The tense disbelief of twenty four hours ago had given way to resignation, but not quite despair. Those present talked in hushed whispers, as if the dead would somehow hear anything louder and be angry that it showed a lack of respect.

An elderly man in a black cassock took to the stage. He wore small round glasses, but no religious symbols of any kind. A lectern had been placed at the front of the stage, complete with microphone. The minister approached and tapped it twice, sending muffled booming noises around the auditorium before clearing his throat.

"Ladies, gentlemen, children, we have come together today, to celebrate the lives of those no longer with us."

Someone in the front row burst into tears. Behind her, a child giggled, nervously.

The minster spoke for ten minutes, trying to cover all bases, all religious beliefs, as well as getting in a word for any atheists and those who might be on the fence about the whole matter. He managed to fill the time with words, yet without saying anything of any consequence. When it was over, nobody seemed quite sure if they should say "Amen", or give a round of applause. So they did neither, and the minister shuffled off, back to wherever it was he had come from.

"That was…weird," a woman at the back said to the person next to her.

"Yes. Maybe it helped some people. Gave them closure."

"Hard to have closure without a burial."

"True. You know what's really weird though?"

"What's that?"

"The captain. I mean, where is he? He announced this service, but he didn't show his face. You'd think he could make the effort to honour those who died on his ship."

Twenty-Nine

The phone rang. Jake had been dozing off, the sound jolted him awake. He looked at his watch, ten thirty. He looked over at Melvin expecting him to say something about sleeping on the job, but the man was slumped in a chair and snoring softly. He picked up the phone.

"Bridge."

"Jake? Martin. We're about to start the engines."

"That's...that's really good news."

"Yeah, whatever. Listen, there will probably be some vibration while we wind her up. Thought I'd better let you know in case anyone thinks the world's ending, again."

"Right, got it. Is there anything you need me to do? Can I help?"

"Nope, we've got it."

A click, and the line went dead.

Jake looked around for Lucya, but she was nowhere to be seen. The idea of getting the ship underway sent a shiver of excitement through him. It was important not to get one's hopes up, that he knew, but now the prospect of moving was imminent he couldn't help himself.

There was a dull thud, Jake felt it through is feet more than he heard it. It was followed a few seconds later by another, then another. Then the vibrations started. Very low frequency at first, and very faint. Concentric circles formed on the surface of the unfinished orange juice in one of the glasses on the table.

"What's happening?" Melvin was awake. He had gone as white as the icebergs outside.

"They're starting the engines. The vibrations are normal."

Jake picked up the handset on his console and his finger reached for the PA button. Another hand pushed it away.

"No," Melvin said. "Let me do it."

"What?"

"I'm here to represent the passengers, but nobody knows that. So we'll kill two birds with one stone. I'll announce the good news."

"Oh I see, hero to the people?"

Melvin ignored him and grabbed the handset.

"How does this work anyway?"

"Speak into it like a telephone. Press this button to talk."

Melvin took a deep breath. The colour was rapidly returning to his cheeks.

"Hello, this is, er, Melvin Sherwood. I am on the bridge representing the passengers on board. I bring you good news. The vibrations you are probably feeling, are those created by the engines which are being restarted. We will shortly be leaving, returning to the land, to find out what has really happened in the world."

Jake rolled his eyes, mouthed at Melvin: "Not shortly, at least another hour!"

Melvin turned away from him.

"We don't know what we will find, and there are undoubtedly difficult times ahead, but I believe that together we will survive..."

Jake flicked off the PA button, silencing the system.

"What? Why did you do that? I hadn't finished!"

"Yes, you had. This isn't the time for any 'I have a dream' speeches, save those for later, when the going really does get tough."

The vibrations had continued to grow in intensity, their frequency increasing too. The consoles on the bridge began to rattle alarmingly. Jake wondered if he should call down to the engine room, but thought better of it. Martin would take it badly, and besides, if there was a problem, the engineers were better off dealing with it than answering phone calls.

There was a knock at the door.

"Max, good morning, how are you?"

"Good, very good. It's been a productive morning."

He walked in and slapped down a sheet of paper on the map table. Jake picked it up and scanned it quickly.

"Ah, I take it this is your new security force?"

"Right. I talked to those ex-army guys and told them the plan and they were up for it before I finished explaining. I had more interest than I needed, so I got to pick the best of the bunch."

"Whoa, whoa, whoa!" Melvin came over, clearly annoyed. "What security force? What plan? You've been plotting behind my back! This isn't what we agreed!"

"Calm down, son," Max said. "You disappeared off this bridge last night, it's not our fault that you didn't stay around to hear what I had to say."

Melvin was turning purple with rage. "You waited for me to leave! The meeting was over. Anything like this should have been discussed openly. You obviously didn't want me involved. Well guess what? I am involved. If you're putting together a security team then you need passenger involvement."

"Now, listen here young man—" Max started.

"Don't 'young man' me, you patronising old tosser."

"Gentlemen, please!" Jake held up his hands, stepped between the two men, who were getting dangerously close. "Let's keep this civil. Max, you probably should have brought this up at the meeting, but I understand your reasons for preferring not to. Melvin, you did leave before Max, you took the chance that something would happen without you being here. So let's all calm down here, okay?"

"I'll calm down when I get passengers as part of the security team," Melvin banged his fist on the table.

"The problem with that idea is Pelagios Line is liable for this ship and its passengers. Having employees take responsibility for security is one thing, we have insurance if anything goes wrong. We can't start handing out that kind of responsibility to passengers, especially with no training."

"Come on, Mr Noah, you know as well as I do that your insurance means shit now. And as for training, your crew aren't trained security agents."

"Actually, the sailors joining my team are all ex-army or navy. They've all got a level of expertise in dealing with difficult situations," Max said, folding his arms across his chest.

"Well, there you go then. I know at least one passenger who's ex-army. He'll be as well trained as any of your lot."

Jake said nothing for a moment, lost in thought.

"Jake, you can't seriously be considering this?" Max looked shocked.

"We've already got a non-crew member on the bridge," Jake said, and began pacing around the table. "There is a certain logic to including non-crew in your team. Arguably it's more important than having Melvin up here. Passengers in the security team would be more visible. It would show we're being inclusive."

"Passengers? How many are we talking here?" Max asked.

"I want one per deck, minimum," Melvin said.

"No way!" Max shouted. "We only have one sailor per deck."

"Perfect, so that will even things out nicely." Melvin grinned triumphantly.

"No," Jake said. "You can have one passenger on the security team. You nominate someone and Max interviews them."

Melvin started to protest, but Jake cut him off.

"It's Max's team, he decides. That's final."

"And when we strike land and see that the company is finished, that you're not employed by anyone? That we're no longer crew and passengers, we're all just survivors?"

"Then we can take another look at the situation," Jake said.

Melvin considered the offer. He walked over to the main console, picked up the handset and pressed the PA button.

"Stacey Martel to the bridge."

Jake and Max looked at each other, surprised.

"You're nominating Stacey for the job?" Jake asked.

"Don't be ridiculous. Stacey's a nice girl, but you've seen the size of her, the only way she could keep the peace is if she sat on someone. I called her up here to keep an eye on you two while I go and find my guy. Make sure you don't plot anything else without me knowing."

"Hey, listen," Jake said suddenly. "You hear that?"

"What?" Max jumped, looked around on high alert, terrified that there was some kind of threat and he had missed it.

"Exactly! It's gone quiet. The engines…the engines are running smoothly."

• • •

Lucya stepped back from the bench and admired her handy work. She was in a store room, down in the bowels of the ship, not far from the engine room. Three of the four walls were lined with metal shelving, the sort often found in warehouses. Every shelf was filled with grey plastic crates bearing the Pelagios Line logo. They were labelled with descriptions such as "flares" and "life jackets". There were several holes where crates should have been. These missing boxes were lying open on the bench in the middle of the room, next to Lucya's creation. Their labels read "beacon spares", "TX equipment", "batteries", and "silicone".

The vibrations from the huge engines starting up had made this delicate operation much more difficult than it should have been. Lucya would have preferred to wait for things to settle down, but she would be missed on the bridge, and she didn't want to bother Jake with what she was doing. There was no point getting his hopes up, it was probably never going to be useful anyway.

She closed up all but one of the crates and put them back on the shelves, then cleared away a soldering iron, solder, and various lengths of wire and some unused connectors. All that remained was a bright orange buoy, a little larger than a football. A flap had been cut into the side. She peered through it and looked at the modified search and rescue transmitter now installed inside. A flashing green LED told her it was working. She put her hand in her pocket and pulled out a piece of folded paper that had been sealed inside a plastic bag, and placed it inside the buoy with the electronics. Finally she closed the flap, took the silicone gun and squeezed the trigger, forcing out a long thin trail of sticky substance with which she sealed the plastic.

Lucya put the silicone gun back in its crate, and then lowered the crate under the bench. She slid it into place alongside the four other buoys she had already prepared but not yet sealed.

A speaker in the corridor outside crackled into life.

"All bridge officers report to the bridge, all bridge officers to the bridge."

"Perfect timing," Lucya said to herself in Russian. She grabbed the ring at the top of now closed buoy, lifted it from the table, and left the room.

Thirty

"Stacey, this is Dave Whitehall, he's our navigation officer. He reports to Lucya, and will be helping make sure we stay on course. And over there is Pedro Sol. He's our lookout and, because we have a reduced bridge crew, is also our helmsman. He steers the ship and makes sure we don't hit anything. Today, I'll be getting us underway and then Pedro will take over." Jake said.

"It doesn't seem like a lot of people to drive such a big ship. Why is the bridge so large if there are so few people?"

"That's mainly because it has to span the width of the vessel so that we have a good visual lookout all around. Nowadays the computers do the driving, as you call it. We're really just here to make sure nothing goes wrong."

Stacey nodded. "So Pedro won't be driving for long, the computer will take over? Like an autopilot on a plane?"

"Actually, no, not today. The computers use GPS, but it seems from our readings that the asteroid took out some of the GPS satellites. If it had hit just a few we'd be okay, but we're not able to get a proper fix on our position so we can't risk it, except for the most basic stuff. We'll get underway manually, and once we're on the right heading, the computer will keep us pointing in the right direction. When it comes to knowing when to change heading, and by how much, we're going to do this the old fashioned way. Dead reckoning, some celestial navigation, and once we get closer to land, we can use the radar to help out. That is if Lucya and Dave can remember how to use that antique equipment they've got out over there." He pointed to the map table upon which were sat charts, compasses, a sextant, and a pile of navigation books. "

"Hey, this was state of the art once!" Lucya called back.

The phone nearest Jake rang, he picked it up.

"Bridge."

"Anchors are up, sir," came the voice on the other end of the line.

"Thank you." He replaced the handset.

"Well then," Jake drew a deep breath, "let's get this ship turned round and get out of here."

He stepped up to a control console near the middle of the bridge, flipped some switches, and took hold of a small joystick. As first officer, he rarely got to pilot the ship anymore, and he felt a thrill as, with the deft movement of fingers, he sensed the vibration of the engines powering up, and the gigantic bulk of the vessel start to move under his control. Turning around a ship of this size was not a rapid operation, and Stacey's excitement at seeing how the bridge operated soon turned to boredom as the slow pace of the manoeuvres became clear. She retired to a chair near a window, and settled in, hoping Melvin would be back soon so that she could go and do something more interesting.

• • •

"So, this is your guy? Older than I was expecting," Max said, looking the man in front of him up and down. He was in his mid fifties, had an unusually red face, and was just the wrong side of average weight. What Max's ex-wife would have called "comfortably rounded".

"Flynn is ex-army. I know most of your men are ex-navy types, but I think Flynn is just what you're looking for," Melvin was trying to sell it, and wasn't entirely sure why. Flynn had been helpful in getting him onto the bridge, his planning had been meticulous and his instincts spot on. Even so, Melvin didn't feel he owed him anything. Yet there was something compelling about the guy. He had the sort of personality that made you feel like you'd known him forever, that he was looking out for you, that you could trust him. Melvin thought that was a good trait, and wished he shared some of that charisma and instant likability; it would be useful when it came to elections, when he would need to beat Jake in being the people's choice to run the ship.

"And is he able to speak for himself?" Max raised his eyebrows.

"Yes, Mr Mooting, sir." Flynn said.

"No need to call me sir; not yet, at least. So, what's your background? What makes you think you'd be useful on my security team?"

"I was in the United States Army for eighteen years. Led fifty men into battle on three separate campaigns, only lost two men in all."

"Why did you quit? And how?"

"Honourable discharge. I felt I had done my duty by my country. It was time for me to move on and put my time into my own projects"

"What sort of projects? What do you do now? Apart from cruising the Arctic I mean."

"Personal…" he paused, unsure how much he should say, "… building projects."

"Ah, home renovation? Yeah, I can understand why you'd need time for that. Do you keep yourself in shape, Mr Bakeman? Do you think you can keep up with my guys?"

"Absolutely. I run at least three miles a day. I've been in the gym every day we've been on the ship, until yesterday of course."

"I see," Max said. He was starting to think that maybe this wasn't such a bad idea after all. Having an outsider on the team might help keep his own men honest. "And tell me, how do you see the role of security officer?"

"First and foremost, to keep the peace. To offer protection and reassurance to everyone on the ship."

"Protection from what?"

"Mainly from themselves."

That did it; Max was impressed. "Well, Mr Bakeman, it looks like you got yourself a new job. Welcome aboard, metaphorically speaking." He shook Flynn's hand enthusiastically.

Flynn smiled at Melvin, giving him a quick wink when he was sure Max wasn't looking.

• • •

Progress was painfully slow. Although the Spirit of Arcadia was now facing away from the icebergs and heading south, a quick look behind through a rear facing window showed just how far they had not come.

Melvin returned to the bridge. Stacey tried to introduce him to Dave and Pedro, but she'd already forgotten their names so she simply said that they were involved in "the driving". With her task out of the way she disappeared quickly, hoping to be first in the queue for the lunchtime service.

Melvin toured the bridge as if he were invigilating an exam. Hands clasped behind his back, taking large quiet strides, he made his way up and down in front of each row of consoles, peering over. He paid particular attention to the map table, and asked a number of questions of Dave. Lucya was all too happy to let her subordinate do the talking. As far as she was concerned the less time she spent around Melvin, the better.

Silvia appeared at lunchtime. With the help of one of her staff she brought up trays of food for the crew. Claude and his team had managed to whip up salt cod and potatoes cooked in milk. It was rich and delicious but, like breakfast, the serving could have been bigger. The bridge crew ate mostly in silence, everyone too involved in their jobs to talk about anything else. Lucya and Dave worked away at calculations, constantly updating their assumed position on the chart. Pedro had taken the helm and was steering a steady course through a flat calm sea. Jake oversaw the operation, checking in with each post regularly. This was his day job and he felt at ease here. Although he was working, it was a true rest from the responsibilities of captain. He longed for things to go back to how they were before. The job wasn't so bad, he told himself. One last cruise and he would have been free to go to Africa. Now though, even once he was done being temporary captain, he realised he was probably going to be required on the bridge indefinitely, given he was the best qualified and most experienced officer of the watch on board.

A ringing telephone broke his train of thought. He answered it, casually.

"Bridge."

"Jake? Martin. We may have a problem."

"What kind of problem?" Lucya and Melvin both looked up. Jake cursed to himself, he knew he should have spoken more quietly.

"Fuel. We're keeping an eye on it, and the rate of consumption is higher than we anticipated."

"By much?"

"Not a lot, but over twelve hours or so it's going to make a difference."

"Are we talking never going anywhere else ever again difference, or won't be able to keep as many lights on difference?"

We're probably going to have reserves for one less full day's cruising than we thought." Martin couldn't hide the disappointment from his voice, and there was something else there too. Shame, Jake realised. He was ashamed they'd got the calculations wrong.

"Okay, keep an eye on it and keep me appraised." He hung up the phone, saw all eyes were on him. "Nothing to worry about, just Martin being extra cautious." The bad news could wait until later, he had a feeling there was going to be more of it when they saw land.

Another phone rang. Lucya answered it, spoke a few words, and hung up. "That was Claude, they finished serving lunch half an hour ago. The restaurants have emptied everyone out, sent them back to their cabins, closed up."

"Right then, time to call curfew," Jake announced.

THIRTY-ONE

LARISSA KNOCKED AT the door to cabin 854. She carried a wide bag over her left shoulder, and a folder under her right arm. The arm was aching from writing, and she decided that whoever was inside 854 was going to fill in the form themselves.

There was a click of a bolt turning, and the door opened inwards.

"About bloody time," the man inside said.

Larissa closed her eyes for a second, told herself to remain calm. "Good afternoon, I'm Larissa, I'm here to complete the passenger census."

"Well get a bloody move on will you. We've been stuck in this cabin for four bloody hours. Just as this ship starts to go somewhere, we're stuck in here."

"Give it a rest, Ken," a woman's voice called from inside. "The poor girl has probably had just as long an afternoon."

Larissa walked into the cabin. It was one of the larger ones, a full suite. She was standing in the sitting room. Opposite her was a huge balcony with a spectacular view of the ocean. There was a plush sofa and two arm chairs, arranged around a low mahogany coffee table. Larissa had polished that table on many occasions, it seemed strange for her to be here in another capacity.

"Do sit down, dear, and I apologise for my husband. It's not as if he can't appreciate the view from here."

"Thank you. This won't take long, there are only a few questions."

The three of them sat down, Ken taking the sofa. Larissa opened the thick file she had been carrying and split the papers inside into two piles. One pile, slightly dog-eared and untidy, went back into the folder. The other pile comprised blank sheets. She peeled off the top two sheets and handed one each to the couple. From the shoulder bag she produced two black ballpoint pens which she set down on the table.

"I need you to fill in your full names, dates of birth, nationality, country of residence, and occupation, all in the boxes as shown. Underneath, please fill in any skills you may have, and anything else you think might be useful to the community if," even after repeating the instructions countless times throughout the afternoon, she still found herself hesitating at this point, "if this community is all that survives of mankind and we have to start over."

"Don't you worry, dear, we're on the move again, look!" The woman pointed to the balcony and the ocean beyond. "The captain says we're going to find a safe harbour."

"Oh, Tracy, you know as well as I do that's just lip service. We're heading for land alright, and when we get there we're going to see what everyone knows full well; that the bloody asteroid has destroyed everything."

Tracy blinked away tears. "I don't believe it, Ken. I won't believe it."

"Um, if you could just fill out the forms?" Larissa was growing impatient. She had seen this same scene played out in countless cabins. In nearly every family or couple she had visited, most were in denial. Most couldn't accept the fact the world had ended, that this was all that was left. The "community" question promoted the same argument, time after time. She just wanted this to be over.

For a few minutes the only sounds were the scratching of pens on paper, and the sound of water crashing against the side of the ship, clearly audible through the open balcony door.

"Well, I don't think I have anything to offer in the way of skills," Ken was sitting back sucking on the end of his pen.

"You're pretty good at painting and decorating," Tracy said.

"That's hardly a skill, is it? Anyone can do a bit of painting and decorating. I think they're looking more for carpenters, stone masons, people who can build a town."

"Actually, painting and decorating would be great. If you've done any of that, please, write it down." Larissa wanted to scream out to put anything down, just hurry up and finish.

Ken scrawled a few words, considered what he had written, and handed back the page.

"What are you writing? You haven't got that many skills!" Ken snorted at his wife.

"I have many hidden talents, Kenneth. Mind you, not as many as you. Like being able to pay for a luxury suite on a cruise liner on a teacher's salary."

"Yes, well, we're not here to talk about that."

"Sorry, teacher?" Larissa's ears pricked up. "Could you list the subjects you teach? That would be very useful." She handed back the paper and pen.

Ken sighed heavily, and started writing once more. Tracy handed her page to Larissa, who scanned through it quickly, then folded over the bottom and tore it off carefully. She rifled through the folder and extracted a page on which were written a long list of numbers. One of the numbers corresponded to that on the slip of paper she had torn off. Against it, she wrote "Tracy Frampton".

"This is your meal ration voucher," she handed the paper back to Tracy. "You've been assigned to the Nautilus restaurant for your meals, second sitting. You'll need to present the voucher at each service. Please don't lose it, no voucher means no meal."

"My mum used to tell me stories about rationing during the war," Tracy looked wistful. "I never thought I'd experience it first-hand."

Ken finished his list and handed back his page. Larissa repeated the same exercise, returning his voucher to him.

"Second sitting, pah!" He didn't look impressed. "So we get the leftovers. Probably cold ones, at that."

"Everyone gets the same rations, Mr Frampton, there's no preferential treatment for the first sitting, I can assure you." Larissa got to her feet. "Thank you for your time. If you could remain in your cabin until an announcement is made, it will make our job much easier."

"So we don't have to stay? We're free to leave?" Ken jumped to his feet.

"I can't force you to stay here, but it really will make things go a lot quicker if you do."

Larissa went to let herself out. At the door, she took one last look at the plush suite. A thought ran through her head. If they were all doomed to live on this ship because the planet was scorched, why should people like Ken get to live in such luxury? He'd paid for a cruise, for sure. But what gave him the right to stay here, in this room, in another week's time, when the cruise was supposed to have finished? And another week after that? And after that? What right did anyone have to any particular accommodation any more, if they were now a "community" of survivors?

THIRTY-TWO

"THIS IS THE captain. I would like to personally thank everyone on board for their cooperation during the census this afternoon. The survey has been completed, and you are free to leave your cabins. Dinner service first sitting will be beginning shortly. Thank you."

Jake replaced the handset and walked over to Lucya's station. She was deep in discussion with Dave, both intensively studying a chart.

"How long until we see land?" Jake asked.

Lucya looked up. "I think we should already be able to see something. Dave thinks I'm wrong."

"If you're not wrong, then why can't we see anything?"

"Because I think we're in the wrong place."

Jake looked confused. Lucya put her hand on his back and steered him round the table to better see the map.

"Look, I think we should be here. In which case, we should be able to see that," she pointed at the land mass. "But we can't. So we're not where we should be."

"Not where we should be if we go by our original calculations," Dave interjected. "But my point is that those calculations are no longer valid. Which means we can't base our position on them. So we are where we should be, we just don't know where we should be!"

"Right now I'm utterly confused," Jake said scratching his head. "What's wrong with the calculations?"

"May I?" Dave looked questioningly at Lucya.

She shrugged her shoulders. "Sure, why not? It's your theory, you explain it."

"When Lucya calculated the route, she took into account the currents. Standard practice, they either carry the ship along or they push against us slowing us up."

"Yes, thank you for the navigation one-oh-one, David. Even I remember that much!" Jake looked put out.

"Sorry, of course. But I think the currents have changed. I don't know how, but it seems like the asteroid changed something. Maybe the heat, or the quantity of ash falling on the ocean, I'm not a scientist, I'm really out of my depth here. But I'm sure the currents changed, and if I'm right then our calculations are void. We're either not as far along on our course as we think, which would explain why we can't see a big chunk of land anywhere on the horizon, or…"

"Or…?"

"Or we're totally off course altogether. We'll know in another fifteen minutes when we can take some more accurate bearings. But gut feeling? I'd say we're on course, just running behind."

"How do you know the currents have changed?" Jake asked suddenly, the question popping into his head.

Dave blushed. "Because our fuel consumption is worse than expected."

Jake looked around, wanted to make sure nobody else was listening. Pedro was busy keeping lookout, and Melvin was falling asleep in his chair.

"How did you know that? I didn't talk to anyone but Martin about that!"

"I've got a mate down in engineering. He called to ask if I knew why we were burning fuel so quickly. He said Martin did the calculations and he never gets them wrong. So I thought about it, and this is the only thing that makes sense."

"Any way to know for sure?"

"Not while we're moving. We could come to a full stop and drop some measuring equipment over the side, but as we'll know in the next quarter of an hour anyway, that idea seems redundant."

Jake sighed. "Okay, well keep me posted. As soon as there's anything new, I want to know."

"You'll see it at the same time as us," Lucya said. "If Dave's right, you'll see a big lump of land out that window quite soon."

• • •

Fifteen minutes later there was a loud "whoop!" from the navigation station. Jake looked over to see Dave beaming from ear to ear.

"Report?"

"Sir, I was right, sir!" came the reply.

Lucya's face was thunderous. "I can confirm we are on course and should see land within the next few minutes."

Jake stood up and walked over to the front facing floor to ceiling window that ran the length of the bridge. He picked up a pair of binoculars and slowly adjusted them, bringing the horizon into sharp focus. It was a grey blur. No sign of land. No sign of ash, either. It turned out the fears of floating ash islands had been without basis. They had passed some patches of the stuff, thin layers floating on the surface like seaweed, or the islands of plastic garbage that they often saw in the Pacific. But it hadn't coalesced into rocks, or if it had, those rocks had sunk without a trace.

"Land ahead!" Pedro called.

Jake adjusted his binoculars again. He still couldn't see anything, just a mass of grey. Were his eyes getting old? Could he trust his own vision? He was beginning to wonder when, right on the horizon, part of the grey appeared to thicken, and then solidify. As he watched, it began to take shape, to form into something with real mass. There was no doubt about it, there really was land ahead.

He walked over to the communications console where he swapped the binoculars for a headset. A thin microphone grew out of the right hand earpiece and curled round under his nose. He pressed a button marked "Channel 7".

"This is Max."

"Max, it's Jake. We're seeing land ahead. You'd better brief your men, people are going to get excited when they see this. Who knows how they'll react or what they'll do."

"Okay, thanks for the heads up."

"Max, how's your new lad doing?"

"Flynn? Yeah, he seems to be a good man. Committed. Good with people."

"Can you assign him to deck ten? Or do you have specific plans for him?"

"Sherwood wants him floating about all over the place, but honestly that's just a pain. I can stick him on ten. Why?"

"Just thinking if there are any more passenger revolts, having a cone patrolling around here might help."

"You expecting trouble?"

"I don't know. I just think that when they see land, a lot of people are going to want to try and get off…"

"No problem, I'll station him on ten. Any sign of trouble I'll call you on the radio."

Jake pulled off the headset and set it down carefully.

Over at the navigation station, Lucya and Dave were busily working the radar, fine tuning the course.

"How are we doing, time wise?" Jake asked.

"Another hour or so and we will pull level with Spitsbergen island." Lucya didn't look up from the radar as she spoke. "Then, we slow down. It's rocky out there, we can't take chances. We have to circumnavigate Spitsbergen and Prince Charles Foreland, then sail up the Isfjorden. We're lucky, at this time of year there will be a lot less ice around, but Pedro is still going to have his work cut out."

A knock at the door, and Silvia entered with more trays of food. The crew settled down to eat, Pedro and Jake taking turns to keep a lookout, and Lucya and Dave alternately manning the radar. By the time everyone had finished their dinner, land was very clearly visible on the port side. Jake tried to get a better look with his binoculars, but the rocky archipelago was so desolate and inhospitable that is was impossible to tell if it was covered in asteroid ash, or was an untouched snowy wasteland.

"I think it's time to get some rest. Lucya, you can take first watch. You're in command, I'll replace you at oh-three hundred hours. Dave, you're taking a break, get some sleep. Pedro?"

"Yes, Captain?"

"Can you find someone to take over from you? I need you rested and alert when we enter the fjord."

"Of course, Captain."

"Be back here at oh-three hundred. Melvin, you organise yourself and Stacy however you want."

Jake looked around at his reduced crew. They were holding up well, all things considered. He himself felt dead on his feet, and he knew the others must be equally exhausted; more so, even. But none of them complained. Even Melvin had held his tongue for most of the afternoon.

He walked slowly back to his cabin, passing Captain Ibsen's quarters on the way. Lucya has asked him why he hadn't moved in there, but after what had happened in those rooms, he had no desire ever to return to them. And anyway, with four or five hours of sleep a night, any cabin was more than adequate for his needs. He kicked off his shoes, undressed, and fell into bed. He was asleep within seconds.

Thirty-Three

Flynn bakeman was wandering the corridors of deck ten. He couldn't have been happier to have been stationed near the bridge. Max hadn't given him any specifics about why he'd been moved up here, but he could guess. Any passenger action would target the bridge. Flynn was in exactly the right place to assist any such approach.

A group of passengers were headed towards him, talking among themselves excitedly. They were two young couples and three children, two girls and a boy. The children were chasing each other round the legs of their parents, the adults didn't seem to mind. One of the women spotted Flynn and hurried over. He'd been issued with a crew jacket, complete with a badge that labelled him as security.

"Hey there, how you doing, honey?" the woman spoke to Flynn as if she'd know him for years.

"Just fine thank you, just fine. And what can I do for you fine people?"

By now the rest of the group had joined them.

"We were all wondering, like, we saw the land outside." She pointed vaguely in the direction of the exterior, although in this windowless passageway it wasn't easy to be sure of one's bearings. "So, are we, like, going to be stopping any time soon? Because we love the cruise ship and all, but we would really like to get off soon."

"Ah, well. Now, I'm not supposed to tell you this, but only a few people are getting off when we get to where we're going."

"Where are we going? Nobody has told us anything about that!" one of the men in the group asked, indignantly.

"Well, again, I'm not supposed to say. I'm not even supposed to know. I don't work for the cruise line you see, I'm a regular passenger like you, just helping out because they need my expertise and experience. But I figure everyone has a right to know what's going on, so I'm going to tell you good people anyway."

The small group looked surprised at this news, and nodded, conspiratorially.

"Okay, well, we're going to Svalbard."

The blank looks told Flynn he needed to elaborate.

"It's an archipelago, a group of islands. It's really just rock and ice, and a few abandoned mines. There's nothing there."

"Well what the hell are we doing going to a place like that?" someone cried. "We need to be going home!"

"I agree, honestly I do. But between you and me, the captain? He's not up to the job. The regular captain didn't make it, got killed by that dust cloud. Even the second in command is gone. So we're left with this kid running the show. He's done exams and crap like that, but he don't know shit about running a cruise ship. 'Scuse me," he added. The children giggled.

"We need to do something," one the men said. He had remained silent until then.

"Hell yeah, you can't have a kid in charge in a crisis!" said the other man.

"Oh, don't worry, we are doing something," Flynn said, seriously. "Once we dock, and we see what's out there—which, by the way, is probably nothing at all—then we're going to have the captain replaced."

"Who's 'we'?"

"The Passenger Alliance. We're a group of passengers who aren't happy about the way this ship has been run these last two days. We've had some success already. We got our top man in there on the bridge, keeping an eye on what's going on. And, honestly, if you knew some of what he's seen? Incompetence on a scale you wouldn't believe."

"Oh, hey, we heard him speak before, didn't we honey?"

"That's right. Melvin someone? But how's that going to help? He sounds like he's just a spy."

"He's much more than that," Flynn grinned. "We have a personal assurance from the captain that there will be an election to choose someone new to run this ship. I mean, we all have a right to decide, right? We all have to live on this ship, so we should be able to choose a leader."

"Damn right!" one of the men said. The women glared at him, but said nothing.

"So when the election comes, and it will be soon, I can count on you guys to vote for Melvin?"

"Er, I dunno." One couple still didn't look convinced. "How do we know he'll be any better? I mean, this kid captain, at least he's got some training. That's gotta be worth something, right?"

"Yeah, but Melvin's got experience. He's managed big teams of people around the world. He's worked in disaster zones, he's been flown in to organise rescue teams and clean-up operations after natural disasters. He might not have fancy certificates and all that, but he's got experience. He can lead us out of this mess, take us home. Keep us safe."

"Well he's got my vote, honey," the first woman said, and the others nodded, although not with any degree if enthusiasm.

"You're making a wise choice. Melvin is our man. Tell others too! It's hard for me, you know, they made me wear this uniform, trying to turn me into one of them. People, they don't always like to talk to the crew. See? Just another way they are manipulating and controlling us. So tell your friends; there is an election coming, and Melvin is our man."

THIRTY-FOUR

THE SECOND NIGHT aboard Spirit of Arcadia following the asteroid was as quiet as the first, for the bridge crew. Jake was woken by his alarm at 2:45am, and made it back to the bridge just on time. Lucya disappeared off for some well earned sleep. Dave and Pedro returned to their posts too. The ship had slowed considerably as it navigated the perilous waters around Prince Charles Foreland. Lucya had made the call that they shouldn't arrive at the fjord too early, it would be safer to make the last part of the voyage during the day. Not for the added light, this far north and at this time of year it was light virtually twenty four hours a day. It was more to do with having a slightly bigger crew on hand. Going slower overnight was a cautious move, but the right one, Jake agreed.

Lucya returned at eight in the morning, just as Silvia brought up breakfast for everyone.

"Silvia, you're an angel," Jake said. "But you must have more important things to do than wait on the bridge crew?"

"Apart from collating the results of the census, I don't have a lot to worry about. With the water rations, we can't clean the cabins, so the housekeeping team are redundant. The bars and cafes are all closed, and Claude is managing the restaurants in the way only Claude can."

"What's Barry up to? I haven't seen him since yesterday morning." Jake felt a pang of guilt that he hadn't caught up with some of the senior staff in twenty four hours.

"Barry is being amazing," Silvia said with a twinkle in her eye. "We've next to no water, everything is rationed, and only the most basic services have power. Even so he's somehow keeping a program of entertainment running. I swear that man could motivate an army single handedly. He's got his team running events all over the ship, taking people's minds off what lies ahead. There's kids' bingo going on in the theatre. The prizes are tours of the engine room. One of the engineers salvaged some solar panels from the burnt out tender and has hooked them up to get the projector in the cinema going. They're showing films all day and the place is packed out. The cafes might be closed, but there's a poker tournament running in three of them. It's proving popular with the older passengers. And the sports instructors are running a whole host of events in the gym now that Grau has cleared out and moved back down to medical. They're such a great team, they haven't left me with anything to worry about."

"Wow, it sounds almost like people are enjoying themselves," Jake was impressed.

"Most people are, I think. There's still the feeling that we've been spared, that we got away with something. I don't know how that will change though, now we're getting closer to land. It looks quite bleak, out there."

Jake and Silvia looked out at the approaching coastline. They were turning in, towards the gaping mouth of the fjord. The landscape was still featureless. Rocks and jagged hills were streaked with snow. Or was it ash? They wouldn't know until they got closer. No signs of life whatsoever. But that was to be expected; this far north settlements were few and far between.

As the land grew ever nearer, the atmosphere on the bridge became increasingly tense. It had only been five days since they were last docked, but it might as well have been five million years ago, so much was unknown. The answers were coming, as metre by metre they closed the distance to Svalbard.

Jake was keeping a keen eye on the terrain. He didn't like what he saw. "Look," he pointed ahead. Lucya and Dave followed the line of his finger. He passed the binoculars to Lucya. "It's hard to tell on the rock, but it looks like ash. And the hills. They're streaked with snow, but it's weird. It's patchy, pockmarked. You'd expect it to be smooth, nobody ever comes here."

"You think it's the ash?" Dave was squinting, trying to see with the naked eye.

"Yes. It looks like it's simply melted away the snow in places. If the ash cloud passed over, it would have done that."

"So why is there still some there? I mean, that is snow, right? It's too white to be ash."

"It was probably thicker in some places. The hot ash would have met the snow and cooled. Where the snow was thin, it melted away and we can see the scars."

On the forward decks below, people were gathering outside, eagerly watching the approaching land. Before long they was passing Prince Charles Foreland, or Prinks Karls Forland as it was officially named on the nautical charts. A long, thin, black and green rocky island, it looked like the spine of a giant sea monster rising up out of the water. Jake had heard stories of the Loch Ness monster in Scotland, and could imagine that the strange outcrop was a huge Nessie, petrified and turned to stone. By now, the ash on the lower lying outcrops was clear for all to see. It was only a thin dusting, but the winds whipped it up into the air, tossed it around, and made swirling grey eddies that reminded Jake of flocking starlings. Where it fell, it amassed into wavelike drifts.

• • •

It took them another thirty minutes of slow cruising to reach the mouth of the Isfjorden fiord. Six kilometres wide at its narrowest point, it was a gigantic natural harbour. As the Spirit of Arcadia slipped between the barren land on either side, Jake felt like an explorer, venturing into a new and undiscovered territory. The sea was calm here. The land that encircled them was low, but further from the sea it swept up into huge dark mountains. It was as if some giant hand had scooped the fjord out of the landscape.

"It's so quiet," Silvia said. She had remained on the bridge for the morning, enjoying the best view on board. "No birds. Why are there no birds?"

Nobody answered her. Nobody wanted to imagine why.

"We should see Barentsburg before long," Lucya said. "To the starboard side."

They kept looking, but didn't see the small Russian mining community. Just ash.

Nobody mentioned it. Nobody wanted to think about where it had gone.

• • •

After what seemed an age, the radar indicated it was time to make the final turn for Longyearbyen. The charts showed that Svalbard airport was located on the flat piece of land to the inside of a ninety degree turn to starboard. The view from the bridge suggested otherwise. There was no trace of any airport buildings, vehicles, or aircraft. Certainly the topography was right, there was no doubt they were looking in the right direction, but there was no sign of life or civilisation.

Jake was at the helm, piloting the ship the last few kilometres to the town. Pedro was not as busy as he had expected. In the relative warmth of June there were no icy hazards floating in the fjord. He was trying to locate the harbour visually, to confirm what the radar was telling them. They had slowed to a crawl, and as they cut through the flat calm blue green water, they created virtually no wake. At this low speed the engine seemed paradoxically louder, the only sound to be heard as they glided through the valley.

"Full stop!" Jake cried automatically, then remembered he was in control. Nobody seemed to notice, they were too preoccupied with the scene outside. It was clear that they had arrived, but Longyearbyen had gone.

Where the town should have been, was ash. Not just the ash from the asteroid, but the ash of burnt buildings. The stubby charred remains of wooden houses rose out of the ground like gravestones. Where once had stood brick buildings, now there were piles of rubble and dust. From the ship they were too far away to see the whole town, but nobody was in any doubt that the rest of the settlement had been destroyed too.

"I can't see the pier," Pedro said, sweeping the bay with his binoculars.

"It's not very big," Lucya called back from the map table. She had a large scale chart of the archipelago and was cross referencing it with the radar screen. "Maybe fifty meters across, tiny really."

"Are you sure we're in the right place?"

"There's really no doubt. Any further and we'll be grounded. The pier must be there. Jake, I think you'll have to just approach sideways on. Cross your fingers until we get eyes on the pier and can guide you in properly."

Jake nodded. He set about manipulating the controls at the helm, diverting the power from the engines to the bow thrusters. The Spirit of Arcadia was a modern cruiser, made to be easily manoeuvrable in the smallest ports. Even so, crabbing into a mooring was always a delicate operation. The ship began to crawl nearer the ruined village, slower than walking pace.

They covered several hundred metres before Pedro spotted something.

"Stop! Stop the ship!"

Jake prodded some buttons and the engine note rose as the thrusters spun up in reverse, arresting the drift coastwards. "You see the pier?" he called over to his lookout.

"Yes and no," Pedro said. "I see some of the pier. It's in the water. The pier is destroyed. We cannot dock here."

Thirty-Five

Out on deck, passengers and crew alike crowded against the railings. Everyone was desperate to see this strange place they had come to. What kind of town was it? Would they be able to stay here? Were there other survivors here? If there were, that meant there could be more in other places too. A glimpse of this Arctic settlement promised so many answers. It promised hope.

But the answers it offered were not the answers anyone wanted to hear. The town was gone, destroyed by the asteroid. The total carnage and destruction visible on the coast was the last scene from the final broadcast. The part that had never made it as far as a camera or satellite feed. The part that many had imagined, but none wanted to believe. And now there was no choice. There was no hiding from the truth. Those last bubbles of hope that perhaps, just maybe, the broadcast hadn't been real, or that the asteroid had not caused such destruction this far north, popped out of existence. Nobody spoke. Nobody cried. The devastation, and the consequences, what it meant for the rest of the world, for the families and friends left behind, it was too much to comprehend.

• • •

Jake gave the order to drop the anchors. He called down to engineering. "Can we cut the engine?"

"We're staying?" Martin asked.

"We have no choice. We stay here or out there, it doesn't change anything. Besides, we really should take a closer look."

"We'll reduce revs to idle. If we don't stay long it will be more efficient than stopping and starting up again."

A click, and the line went dead. Jake looked at the silent receiver in his hand, replaced it slowly.

"I'm sending Stacy with you," Melvin said. Until that moment he had remained silent.

"I didn't say I was going," Jake replied.

"Of course you're going. You're really going to delegate this?"

"I'm coming as well." Lucya joined Jake at the helm.

"No. If I go you have to stay here. You're next in command, we can't both leave the ship. If anything happens to me…"

"I may be being a bit stupid," Silvia said, "but why is anyone going over there? I mean, look. Just…look. What do you expect to find?"

"We have to keep an open mind, Silvia." Jake was trying his best to sound positive. "For one thing there could be survivors. We might be able to help them."

"We don't have enough food and water for the people we've already got!" Melvin looked unhappy. "We can't go taking on any strays."

"For another thing," Jake ignored him, "there was fuel here. I know it's a long shot, but we've spent nearly twenty four hours cruising time getting this far. Without fuel we are dead. If there is even the slightest, most remote possibility there is diesel here, perhaps in a shelter or basement or something, then we have to find it."

"There's the airport too, don't forget," Lucya added.

"Lucya, the airport…we didn't see it. It must have met the same fate as…." Jake looked out over the missing town.

"Undoubtedly. But isn't it worth checking out anyway? It's three kilometres, you could walk there in half an hour, once you've landed."

"Maybe. Let's see how we're going to get to Longyearbyen first." He picked up the phone and dialled.

"Martin? Jake."

"Look, I've done the math. It really is better to keep the engine idling." He sounded irritated.

"Sure, whatever. That's not why I'm calling. The tenders, they were badly damaged in the fires. How quickly can you get a team to repair one, get it seaworthy?"

"Some of my guys already checked on them. One is a write off, total wreck, not worth pursuing repairs. We're cannibalising it for spares though. The other was less badly burnt. Some damage to the hull, quite a lot to the engine."

"How long before she can be ready?"

"Probably a day or two of work."

"You have two hours."

"That's impossible!"

"We can't sit around for a day waiting here, looking at…that. We have to get over there and take a proper look around, the people are going to demand it."

"People demand all sorts of things, it doesn't mean they can always get what they want."

"Two hours, Martin. She doesn't have to be perfect, but she needs to be ready to go in two hours at the latest." He clicked the phone down. He knew he was pushing his luck with Martin, but he would rather suffer the complaints of one engineer than the wrath of thousands of angry passengers.

He made two more calls.

"Grau, how's the leg?"

"Further improved, thank you for asking. How is the captain?"

"As well as can be expected. Listen, do you think you'd be up to joining me in a landing party?"

"You think there could be survivors over there?"

"Honestly? No, I don't. But if there are, we need you with us."

"I don't know, Jake. Getting round this ship is one thing, but that is rough terrain, and it's cold. I would slow you down, be a liability, and not much use to you even if you did find anyone. I can send Kiera, though. David is sleeping, he ran the night shift."

"Fine, Kiera's a great nurse, she'll be perfect. Tell her to be on deck two in a couple of hours, by the exit for the tender."

Click. He swapped the phone for a radio headset, and punched in the channel number he wanted.

"Max, I'm taking a landing party over there. I could use one of your security guys. Someone strong. If we find fuel, or food, or anything we can salvage, we could use help bringing it back."

"There must be a hundred sailors twiddling their thumbs, why not take one of those?"

"I'm bringing a couple of sailors too, but this isn't just about carrying stuff. We don't know who or what we might find."

"Alright, what about the new guy?"

Jake considered this. "I'd rather take a company man. I've already got a passenger representative, I don't want to be responsible for more than one cone."

"Okay, I'll send Reeve. You can't miss him, he's six foot six and bald as an egg."

"Thanks. Have him meet me on deck two, by the tender exit, at oh-two hundred hours."

"Will do."

Jake sat back down in the captain's chair, stared out over the mountains ahead, trying not to look at Longyearbyen.

"It's midday," Silvia said. "I'll bring up some lunch. You need to eat before going over there."

"Maybe," Jake said. But nobody really felt like eating.

Thirty-Six

"You must be Reeve," Jake looked the man up and down. Mostly up. He looked more like a vigilante than a security officer, but he'd got through an interview with Max, so that was good enough. "Stacy, Reeve is our other regular security guy. Reeve, Stacey is here representing passenger interests." Reeve raised an eyebrow, nodded at Stacy. Jake finished the introductions.

The group were standing by a large square opening. The chunky metal door cut into the side of the hull had been lowered outwards, and icy arctic air whistled in. The opened door formed part of a staircase; five white steps to where a telescopic stairway descended to the right, down to a platform that hovered just over the sea. Moored at the bottom was a bright orange tender. It looked like a bigger lifeboat, and indeed could double as one in an emergency. Jack stepped outside, the cold air hit him full in the face. He reached the bottom of the stairs, and stepped on board the little boat through a sliding door in the middle.

An engineer was waiting for him. "We've patched her up the best we can, Captain, but she really needs more work." He gestured towards the side. "She took quite a bit of fire damage, parts of the hull were melted away."

"So, when you say you patched her up, you really patched her, that's not just a turn of phrase."

"Very much so. Martin isn't happy, he wanted me to pass on his feelings that this boat was not ready to be lowered into the sea and that he won't take responsibility for anything that happens to it." The young man clearly felt embarrassed relaying Martin's words, and seemed glad he'd got it out of the way.

"Well, she's floating, isn't she? So I think we'll be fine. Thank you, er…"

"Rigg, sir, Bryan Rigg."

"Yes, thank you, Rigg." He waved at the others at the top of the steps. "Are you coming, or are you all just going to stand there?"

Reeve came down and boarded the tender, followed by Stacey, Kiera, and two sailors, Horace and Dante. Rigg was standing in the tiny wheelhouse at the front. He pressed a combination of buttons to start the engine. A puff of diesel smoke and the starter turned twice, three times, before bursting into life. From somewhere behind them came the sound of dirty water being spat out in puffs and wheezes as the bilge pump got going. The engineer retreated back through the boat, and stepped outside onto the platform. He untied the two thick blue ropes that secured the orange vessel to the Spirit of Arcadia, coiled each one individually and tossed them onto the little boat, casting them adrift.

"Horace, would you?" Jake asked.

The sailor took the wheel. Dante went back to the door, clasped a grab rail on the roof, pulled himself up and outside, where he walked carefully round to the front. He sat on the roof and took up a watch. The tender eased away from its mooring and set off across the last kilometre to the shore.

Despite the breeze the water was calm, which was fortunate because there were obstacles to avoid. Before long, Dante had spotted something dark and straight edged lurking just beneath the surface. All the while looking forwards, he tapped on the window below him and signalled to Horace to steer clear. The tender was easily able to change direction quickly, and it glided past. Looking down on the menacing shape hidden just below the water, Jake saw it was a huge chunk of the concrete jetty that they had been hoping to tie up to. He looked on in awe as the little boat tiptoed around more pieces of the pier. Some were hidden below the water line, others rose out of the sea like sheer sided rocks.

"What could do this?" he said to nobody in particular. "What kind of force could rip apart something like that?"

"I once saw a tornado," Reeve said. "Blew right down the other side of the street in front of me. Picked up the roofs of houses and sent them flying into backyards half a mile away. Picked up cars and dumped them down again, a block later. It was an awesome sight, the power of that twister. But even that couldn't have done this kind of damage. Man, if that asteroid did this, then how the hell did we survive?"

"It was higher. When it went over us, it was going up. Something made it change direction, and it happened before it reached us. Who knows, maybe it was gaining altitude the further north it got? We were anchored very close to the magnetic pole, perhaps the earth's magnetic field interrupted its orbit and sent it spinning off back into space?" It was a pet theory Jake had been toying with for a while.

"If that's right, Captain Noah, and it levelled a town like this from a higher altitude, then I can't even begin to imagine what damage it did further south when it was lower."

Jake closed his eyes, swallowed hard. He saw Jane, couldn't get her out of his head. He'd avoided thinking about home, had been too busy when on duty, and too tired in his brief rest periods. But seeing the destruction, he could no longer hide from the truth, the inevitable truth that Jane must be dead. His parents, dead. Everyone he knew, everyone he had ever known, they were all dead. He felt tears welling up in his eyes, was fighting for breath, tried to open his eyes but they felt like they were glued shut. His legs gave way underneath him, and that was the last thing he remembered.

• • •

"Captain Noah? Can you hear me?"

Jake tried again to open his eyes. The light was strong, they stung. He was lying on his back, but wasn't sure where. A figure was bent over him, looking at him. A woman.

"Jane? Is that you?"

"Captain Noah, it's Kiera. No, don't try and move, not yet. You fainted, Captain, you hit your head on a bench."

A tiny light flicked on, shone directly into his left eye, then the right. A pair of hands turned his head to one side, very gently.

Fingers probed around the back, carefully, gently. A jolt of pain stabbed at his skull. He cried out.

"Sorry, Captain, I didn't mean to hurt you. There's some blood, and you're going to have a heck of a lump there for a while, but I think you'll live."

The pain had somehow brought his vision back into focus. He looked up at the nurse. She actually looked a little like Jane, he thought. Similar short blond hair, thin face, long neck. He didn't feel so bad about having said the name of his wife. He did, however, feel intense embarrassment at having passed out, and in front the others. Not Kiera, she was a nurse, she'd seen it all before. Not even the sailors, not really. What really upset him was that Stacey would have witnessed it. A moment of weakness. He had a nasty feeling he wouldn't be allowed to forget it.

"Can you try and sit up for me a bit, Captain?"

"Only if you stop calling me that and call me Jake."

"If that's what it takes. Come on, let me help you."

She put her hands behind his shoulders and helped him lift his back from the floor. Another jolt of pain shot through his head. He winced, but didn't make a noise. Once in a sitting position he shuffled back until he was propped against a bench. The opposite bench bore a dark red stain. His blood. His eyes swivelled around as he scanned the interior of the boat.

"Where did everyone go?"

"Horace and Dante went to tie us up. The other two have gone ashore."

"Damn. Damn! Ouch!" his hand flew up to the back of his head.

"Careful, no sudden movements, Jake!" Kiera smiled cheekily. "I need to dress that, then you can go out and play too."

"They shouldn't have gone without me. Oh, what the hell, I never asked to be captain anyway. So what if nobody listens to me?"

"To be fair, I don't think you gave any orders to remain aboard while you fainted." Kiera regretted the words the instant they left her mouth. She looked nervously at the captain, worried she had overstepped the mark. He started back at her, and a grin spread across his face.

"No, I don't suppose I did. Now, about that dressing."

The nurse pulled out some sterile swabs from her medical kit, doused them in antiseptic, and dabbed at the wound on the back of his head. It stung when she touched it, but not as badly as before. Once clean, she did her best to bandage it. She looked at the dressing on his hand.

"Well, you've got matching bandages now."

"Don't. I must look like some kind of confused pirate with this stuff wrapped round my head."

"I don't think anyone is going to worry about that. Do you think you can stand?"

"I can try."

There was a blood curdling scream from outside. A woman's voice. Stacey's. It wasn't just a single scream, it went on and on.

"What the...?" Jake tried to scramble to his feet, but the sudden movement sent more shockwaves of searing pain through his head, causing him to fall back onto his backside. "What's happening, what's going on?"

Kiera rushed to the open sliding door and looked out. At the exact same moment there was another scream, a man's.

"What can you see?" Jake was still trying desperately to get to his feet. He hauled himself onto the bench and looked out the window. They were tied to the remains of the pier. Horace had found a spot between the broken concrete that littered the sea just large enough to nestle the tender in. The pier was much higher than their little boat. It had been designed for cruisers and tankers, not small craft like this. Most of the window was obstructed by concrete, just a thin slot at the top was clear. Through it, Jake thought he could make out Stacey. She was on her hands and knees, screaming, apparently in pain. It was hard to tell why, she was too far from the boat to see. In front of her was one of the sailors, he had also been on his hands and knees but as Jake looked on he saw him roll over onto his back.

"It's Stacey," Kiera called back from the window. "Wait there, I'm going to try and help." She grabbed her medical bag and climbed out of the boat onto the roof, and from there jumped onto the broken pier.

Another scream, but this time not pain. It was Reeve, he was running towards Kiera.

"No! Get back on the boat! Don't go any further! Get back!"

Jake tried again to get to his feet, this time successfully. Adrenaline was coursing through his body, and it blocked out much of the pain in his head. He wobbled over to the door. From behind him came a terrible cracking sound, and then another noise, like someone had opened a gas bottle. He turned to see a crack opening up in the hull. Just a hairline fracture, but enough that seawater was spurting through at high pressure. The force of the water was opening the crack wider. The hastily applied patch was breaking apart. He steadied himself, climbed through the door and grabbed the thick concrete of the pier. His shoulders were level with the ground outside and he didn't know if he had the strength to pull himself up.

"Get back on the boat Kiera, now!" Reeve had nearly reached them. Stacey and the sailor were now both writhing around on the ground, still screaming.

"No, Kiera, don't get on the boat!" Jake called up to her as she turned round to jump onto the roof. She looked down at him confused, and turned back to Reeve. He was beside her now.

"Captain! Stay on the boat, it's too dangerous," Reeve called.

"Get me out of here Reeve, this boat is sinking!"

The security man looked over at the others on the ground. Their screams were weakening. He sprinted to the end of the pier, grabbed Jake's hands. As he pulled, Jake pushed off as best he could. He landed on his knees, felt he was about to collapse.

"Get up, now!" Reeve cried, adding, "sir!" Without waiting, he pulled Jake onto his feet. "Don't move. Either of you. Don't move from this spot."

The wailing had stopped, and the only noise was the sound of water flooding into the failed tender. It groaned, creaked, then lurched over onto its side, sinking until just the upturned side protruded from the water. Air bubbles gurgled up and popped on the surface, and then, there was silence.

• • •

"Reeve, what the hell is going on here?" Jake's head was throbbing, and he was bruised on his chest where he had been pulled out of the boat so quickly and aggressively. "What's happened to Stacey and whoever is with her? Kiera should go and help!"

"No, nobody should move. It's the dust, the ash. It's dangerous."

"What do you mean? It can't still be hot, not after all this time."

"It's not the heat, there's something else. Look around, it's not the same ash. It's thicker, we didn't see this on the ship."

Jake and Kiera did as instructed. Where they were standing, on the very edge of the broken pier, there was no ash. It had been blown away, probably into the sea. The pier opened onto a wide flat area. Jake could imagine how normally it would be filled with vehicles, coaches taking cruise parties on tours of the town, or trucks loading and unloading supply boats. The ash gradually increased in thickness in this area, until it became impossible to tell where the hard standing ended and the road up to the town began. Stacy was about fifty metres away, where the ash was several centimetres thick. Something was wrong with her though, something more than the fact she wasn't moving.

She was shrinking.

Jake stared, his mouth open. There was no doubt about it. She was lying on her front, and she was deflating like a balloon. The sailor next to her was the doing the same, it was just less obvious due to the size difference.

"That ash," Reeve said, "is dissolving her flesh."

"I don't...how...what?" Kiera seemed unable to say any more than that.

"I told her to wait for you two, but she ignored me, said she was going up to where the wreck of the town is. I sent Horace after her and waited here awhile. Then I sent Dante to try and find the airport, and I followed after the other two. She screamed, and when I got to her, her feet were...melting." Reeve had one hand on his hip and the other on his forehead. He was swinging slightly from side to side, like he was debating with himself about whether to continue.

"Go on," Jake said.

"I could see it was the ash. She was wearing flip flops, she must have just kicked through the ash like sand on a beach. And it dissolved her feet, I mean, it just ate away at her flesh. I've never seen anything like that, not like that…."

"And Horace?"

"He tried to get it off her. Brushed it off with his hands. His bare hands. As soon as they touched it, the same thing happened. It's… it was…I've never seen anything like it. That's why we can't go any further. If that stuff touches your skin, you're dead. I don't know what the hell it is, and I don't want to know. We need to get away from here."

"We need to find Dante," Jake said, looking up at the security officer. "Which way did he go?"

"No! It's too dangerous."

"Reeve's right, Jake. Besides, you're in no state to go after anyone."

"We can't just stay here and wait for him to find out for himself what that ash can do! Besides, look at that." He pointed to the partially capsized tender. "We're not going anywhere, we can't!"

Reeve reached inside his jacket pocket and extracted a radio. He pressed a button and it crackled into life. "Max, this is Reeve, over."

A tinny voice replied. "This is Max, go ahead."

"We have a problem. This environment is extremely hostile, I repeat, hostile. Too dangerous to stay. Our transport is no longer functional, we require alternative transport back to the Arcadia A.S.A.P., over."

"Understood. I'll get on it. Standby, I'll come back to you. Out."

"Maybe we could swim it?" Kiera suggested. "Although," she looked at Jake, "no, maybe not."

"We don't know if the water is toxic. There must be ash in there too, who knows what it could do to us?" Reeve shook his head.

"We've been drinking water from the desalination plant since that ash cloud hit. We haven't had any reports of anyone melting in medical."

"Yes, but like I said, this isn't the same ash that we saw further north."

"Well I think we might have our answer," Jake said. He had turned and was looking at the water. About a hundred metres away he could see Dante, swimming towards them.

THIRTY-SEVEN

"WHAT DO YOU mean, dangerous? What is happening over there?" Lucya was trying not to panic, not very successfully.

"I don't know, and it's not important right now. We need to get them back over here. What other transport do we have?" Max asked.

"All the lifeboats burned. The other tender has been broken up for spares. That just leaves the rafts. We'll have to send someone over in a raft." She paced back and forth, thinking hard, then picked up the phone and dialled.

"Engineering?"

"Martin?"

"Yes. Lucya?"

"We have an emergency. The tender sunk and there's something going on over there, something dangerous. We have to get them back, fast. I'm going to launch a life raft. Dave will take it over and bring them back."

"I will?" This was news to Dave, and he wasn't very happy about it. "I'm a navigator, not a raft...driver!"

"Fine, then find me a sailor who can go instead. But you'd better hurry, because as soon as that raft hits the water someone is going, and it could just as easily be you. Go!"

Dave rushed off to find someone better suited to the mission than he was.

"Sorry, Martin, anyway, so how do we propel the raft? Those things don't have motors."

"There are spare oars in the stores. I can send someone up with them."

"No! No, I'll come and get them. Thanks."

She hung up.

"Pedro. Listen, you need to try and take us in closer. It will take too long for them to row over. The closer we can get, the better."

"This is very risky. There are bits of concrete pier in that water," Pedro said carefully.

"I know. So don't hit them. Melvin, time you earned your keep around here. You need to stand there." she pointed to the far end of the bridge, with windows that extended beyond the beam of the ship. "You're on lookout. If you see anything in the water, shout at Pedro."

She turned to leave, but Max called after her.

"Lucya! I don't know what's going on over there but it doesn't sound good. Reeve said the environment was hostile. He's a good guy, wouldn't exaggerate. If there's a danger to this ship then we need to be prepared."

"Agreed."

"By which," Max could see she hadn't got the point, "I mean armed."

"I see. I think that's really a decision for the captain to make."

"The captain isn't here. He's in the hostile environment. Maybe he can't make a decision. He left you in charge, you need to make the call." Max looked over to the secure weapons cabinet.

"Fine, yes, you are right. Do what you have to do."

Lucya raced out of the bridge, down the corridor, and down ten flights of stairs to deck one, cursing the decision not to switch on the elevators with every flight. She wound her way through the labyrinth of passageways on the deepest level, until she found the store room. Once inside, the oars were easy to find, they were stacked on a top shelf, above the grey crates. She looked at them, then bent down under the table and looked at her special buoys. She picked one out, grabbed two oars and left for deck seven.

• • •

Martin Oakley was fuming. One minute he was having a perfectly normal conversation with one of his engineers, and the next he couldn't hear himself think as the engine he was stood next to started to rev up.

"What the….? What's going on?" He threw his hands in the air, looked to his colleague for an answer, and realised one would not be forthcoming. "We've dropped the anchors for goodness sake, we're not supposed to be moving anywhere. What are they playing at up there?"

"Actually, according to the computer, the anchors were pulled up two minutes ago."

"Who ordered that? Lucya said she was leaving the bridge to go down to the stores. Right, that's it. They can't just move off without telling us first."

Martin picked up the phone and dialled the bridge. He let it ring for a good minute, but nobody answered. Even though he was below the waterline and there were no windows, he could feel the ship moving slowly, although he couldn't be sure about the direction.

He slammed the phone down, angry that nobody would pick up on the other side. After pacing up and down, muttering to himself, he picked it up again and started to dial another number.

"Maybe Silvia knows what's going on here, she…"

He didn't complete the sentence because there was an ear splitting crunching sound, the ship shuddered, and he was thrown from his feet. The telephone handset fell to the floor where it cracked in two. Martin's colleague was toppled off balance, but caught the edge of a console and steadied himself. The ship had come to rest. The engine revs died down, and it was then that Martin became aware of another noise. He knew that sound, he had heard it once before, but only once. That was the sound of water pouring through a hole in the hull.

• • •

"You know how to handle one of these?" Max asked.

"Of course. I told you, I was a solider. Once a solider, always a soldier."

Flynn took the gun. Holding the cold metal barrel upright in both hands, he looked it up and down, then held it to his left eye, checking the sight.

"I do not expect any weapons to be discharged on this ship, you hear me? This security team is here to keep the peace, not to terrorise. This is a deterrent. A last resort."

"I understand, sir." Flynn pushed the strap of the weapon over his shoulder. "A last resort."

"Glad that's clear. Now, back on patrol."

Max left for the bridge to pick up more weapons. He needed to arm the rest of his security team.

• • •

Lucya arrived at deck seven at the same time as Dave. He was accompanied by a young looking sailor. Lucya stopped and stared at him for several seconds, she couldn't believe he was old enough to be working.

"This is Chuck, he's going to take the raft across," Dave said.

"Chuck? Really? There are actually people called Chuck?"

Chuck turned scarlet. "Ma'am," he said simply.

"Right, Chuck. Tell me, once we open one of these capsules, the thing flies off, inflates, and lands in the water, right?"

"That is correct ma'am."

"Okay, so two things Chuck. One, my name is Lucya, forger the ma'am thing, right?"

He nodded.

"The second thing is, once the raft hits the water, how do we get it back here so you can get in?"

The two men considered the question. They were standing outside next to a metal framed construction on which nine large white capsules, like giant pills, were tied down. The frame was angled in such a way that when a capsule was untied it would roll down and into the sea.

"Maybe I'm missing something," Dave said, "but can't he just use the escape slide?"

"No. We're not deploying that for one person. It's single use, what happens in a real emergency when the slide has gone?"

"See? I knew I was missing something."

At that moment there was a huge crunch, the sound of metal being ripped, then a groaning sound from below. The ship came to a sudden, jarring halt. Lucya, Dave and Chuck were thrown against the side railings. All three exclaimed in surprise and pain.

"Jesus! What the hell?!" Dave looked around, confused.

"I think we hit part of that pier. Fuck! Jake is going to kill me." Lucya, rubbed her side where it had connected with the handrail. "You, get down there." She pointed to the sea. "Take the steps for the tender. I'm launching this thing and you're going to have to swim for it. I have to get back to the bridge."

The sailor looked at her as if he must have misheard.

"Now!" she screamed at him.

He nodded, and ran back inside for the stairs. Lucya reached under the first fibreglass capsule, wrapped her hand around the release buckle, and pulled hard. The strap holding it to the metal frame snapped in two. The capsule rolled slowly to the end of the metal ramp, out over the handrail, over the water, and fell. As it did so, it split open. There was a whoosh of compressed air being released, and a mass of black and red material pushed its way out, separating the two sides of the capsule. Within seconds it had inflated to form a giant raft. It popped into its final shape just as it hit the water with a slap. Fully inflated, the raft looked like it could never have fitted into the capsule. It was made to hold up to thirty passengers. Rectangular in shape, and slightly tapered at the front and back, the outer edge was made of sausage like air chambers. Three more chambers within the raft provided seating. A bright orange hood that could be deployed to provide shelter from the elements was rolled up on one side, out of the way of anyone in the water trying to clamber aboard. Lucya watched the raft hit the water, threw her pink buoy after it, and jettisoned the oars over the railings. Before they had splashed into the sea, she had already turned around and run back inside, in the direction of the bridge.

THIRTY-EIGHT

SOMETHING WAS WRONG with Dante. At first, it was hard to see exactly what, but as he approached it became clearer. He had no hands. His arms splashed in and out of the sea, but without palms and fingers to pull against the water, he was limited in his ability to generate propulsion.

Reeve took a step back then ran two steps forward and jumped off the end of the pier and onto the side of the upturned tender. As he landed his feet slipped beneath him and he fell onto his read end, slid towards the now vertical roof. With a grunt he rolled over onto his front and grabbed at the window frames, arresting his slide just as his feet and legs disappeared over the side. He hauled himself back up, got to his hands and knees, and proceeded to crawl to the rear of the craft.

Dante was approaching, slowly. Reeve called to him. He seemed to hear, changed direction slightly, and with a few more strokes reached the back of the boat. The security man reached out and grabbed the end of his right arm, pulled hard. The boat was low in the water, only half a metre or so was exposed, so it wasn't too difficult to pull Dante out and onto the side, and relative safety. He lay on his back, panting, coughing.

"Dante, what happened? What the hell happened to your hands?"

"The ash…" he was still out of breath, struggling to get the words out. "It was the ash…"

Everyone stared at the stumps at the ends of Dante's arms. Blackened, fused by the burning ash.

The awkward silence was broken by the sound of tearing metal echoing across the fjord.

• • •

Martin charged from one end of the engine room to the other, through the open door and into a passageway. A quick left turn and through two vast chambers. Both housed gigantic tanks, each bigger than the sixty person tender that was, unbeknownst to him, now lying wrecked in the fjord. As he ran, the sound of gushing water grew ever louder. By the third chamber, he was running through sea water. The noise was now deafening. It was coming from the fourth chamber ahead, a chamber that was filling rapidly with water, spilling over the threshold of the bulkhead. When he reached it, he tried to push the heavy metal door shut. But the water was rising, pushing the door back out towards him.

"Richard! Where are you? Get your arse down here now!"

He could hear the sound of his colleague's steps running towards him. Then the clicking of boots on the metal floor turned to the sound of feet splashing through water, and suddenly Richard was there, pushing the door with him. Martin turned and pushed with his back. It was as big as the side of a bus shelter, and thick steel. On its well-oiled and balanced hinges, it was normally simple enough to swing shut, but the pressure of the water coming through made the task almost impossible. The two men heaved with all their might, feet slipping and sliding in the sea water. With an almost herculean effort, the edge of the door finally reached the frame. Martin's foot hit on something under the water. A ring in the floor, used to tie down equipment when the going got rough. He dug his heel against it and pushed with all his weight. The extra purchase was just enough, and the door thudded into place.

"Lock it!" Martin couldn't hold the force of the water much longer.

Richard took his hands off the door and spun the wheel mounted in the middle. Almost immediately, Martin felt the pressure release from his back as the locking bolts moved into place. He dropped forwards, his hands on his knees, head hung low, panting.

"We did it!" Richard exclaimed. "Hey, it's okay, we got it closed, we're safe."

"No," Martin said.

"No really, we'll be fine!" Richard tried to reassure him. "That bulkhead is designed to withstand the chamber being completely flooded. We can pump out these others and we'll be okay. We might need to pump some ballast into the tanks to balance us up a bit."

"No. Shit, no, not that." Martin was staring at the water.

Richard looked down. He understood the problem. It wasn't just water they were standing in. There was diesel fuel mixed in with it too.

• • •

Chuck ripped off his jacket, kicked off his shoes, and leapt into the water. The icy cold nearly stopped his heart, but he didn't have time to worry about that. He swam as fast as he could in the direction of the raft. Fortunately it hadn't fallen far from the ship, and there was no current to speak of, so it hadn't moved far. Within a minute of hitting the sea he swam right into one of the oars. Stopping to tread water, he picked it up and threw it as hard as he could manage in the direction of the raft. He swam on, stopping twice more to throw the oar further, before finally it landed inside the inflatable. Shortly afterwards he arrived there himself. Using the orange rope tied around the outside to pull himself up, he rolled into the emergency vessel. He got to his knees and looked around for the second oar. It had floated off towards the shore. Positioning himself at the front of the raft he began to paddle. A stroke to the left, pull the paddle out of the water, then a stroke to the right. It wasn't quick, but he was going in the right direction. When he reached the second oar he retrieved it and set it down beside him. The raft was too wide for one person to row conventionally, but the oar would be useful when he had help coming back.

• • •

"What just happened?" Jake was desperately trying to see where the noise had come from, but the ship was too far out to see clearly. From his position on the shore, everything looked fine. "Get Max on the radio, find out what's going on!"

Reeve put his hand in his inside pocket. His expression changed. He pulled out an empty hand, tried the other pocket. "Shit."

"Where's the radio, Reeve?" Jake already knew the answer.

"It must have fallen out when I slipped. Damn it!"

"Well, there's not much we can do about that, so I guess we'll find out what's happened when we get back over there." Jake was starting to feel a certain sense of detachment. This landing expedition had turned into a disaster. If he didn't know what had just happened on the ship, well at least it was one less thing to worry about. For now.

Dante had got his breath back. He and Reeve were perched on top of the tender. Jake and Kiera were sitting opposite on the very edge of the broken pier, as far away from the deadly ash as they could.

"I hadn't got far, but I wasn't sure I was going the right way. On the map we looked at, there was a road from here to the airport. I couldn't tell if I was on the road or just some rock, it was all covered in ash. So I was kicking the ash with my feet, trying to see what was underneath, you know, like you do in the snow sometimes? And I saw something shiny, where I'd cleared a bit with my foot. So I crouched down to get a better look. I started pushing the ash away to the sides with my hands. And then," he raised the stubs of his forearms in the air, looked at them like he still couldn't quite believe it.

"How did you stop it going any further?" Jake asked. "With Horace and Stacey it…well, you know."

"I ran to the sea and shoved my hands in. I thought they were burning, it felt like they were on fire. I just wanted them to stop burning! And when they hit the water they just…they just kind of disintegrated."

"Jesus," Reeve said, shaking his head.

Kiera wore an expression of deep sympathy, but didn't know what to say.

"I'm sorry. I'm so sorry," Jake said. "This is my fault. We should never have brought so many people over here. We should have taken it slower."

"No," Dante said. "This is nobody's fault."

"Look!" Kiera was pointing out towards the fjord.

Reeve and Dante turned their heads. Paddling over the water was a black and red inflatable life raft.

• • •

"The fuel tank ruptured?" Richard hadn't moved, he remained rooted to the spot.

"Impossible. It's too far from the hull. Whatever we hit couldn't have pierced that deeply." Martin shook his head.

"But that's oil, diesel oil. Floating on the water."

"Yes. But it can't be. Unless…oh shit!"

Martin flew forwards, trying to run around the massive tank in the chamber. But his legs had to fight against the water, slowing him down. Richard watched as the chief engineer appeared to advance in slow motion. On the other side of the tank was a thick white pipe that ran the length of the chamber. It passed through the walls at each end, and at half a meter from both walls, a red wheel protruded from the pipe. Martin spun the wheel nearest the flooded chamber.

"Of course," Richard said looking on. "The fuel line. It didn't puncture the tank, it broke the fuel line."

"That's shut off the line," Martin said panting from the effort. "That'll stop any fuel from tank three leaking out."

"You realise, of course you do, that it means we lose access to tank five?"

"I know. But it's going to leak out of the broken line too. One and two are already empty. We've just lost the use of two thirds of our remaining fuel supply."

• • •

It took a considerable time for the raft to reach the pier. For one thing, paddling from the front with a single oar was slow work. For another, Chuck had to try and steer round the giant lumps of concrete protruding from the water, and the even more dangerous ones, hidden just beneath the surface. When he did eventually reach the upturned tender, Dante had lost consciousness. The pain and the cold had been too much.

"I'm going to lower him down, grab his legs," Reeve called to Chuck. He had his hands under the unconscious man's arms and was dragging him nearer the raft. He pulled him round so that his legs hung over the side facing the Spirit of Arcadia. Chuck grabbed the Dante's ankles and pulled them into the raft as Reeve lowered him down.

"One down. Now you two," Reeve said looking over at Jake and Kiera. "Whoa!"

All the movement had unbalanced the capsized boat. They had assumed it had come to a rest on the sea bed, but in fact the water was much deeper. The underwater side of the tender was actually stuck on a pointed piece of concrete below the surface. The shifting weight of Reeve and Dante had caused the tender to tilt towards its back. With a creak, it upended, launching Reeve headfirst into the fjord. He disappeared from view, then popped out of the water a few metres away, spitting and coughing. He was just in time to see the remainder of the boat disappear with a glugging sound and a muddle of air bubbles. Chuck was already paddling towards Reeve, who reached out for the rope and pulled himself onto the raft. He understood why Dante had lost consciousness; the cold water had sucked the feeling from his hands and feet. Dante had the added problems of blood loss and shock to deal with. Passing out was probably he best he could have done, under the circumstances.

With the tender gone, it was actually easier for Chuck to get up close to the pier. Jake and Kiera lowered themselves into it with relative ease.

"Okay, Reeve, ready to help me row?" Chuck said, holding out a plastic oar.

Thirty-Nine

THE LIFE RAFT made quick time back to the ship, aided by Reeve. Max was waiting at the bottom of the steps, along with one of his new recruits. Jake noted, with dismay, that they were both bearing arms.

Chuck jumped onto the platform with a rope and secured them. Dante was helped off first, and the others followed.

"Come with me, I'll take you down to medical. Grau is going to need to look at this," Kiera said, and disappeared with Dante.

"Reeve, what's the situation? Any immediate danger to the ship?" Max asked.

"No, sir. I believe we are safe here. But the environment on land is extremely dangerous." He outlined what had happened with the ash, and the fate of Stacey and Horace. Max was clearly shaken, but he was a professional and hardly let it show.

"Max, you should get back to patrolling, keep an eye out." Jake said, scrambling to the platform. "Who knows who saw what, or what rumours are going to spread. Things could turn nasty. We'll talk about the guns later."

"I sought authorisation, Captain," Max said defensively.

"I'm sure you did. Like I said, we'll talk about it later. Can I borrow Reeve for a bit?"

Max nodded. He turned and headed off, one hand on the rifle slung over his shoulder.

"What do you want me to do with the raft, Captain?" Chuck asked.

"Leave it tied up, for now. We might need it." Jake couldn't immediately think of any reason why that should be, but he thought it best to keep his options open. "Reeve, I think you'd better come to the bridge with me." He turned to Chuck. "Thank you, sailor, you did a good job there."

Reeve and Jake started on the long walk up the stairs towards deck ten.

• • •

"Where's Stacey?" Melvin asked, as soon as Jake had shut the door to the bridge behind Reeve.

"Jake! How are you? What happened? Are you okay? Max said it was dangerous!" Lucya threw her arms around him, then remembered his rank and the fact there were others present, and stepped back.

"I'm fine. What happened to the ship? We heard a sound, like…" Jake wasn't sure what it was like.

"I asked you where Stacey is?"

"Lucya?" Jake said, ignoring Melvin.

"I screwed up, that's what happened." She looked away, embarrassed. "I ordered Pedro to take us in closer. I thought the raft would get to you quicker. But we must have hit one of those submerged bits of concrete pier. Shit, I'm sorry Jake, it was my fault, I take full responsibility."

"Do we know the extent of the damage?"

"Martin is on his way up here. He said it's pretty bad, but under control."

"Captain Noah, are you going to tell me where Stacey is?" Melvin stepped between Jake and Lucya, making himself impossible to ignore any longer.

"Melvin, you should…perhaps you should sit down," Jake sighed.

"Why? What's happened?"

"There was an accident. Well, not so much an accident. It's more that we didn't know about the ash. But Stacey went off without the rest of us, she should have waited and…"

"What are you saying man? Pull yourself together and give me a coherent explanation. Where is Stacey?"

"She's dead, Melvin, okay? She's dead!" Jake shouted. "And so is Horace. He tried to save her, and now he's dead too."

"Oh my God!" Lucya's hand flew to cover her open mouth.

"You absolute…!" Melvin flew forwards, wrapping his hands around Jake's neck and squeezing. "I'll kill you! You bastard, do you hear me? I'll kill you!"

"No! Stop! Get off him!" Lucya screamed, looked around, panicked. "Somebody stop him!"

But Reeve was already there, pulling Melvin away from Jake's neck. The instant the two men were separated, Melvin's hand curled into a fist and powered into Reeve's belly. The two men were of a similar size, but Reeve was fitter and stronger. He was winded, but far from beaten. He locked a powerful hand around Melvin's wrist, twisted it up and around behind him. With his free hand he pushed on his shoulder, sending him to his knees. Jake was staggering backwards, still clutching at his throat. Lucya ran to him once more, but he backed away from her, trying to shake his head.

Someone hammered on the door. Nobody moved. Reeve had Melvin pinned to the floor, Jake was still recovering, Pedro and Dave were looking on in stunned silence, and Lucya seemed to be in shock. More banging, and the sound of someone shouting snapped her out of it. She undid the security bolt and let Martin in. His face was thunder. Seeing Melvin on the floor didn't seem to worry him in the slightest.

"You've really done it now, Jakey boy. Oh you have gone and royally screwed us. Leaving her in charge," he almost spat the words out, "while you fuck off on your jolly. One incompetent leaves another to run the show. And oh, what a performance she puts on. Crashing, Jake. Crashing the ship and rupturing the hull."

"Oh Jesus," Lucya whispered.

"I don't think Jesus is around, love. Or if he was, he would have obliterated our sorry arses with that asteroid, because that would have been kinder. Now we're doomed to die on this ship because, and get this because it's great, it's abso-fucking-lutely marvellous, she not only ruptured the hull, but she took out the fuel line. Oh yes, you heard me right. Fuel tank four is, right now, spurting its contents into the fjord. The fjord is returning the favour by filling the tank room with water."

Having got his rant out, Martin deflated somewhat. He found a chair and collapsed into it, covering his face with his hands.

"If I understand you correctly, we've lost one fifth of our fuel?" Jake croaked, recovering slowly. "We have five tanks on board, no?"

Melvin had stopped struggling and was now listening intently to the engineer.

"No, Jake. No, we didn't lose one fifth. Two tanks were empty. Two are now leaking out through the broken pipe. We have one tank left. The tank we've been running on the last two days. Our fuel is at less than twenty percent."

• • •

In a dark corner of the casino, a group of passengers were talking in hushed voices.

"What's happening? What did they find over there?"

"I heard that the asteroid turned everyone into zombies, that they ran into a load of Norwegians who had become the walking dead."

"That's stupid. But they definitely found something bad. The security men were running round in a panic. And we saw them come back in a life raft. What happened to their boat?"

"My wife said a security guard told her the land was toxic, that it makes your skin melt."

"That's as stupid as the zombie thing!"

"Well whatever happened, I don't reckon we'll be getting off anytime soon."

"If you ask me, it's time for that election."

"What election?"

"Apparently the captain promised an election if it turned out there are no other survivors."

"I reckon I should stand."

"That Melvin guy is going to stand. He sounds amazing, he led a mutiny and got them to let him stay on the bridge. He's looking out for all of us, because otherwise they want to control us."

"Yeah, enslave us."

"We have to vote for Melvin. Pass the word on."

On every deck, the same whispered conversations were taking place.

• • •

"If he lets you go, are you going to behave?" Jake asked Melvin.

"I ought to kill you."

"I take it that's a no, then. Reeve, you're going to have to tie him up."

"No! Wait. Think about Tania Bloom. If you tie me up then the others will know. When I don't make contact, they'll kill her. Do you want more blood on your hands today, Captain?"

Jake groaned. He knew his hands were tied, therefore Melvin's never could be.

"Okay, let him go. But if he tries anything, we're rounding up all his cronies and searching this ship top to bottom for Tania."

"You'll never find her," Melvin said, getting to his feet as Reeve released his grip. "You couldn't find her during the census, you won't find her now. We're not dumb."

Melvin walked towards the door.

"Where are you going now?" Jake asked.

"To check in with my friends. And to find someone to take over the second watch. You might have killed Stacey, but we're going to damn well make sure we keep a presence up here."

He pulled the door open and stormed out.

"Reeve, follow him, I don't trust him."

"Sure thing, Captain."

Jake staggered over to the captain's chair and slumped down. Lucya followed.

"You guys should go and get some rest," she said to Pedro and Dave.

"I don't mind staying," Dave said. "I was scanning the radios, you never know."

"No, it's fine, I can do that. You go on, take the opportunity to catch up on some sleep."

Dave nodded. Pedro followed him off the bridge, leaving Jake, Lucya and Martin alone.

"What do we do now?" Jake said. "I mean, I really thought, hoped, there would be something or someone. That it wasn't as bad as on the television. But it's all gone, Lucya. All of it. There's nothing, just ash. Toxic ash."

"We don't give up!" Lucya sounded defiant. "So there's nothing here, it doesn't mean that it is the same everywhere. We go further south. Norway. Scotland. We keep going until we find somewhere that escaped, like we escaped."

"No," Martin said. He walked over to join them. "You saw that broadcast. That asteroid destroyed everything. We escaped because we were so far north. The further south we go, the worse it will be."

"What about the south pole?" Lucya wasn't about to give up. "We escaped at the north pole, maybe the south pole did too?"

"Lucya, there's nothing at the south pole. It's ice, snow. It's the harshest conditions on the planet. Even if it wasn't touched, what do you think is there for us?"

"I don't know! But surely it's worth a try?"

"We don't have the fuel. We have maybe enough to reach Scotland, if we turn off the generator and one engine, just run the other engine. And then what? When we arrive there and find exactly the same thing as here? Then we'll have no fuel left, no power."

"We can't just stay here!" Lucya was starting to panic.

"Lucya, we have no choice," Jake said. "That asteroid has killed us like it killed everyone else in the world. It's just that it's going to take longer for us to die. We thought we were lucky, that we'd escaped. But they were the lucky ones. The people who never saw it coming. The people who were wiped out in the blink of an eye. Most of them probably never knew what hit them. Even those who did, they only had a few hours warning. Time to panic a little, to pray a little, to say goodbye to those they loved." An image of Jane blinked before his eyes again. "We don't have that luxury. We're going to die slowly. Painfully. Of cold, of dehydration, of starvation."

"We don't all have to die," Martin said coldly.

"What do you mean?" Jake looked at him.

"This ship can't sustain three thousand people, not with the little fuel we have left. But it could keep a few hundred alive. Long enough to find a way to survive."

"You can't be serious?" Lucya stared open mouthed.

"Why not? It makes sense to me. Decimate the population on board. No, not decimate, more than that. Sacrifice, say, nine out of every ten people on board. The resources on the ship can keep three hundred people alive for ten times as long as they can keep three thousand alive."

"Martin, quite apart from the fact that what you are suggesting is completely and utterly morally repugnant and out of the question, it would only prolong the inevitable. The ten percent you let live, will just live a bit longer!" Jake couldn't believe he was having this conversation. He couldn't look at Martin, got up and walked to the window, stared out at the fjord.

"On the contrary," Martin was getting into the flow of his thinking. "That extra time would make all the difference. We could create a farm in Palm Plaza. Rip out the plants, grow food. It wouldn't be enough to feed three thousand. But three hundred? Maybe, if we were clever about it. And we can fish, too. Heck, we could even freeze those we sacrificed and eat them. Like those guys whose plane crashed in the Andes, years ago. There are other ways of generating power as well, given enough time. This ship could be made self-sufficient. If the population were reduced."

"You're disgusting. I can't believe you would even say something like that!" Lucya slapped Martin in the face and stormed out, slamming the bridge door behind her.

"And then there were two," Martin said.

FORTY

EILEEN BAKEMAN STOOD outside her cabin, the tips of her fingers on the door handle. She had been about to enter, but a sound from inside made her stop. It was her husband's voice. She found this strange, because he insisted on never letting anyone else into the cabin. Eileen had made some friends on board, before the asteroid, but Flynn had made it very clear that they were not welcome in their private space. So Eileen was curious; who was he talking to?

Slowly, quietly, she put her ear to the door. Apart from the distant hum of the engines still idling far below, there was no other sound. She could make out his words quiet clearly.

"...so I beg you Lord, give me the strength to carry out your work. The first of many sacrifices is soon upon me. The end draws near, the beautiful day approaches. I am the instrument of your will on Earth, your humble and faithful servant. Amen."

Eileen gasped, took a step back and turned to leave. The door opened and Flynn filled the frame.

"Hello, my love. It is time for you to come inside."

"Oh, Flynn. Hi honey. I was just going to see if the dinner service had started." She took another step away from the cabin.

He reached out, grabbed her arm and pulled her towards the door.

"Flynn! You're hurting me!"

"I said, it is time to come inside now."

He yanked her arm sharply, and in one movement pulled her through the door and flung her onto the bed.

"Flynn, I don't understand? What did I do wrong? Tell me

what I did, Flynn, I'll put it right, I promise!" Tears began to streak down her face.

"Me, me, me, it's always about you, isn't it? You think you did something wrong? You did nothing. Nothing! You are a waste of space, and a waste of resources. This ship doesn't need people like you. People like you are what caused the problem. You consume relentlessly. You take without giving back. You suck the world dry. He gave us a beautiful, abundant world. A world of balance and harmony. And now that balance will be restored."

"Flynn, you're scaring me!"

She dug the heels of her shoes into the bed, pushing herself away from him, but in vain. He was far stronger than she, and he simply tugged her back towards him. He reached over her head, picked up a large white pillow. It was embroidered with the name Spirit of Arcadia, and the logo of Pelagios Line.

"Hush now, my love. It's alright, I forgive you. And He forgives you, too. He loves all of his children, you will find peace in Heaven."

"Flynn, no!"

But her words went unheard, as the pillow covered her face. He held it down, a hand on each side. She writhed and kicked, and nearly broke free. But he sat astride her, pinning her down. It didn't take long, her struggling quickly abated, and then she lay motionless.

FORTY-ONE

THE SILENCE THAT had engulfed the bridge since Lucya had left was broken by a knock at the door. Neither Martin or Jake responded. Then a second knock came, more insistent.

"Who is it?" Jake asked wearily.

"Melvin."

He got to his feet with great effort, still feeling somewhat groggy from having fainted earlier. The subsequent events had taken any energy that might have been left, right out of him. He shuffled to the door, pulled it open.

Melvin strode in, followed by another man that Jake didn't recognise. An older man. He was carrying a gun.

More men filed in behind him. Including Melvin, Jake counted fourteen in total. There were no women. The man with the gun shut the door to the bridge and sprang the bolt, locking out anyone who might have a key.

"Sit down, Jake," Melvin said.

He didn't really understand what was going on, but he was in no mood to argue. He went back to his captain's chair and sank into it.

"So, is this mutiny?" he asked.

"No, it's more democratic than that." As Melvin spoke, the man with the gun stepped up to his side. The others remained silently at the back of the room. "You made a promise. If there was no longer any chance that the owners of this ship had survived, there is to be an election."

Martin looked on, saying nothing.

"From what you and your men have reported from your landing expedition," Melvin continued, "we understand that time has come. There are no more survivors. The world, as we know it, is gone. You and your crew are no longer employees. We are no longer customers. We are all equal. We are all simply survivors. And it is therefore right that we choose who is to be in charge, a leader."

"You're right," Jake said.

"The election is to be held today, immediately. You will put out a call instructing anyone on board who wishes to participate to go to the theatre, cinema, and casino. We have people in all three locations ready to hand out ballot papers."

"No," Jake said, simply.

"I'm sorry?"

"I said no."

"What happened to 'you're right'? Do we need to force your hand?" Melvin glanced at the men behind, and the man with the gun stood next to him.

"Nope. No force necessary. And no election, either. Well, unless you want to run against anyone else. But not me, you're not running against me. I'm done. You're right, I'm no longer an employee, I no longer represent the owners of this ship, there are no owners now. I have no more right to be in this chair than you, him, or anyone else." He pointed at Martin, who continued to remain silent. "To be honest with you, Melvin, I didn't want to be in charge. I never had any grand aspirations to climb the career ladder as far as captain. I certainly don't want the responsibility for three thousand souls given what's out there now. Our days are severely numbered, and you are more than welcome to see out those remaining few from this seat."

He got up, walked towards the door, patting Martin on the shoulder as he passed by, but without looking at him.

"Wait!" Melvin stepped to the side, blocking Jake's exit. "You can't leave the bridge. I need a pilot, and you're the best qualified."

"Well it's like you said, Melvin, there are no employees any more. I don't work for you, or anyone. You're in charge now, so that can be your first decision can't it? Choose who you're going to hire. I'm not applying for the job, by the way. Pedro's good, and I think a couple of the junior seamen survived. I'm sure they'd be happy to interview for the position, or ministerial post, or whatever you decide to call it. Have fun."

He walked around Melvin, unbolted the door, and left without looking back.

Forty-Two

"Ladies and gentlemen, can I have your attention please. This is an important announcement that concerns everyone aboard this ship. My name is Melvin Sherwood. For the last two days, I have been representing the interests of passengers on the Spirit of Arcadia. Today is one of the most important days in the history of the human race. Today, we start over. A new community. A community of survivors.

"You will no doubt already have heard certain rumours regarding a landing party that was sent to the town of Longyearbyen today. Their mission was to discover the fate of the world. What they found, was not good news. I will not lie to you, and this is difficult to hear and to accept I know, but the town and everything in it have been destroyed. The landing party's findings show beyond all shadow of a doubt that, as we feared, the world as we know it has ended. Anyone who survived the heat and storm of the asteroid itself, must surely have perished in the highly toxic ash that it deposited. Maybe, somewhere, there are survivors who made it to some kind of shelter. But even they are unlikely to survive an encounter with the ash, when they resurface. We are forced to conclude that the population on board this ship are the sole survivors of the human race."

Melvin paused, partly for effect, and partly to gather his own thoughts, unaware that every corner of the ship had fallen silent as people listened to his crackling voice on the PA, hanging on his every word.

"Most of us joined this cruise as paying customers, passengers. We were looked after by crew members. Now, there is no distinction. We are all survivors. As many of you know, it was my intention to stand in an election against Acting Captain Jake Noah, as the person who would represent the people, and lead us in our quest for survival. Captain Noah has chosen not to stand. Indeed the captain has, I am sorry to say, abandoned his seat with immediate effect.

"Every community needs a leader, and we must choose one as quickly as possible. I am therefore calling for a debate about the immediate direction we should take, and for and an election to choose a new captain. Anyone who believes they are the right person for that role, may present themselves. Everyone over the age of sixteen years should have a vote. I extend an invitation to all aboard to join with me in the theatre this evening at nine, where those wishing to stand can make their case, and we—as a democratic community—can decide our destiny.

"Make no mistake, the times ahead will be difficult for us all. We will have to make some tough choices, unimaginable choices. History may not look kindly on the decisions we will make, but we must do what is necessary in order to survive.

"Thank you for listening."

FORTY-THREE

JAKE LOOKED AT the speaker inset in the ceiling above his bed. It had just fallen silent.

"Hardly Churchill," he said to himself.

He rolled over and tried to go to sleep.

Someone had other ideas though, and within minutes, a rapid knocking at his door arrested his slide into unconsciousness.

"Go away." He didn't want to see anyone.

"Jake, you'd better open up and tell me what on Earth is going on."

Maybe, he decided, he could make an exception for Lucya. Besides, she was the most stubborn person he knew; there was no way she would leave him in peace. He forced his eyes open and went to let her in. She barged past him and stood at the end of the bed, hands on her hips.

"What are you doing in here? I mean, I am assuming you did hear what Melvin just said? Why aren't you going upstairs to kick his ass? Come on! Jesus, Jake, if you're worried about Tania, don't be! She'll have to look out for herself!"

"Lucya, calm down."

"Calm down? Have you completely lost it? Kiera said you got a bump on the head. Did it knock all sense out of you? We need to go and stop him! Set the record straight!"

"The record is straight. There's nothing to get worked up about."

"He thinks he's in charge!"

"He is in charge."

A stunned silence. Lucya dropped to the bed, mouth open. She tried to speak, realised she didn't know what to say, so stopped again.

"Melvin's right," Jake said. "I have no more right to be in charge than him or anyone else. So I let him take over."

"Oh, really? No more right, perhaps, but a lot more qualification! What does he know about running a ship? You think he understands everything it takes to keep this place going?"

"Of course not. But he doesn't need to, there are plenty of people who do. Martin, Silvia, Claude, you."

"Don't count on me, I'm not spending a second helping him out."

"It doesn't matter, Dave probably will. And even if he doesn't, we can't go anywhere, anyway. You know we're all dead, it's only a question of time now."

"So that's it? You're just giving up?

"What else can I do, Lucya? What else can any of us do?"

"We fight! We work together! We find a way! We have the census. You know who's on this ship? I've seen the lists! There are builders, carpenters, teachers, chefs, farmers, fishermen, mothers, doctors. We have every skill we need start again. We could build a home, a town. A city!"

"Where? The land is poisoned. There's nowhere left to go. If the land this far north is like that, there is no more hope."

"But there must be!" Lucya was crying now. She stood, looked up into Jake's eyes. "I don't want to die, Jake. I don't want you to die! I love you and I can't let it end like this!"

The two of them looked at each other, motionless, neither sure what was about to happen next. They made up their minds at the exact same instant as they flung themselves together, the stress of the last few days fuelling their frenzied and passionate embrace. Two bodies sank onto the bed, and Jake knew he was no longer afraid of dying.

• • •

He awoke to the sound of Lucya getting dressed.

"No, don't get up," she said from the end of the bed. "I'm just going to my cabin to get some things. I'll be back in five minutes. If you want me back, that is?"

He smiled. "Of course I want you back."

She slipped out the door and was gone. Jake lay staring at the ceiling, trying to work out how he felt. He had loved Jane for as long as he could remember. They had met at university, got together in the first week. He was devastated when they had separated. But deep down, he knew it was over. He had always known, if he was honest with himself. They wanted different things and had been growing apart for years. He had tried to blame it on the fact he was away at sea for so much of the year, but that was merely an excuse, things were no better when they were together. If anything, they were worse, the cracks were all too obvious. And then then was Lucya. Of course he had known how she felt about him; everyone knew, she was hardly subtle. And he was deeply attracted to her. But their rank on board, and their professionalism, not to mention Jake's residual feelings for his wife, meant that nothing could ever come of their feelings.

But now? Now the world had changed, in so many ways. Time was running out, they were surely going to end their days on the ship in the weeks to come. So here it was, his last shot at happiness. He had shed his responsibilities, and he knew Lucya would never set foot on the bridge as long as Melvin was in charge. No, they would see out their remaining time as passengers on a cruise ship. They would savour every moment as though it was their last, knowing it really could be.

With that thought in mind, and a smile on his face, he got out of bed and strode into the tiny shower room. A heavy hammering on the door brought him out again.

"Okay, coming. Don't break the door down! I know you're eager to get back into bed." He clasped the handle, swung the door inwards.

It wasn't Lucya. Instead, he came face to face with two men. One looked Chinese. Shorter than himself, older too, with thinning hair. He was dressed in a Hawaiian shirt and Bermuda shorts. The other man was about the same height as Jake, but was of a more substantial build. He was blond and blue eyed, with sharp features.

Both men were carrying guns. Jake recognised them as the semi-automatic weapons from the secure cabinet on the bridge.

"Get some clothes on, you're coming with us," the blond man said.

He spoke with a clipped accent. German, Jake thought, or maybe Austrian. His mind was set racing. What could they need him for? He'd relinquished control. Did they need someone to pilot the ship? Pedro could do that, or any one of a number of sailors aboard.

"Why?" He asked.

The two men looked at each other, then back to Jake.

"Melvin said you weren't very intelligent. Let's see, two of us, armed. One of you, naked. I think we give the orders, and that you follow them, yes?"

"Or what, you'll shoot me? I assume from your being here that you need me, so shooting me isn't going to help, is it?"

"Not you. But your girlfriend? Ja, I could maybe shoot her." The blond man smiled, just a tiny bit. "I mean, after I've had some fun with her first."

Jake felt the blood drain from his face.

"Ja, that got your attention, no? So now you're thinking, maybe we're bluffing?"

It was precisely what Jake was thinking, or at least hoping.

The blond man continued. "But I can tell you that she left this cabin four minutes ago. He hair was a messy, and she was not wearing shoes."

"Where is she now?"

"She is enjoying the company of my colleagues. Being reunited with Tania Bloom. So, if you want to see her alive again, I strongly recommend that you follow my earlier instruction." The smile disappeared. "Get dressed and come with us."

The Chinese man nodded once. Jake turned and scrambled to find his clothes. They had been removed in haste, and were spread around the small cabin. A sock here, a shirt over there. With panic rising, he pulled on his trousers and shirt.

"Take me to her, now!" he shouted.

"No, not yet. You need to be dressed properly, Mr Noah. Put some socks on, tuck your shirt in. Take your time."

"What?"

"I said take your time. Your girlfriend is not going anywhere, she can wait."

Jake didn't understand, but he was in no position to argue. He put on the rest of his clothes and tidied himself up the best he could, his hands shaking.

"Shoes," the blond man said. "And your jacket, too."

As soon as he was fully dressed, the Chinese man gestured with the barrel of his gun that Jake should step outside. He took one last look back at his cabin, he had a feeling he would never see it again. It wasn't much, but it was home for much of the year. The clock radio next to his bed showed the time was 21:30. He and Lucya had slept for longer than he thought. He swallowed hard, shut the door, and looked at the blond man.

"Where now?" he said.

"Follow me."

FORTY-FOUR

THE THEATRE WAS almost full, not quite as packed as it had been three days ago, when everyone had jammed in to witness the end of the world, but considerably busier than for the memorial service. A few seats remained empty, and there was plenty of standing room. Conversations were being held in hushed voices, there was a real air of anticipation, if not quite hope. On the stage stood a tall, red haired man, and an equally tall but much more muscular somewhat older man. It was the latter who spoke first. He had no microphone, but the acoustics were excellent in the well-designed auditorium, and he projected his powerful voice into every corner. As soon as he began to speak, the crowd fell silent, devouring his every word.

"Ladies, gentlemen, allow me briefly to introduce myself. My name is Flynn Bakeman. I'm here this evening as an independent moderator. The purpose of our time here is to elect someone to take charge of this ship, now that the captain has stepped down. I think everyone will agree that this should be done quickly, efficiently, and democratically. This gentleman to my side is Melvin Sherwood. Many of you will already have met Melvin, he has been working with the bridge crew representing passenger interests. Now, if we can get things underway, can I ask anyone who intends to stand against Melvin to come and join us on the stage. If there are too many candidates we will probably need to hold two rounds of voting. So please, come and join us if you wish to stand for election as captain."

A voice from the back called out "What is this, the X Factor?" It was met with a few sniggers, but the noise quickly abated, as those present looked on intently, waiting to see how many people would get up onto the stage.

Only one man did. He had been sitting in the front row. Those who arrived earliest in the theatre would have seen that he was the first person seated. In fact had anyone gone to the theatre hours earlier, when Melvin had finished his announcement, they would have found this man's seat occupied.

The man made his way up the four steps at the side of the stage. He was short, a little hunched over, and rather scruffy. He wore grey trousers, a blue shirt, and a beige jacket. The untidy thin brown hair on his head seemed mismatched with his wiry and bushy beard. Guided by Flynn, he took up position next to Melvin. The two men shook hands, then turned to look out to the auditorium.

A few minutes went by, but it had become clear that nobody else was going to take the challenge. Melvin had to try and suppress a grin. The competition was even less than he had expected. Finally, Flynn spoke again.

"Thank you, sir, for your courage. Now, I would like to invite our two candidates here to speak for a few minutes. Each can present their ideas for exactly how we should proceed in the coming days. In order to keep things fair, I will allow each man a maximum of five minutes in which to speak. When both have had their turn, we will open the floor to questions for a period of thirty minutes During this time we will all have the opportunity to cross examine these men. I will then call for a vote by way of a show of hands. If it's too close to call, we will take a count by asking you to leave through one of two exits. So if that's all clear, then I give the floor to our first candidate."

Flynn took a couple of steps back, and Melvin stepped up to the front and centre of the stage.

"Thank you Mr Bakeman, and thank you, sir, for presenting yourself," he nodded towards the scruffy man. "And thank you to all of you for coming here and supporting democracy. My name is Melvin, and until three days ago I was a passenger, an entrepreneur, a son, and a brother. This was my first vacation in more than five years. The last five years I have created a business. I was out of work, but I didn't want to live off the state. So I borrowed money from friends and family, and I started a business. I worked every single day of the last five years, many days I worked sixteen or seventeen hours. My hard work paid off, and I was able not only to support myself, but also to take on employees and support them and their families too. I tell you this for one reason. That reason is this. To show to you that I know how hard work and commitment pays off. I understand what it takes to get through the hard times, the times when you can't see the light at the end of the tunnel. I know that if you make a plan, and stick to it, keep doing what you believe, then eventually, inevitably, that work will reward you.

"This ship needs a plan. To say there are dark days ahead would be a massive understatement. I think we all comprehend the enormity of the problem here. We are a floating city, with severely limited resources. We have to act decisively and quickly, before those resources come to an end. If you elect me tonight, to take the captain's chair, then I will immediately order this ship to sail for Scotland. It is well within the range of our fuel reserves, and it has one unique feature that I believe will be our salvation. There is a hardened military facility in the north of Scotland, a place that was designed to withstand nuclear attack. If anyone has survived this disaster, they will be in such a facility. Moreover, the bunkers in this base are kept stocked with supplies to last months or years.

I am not suggesting this trip will be easy or without danger. The facility is inland and will require an expedition through dangerous toxic ash. As your captain, I will lead this expedition. I will take on the risk, because I believe that the reward will be survival for us all. That is all I have to say, thank you."

Melvin stepped back. There was silence. Then somebody, one person near the front, began to clap. They were joined by another, and then another. Soon the whole auditorium was resonating with the sound of a thousand people clapping and cheering, and shouting Melvin's name.

Flynn waited for the excitement to calm down before once again taking centre stage.

"Thank you, Mr Sherwood. A passionate speech indeed. So now I would like to ask our second candidate to take the floor." He looked at the bearded man. "If you would like to step forward, you have five minutes."

Flynn once again stepped back, taking up position next to Melvin. The scruffy man moved to the front of the stage.

And that was when all hell broke loose.

Forty-Five

The blond man led Jake down the corridor to the stairs, the other man brought up the rear. They climbed three flights, emerging on deck six. The men made no attempt to hide their weapons, but the ship appeared deserted anyway. Jake assumed that most people had gone to Melvin's election meeting, and anyone who hadn't was staying put in their cabins, awaiting the outcome.

"This way," the blond man grunted. He set off in the direction of the theatre.

The theatre was huge, spanning three decks. There were several sets of doors on each deck, giving access to the different tiers and blocks of seating. They didn't use any of them. Instead, they stopped at an innocuous white door. It was not labelled. The German waited to one side, watching Jake, while the Chinese man pulled out a key, inserted into the lock, and turned it with a click. He pulled down on the handle and the door opened with a squeak.

"In," the blond man pushed Jake towards the room.

He stumbled forwards and found himself in a small dark space. The back wall, to Jake's left, was filled with racks of technical looking equipment. The far wall had more of the same. The front wall, to the right as Jake entered, had a window inset into it. The window was directly opposite the very centre of the theatre stage, and gave an excellent view of the whole theatre. Underneath was a very wide black desk, covered in knobs and sliders. Jake had never been in this room, but he could see that it was used to control the stage lighting and sound.

His captors exchanged a few quiet words, then the Chinese turned and left, closing the door behind him.

"Sit down, relax a little. We have some time to kill." The blond man pulled up a chair and positioned it so that he was looking out over the stage. Jake remained defiantly on his feet.

"As you like," the man said shrugging. The gun lay across his knees, its presence a constant threat.

Jake looked out of the window. He could see Melvin standing on the stage, and another man too. He recognised that man, he had been with Melvin when he came to the bridge earlier. He had been armed. Another of those guns from the cabinet. A third man joined them on the stage. He was much smaller than the other two, scruffy looking, bearded. There was some more talking and then Melvin stepped forward to speak.

The blond man in the small room set the gun down and got to his feet, extracting something from his pocket. It was a thin black plastic tie, the kind used to attach cables together.

"Sit," he said, pointing at the chair.

Jake briefly considered refusing, but it was pointless. Screaming for help would be a waste of time, as the room was clearly soundproofed. Fighting back was also not an option, given the size of the other guy, and the fact he had that gun, of course. He took a deep breath, thought of Lucya, and sat down.

The blond man pulled Jake's arms around behind his back and wrapped the cable tie around his wrists, as well as the central column that held the back of the chair to the base, securing them tightly together. He produced another tie from his pocket and used it to bind Jake's ankles. There was no way he was going anywhere, now. The man walked back to the window and looked out. Jake could see that Melvin was still speaking.

The gun was propped up against one of the equipment racks. The German sauntered over and scooped it up. He unclipped the ammunition cartridge and popped out a number of bullets, which disappeared into his pocket. After slotting the cartridge back into place, he returned to the window, and raised then gun sight to his eye.

"What the hell are you doing? You're going to kill Melvin?" Jake said incredulously. He struggled against the fastenings, trying to get free, but there was give, he was stuck fast.

"Shut the fuck up, if you don't want to see your intestines ripped out and spread across this desk," the blond said without looking around.

Jake did as he was told.

Forty-Six

THE SCRUFFY MAN opened his mouth to speak. If any words escaped his lips, they were never heard. The crack of the gunshot rang out from the back of the auditorium. The noise bounced off the walls, the stage, and the specially placed acoustic surfaces suspended from the ceiling, deafening everyone present for a split second. A red dot appeared in the forehead of the election candidate. The back of his head, along with his brain, was spread over the black curtain that lined the rear of the stage. He crumpled to the floor as if someone had let the air out of him.

Somebody screamed. Then, everybody screamed.

"Everybody get down!" Flynn shouted from the stage. His words went largely unheard. Anyone who could get to an aisle was already running for a door. Those sat further from the exits either cowered in their seats or curled up on the ground.

A second shot rang out. It hit Melvin's right arm. He cried out in pain, grabbing the wound.

"No!" Flynn shouted. He threw himself in front of Melvin, pushing him out of harm's way, just as a third shot was fired. It caught him in the shoulder, and he fell to the ground with a squeal of pain.

The fourth shot found its mark and Melvin's head exploded, his brain tissue and bone mixing with that of the scruffy man on the black curtain. His body fell backwards, crashing to the floor.

Flynn struggled to his knees. It was pandemonium. More people were scrambling to get out. But they couldn't, because all of the doors had been locked. Those people nearest the exits were being crushed by the weight of the mass of bodies pushing forwards.

"Quiet! Everyone stop pushing!" Flynn shouted as loud as he could. He got some attention, but it hardly made any difference.

The four shots had all been fired within a few seconds. When a minute had passed with no further gunfire, Flynn managed with some effort to get back on his feet. That got the attention of some more people, and the panic abated a little. He looked around and spotted a couple of big guys who had been sitting in the front row. They were crouched on the floor, but were not hysterical, they appeared to be holding it together.

"You two, with me!" Flynn called out to them, pointing. Clutching his wounded shoulder he jumped from the stage and started to run up the central aisle of the theatre.

"He's in the lighting room, look!" he yelled breathlessly.

The two men looked in the direction of Flynn's outstretched hand and finger, and sprinted after him. Other people also stopped what they were doing and watched the election moderator charge towards the back of the theatre.

"Watch out! He's got a gun!" someone shouted near the back.

As all eyes followed Flynn, he galloped towards the lighting control room window. Framed within was a man holding a semi-automatic rifle.

Forty-Seven

From his position, tied to the chair, Jake had a perfect view of events as they unfolded. He watched his blond captor shoot the scruffy man on the stage. He saw him shoot at Melvin. He watched the moderator dive to protect Melvin, and the two subsequent bullets which injured the moderator and killed Melvin. He waited for one last bullet which would surely kill the moderator, but it never came.

As soon as Melvin was down, the man stepped back from the window and turned to Jake. His hand went into his jacket pocket and came out grasping a something thin and black. He squeezed it. A steel blade shot out, perfectly polished. He took another step forwards.

Jake, who only hours before thought he was no longer afraid of dying, found himself very afraid indeed. He closed his eyes, and waited to feel the blade on his neck, or through his heart. But he felt neither. Instead he heard a light snipping sound, and the tension around his ankles was gone. He opened his eyes but the blond man was nowhere to be seen. Then, another snip, and his hands fell free. He jumped to his feet and whirled around.

"Congratulations," the blond said, "you just committed double murder. Catch!"

He threw the gun at Jake. Instinct kicked and he caught the weapon in both hands. The man opened the door, released a catch on the lock, exited the room, and pulled the door closed behind him. Jake stood for a second, stunned into silence. He had no idea what had just happened.

It was then that he became aware of the noise coming from the window behind him. There had been screaming since the first gun shot, but the commotion had changed, it was less screaming and more shouting. He turned to look.

"Watch out! He's got a gun!" he heard someone near the window scream out.

He looked down. He was still holding the weapon. He looked up. The election moderator was headed his way at a charge, followed by two burly men.

• • •

Flynn reached the window. The glass had been shattered by the bullets, leaving a carpet of tiny sparkling granules covering the floor.

"Son, don't do anything stupid. Give me the gun," Flynn reached out a hand tentatively.

Jake looked at the gun in his hands as if he couldn't believe it was real. He dropped it like a hot potato, jumped backwards, away from the window.

"Get in there and pin him down!" Flynn shouted at the two men who had followed him. They scrambled up through the opening and across the lighting control desk. Jake didn't move, didn't fight back as the men grabbed an arm each.

Back in the theatre the panic was subsiding. The gunman had been stopped, there was no longer a danger. Now the people were migrating towards the back. Everyone wanted a glimpse of the madman who had just killed the two candidates in cold blood.

"Jake? Is that you?"

The voice came from behind Flynn.

"You know this man?" Flynn turned and asked him.

The man stepped forwards, to better see through the window. Jake recognised him at once.

"Know him? That's Jake Noah. He is, was, the captain," the man said.

"Martin! No! This isn't what it looks like!" Jake cried out. Seeing his chief engineer had snapped him out of his state of shock.

"This is Noah?" Flynn asked. "This is the man who walked

away from the captain's chair? The man who left us without a leader in our time of greatest need?"

"No, that's not true and you know it," Jake protested. "Melvin came to depose me. You were there, one of his heavy mob, I saw you!"

"I've never set eyes on you in my life," Flynn all but spat the words out. "And now what? You've decided that you want your old job back? Decided to wipe out anyone who could stand against you? You think that with Melvin and…the other candidate whose name we never even found out, you think that now they're dead you can just reclaim your position on the bridge?"

"What? No! No of course not. I didn't do this! There was another man, a German!"

Flynn raised an eyebrow. "Is there anyone else in there?" he asked the two men who were still restraining Jake.

They looked around the tiny room, as if someone could somehow have hidden away, and shook their heads.

"Mr Noah, you are a murderer. Your fate is not for me to decide though. Men, hold onto him."

Flynn walked back down the aisle, still with one hand pressed against his shoulder. It was soaked with blood, but he didn't seem to be letting the wound stop him. He reached the front of the auditorium and took the small flight of steps at the side of the stage. All eyes were on him as he stopped in front of the two bodies.

"Ladies and gentlemen, as if we were not already in dark times, we have experienced a true atrocity here. But we must not let these actions stand in the way of democracy. We need a leader now more than ever before." A thousand people were hanging on Flynn's every word. "Clearly the position is not without risk, there will always be elements who are opposed to the democratic process. So, I urge you again, would anyone who thinks they could lead us, please come up to the stage. Time is short, we have to act decisively and act now."

Silence.

Of the thousand or so passengers and former crew packed into the theatre, not one moved.

"Anyone? Please?" Flynn pleaded from the stage.

"Why don't you do it?" someone called out.

"Yeah! You're already up there!" another voice shrilled.

There was a murmur of agreement from the crowd.

"I wouldn't consider myself the man for the job," Flynn said modestly.

Several people shouted in response to that.

"You're a bloody hero, mate!"

"You're clearly a born leader!"

"You've been in charge all evening, why not keep going?"

"Captain Flynn!" somebody screamed from one of the balconies. "He's our saviour!"

That prompted cries of encouragement. The mood in the room was changing. The sense of panic and fear had been replaced by a feeling of anticipation, almost excitement. There were more cries of "Captain Flynn". The cries united and became a chant.

"Captain Flynn! Captain Flynn! Captain Flynn!"

They reached fever pitch, Flynn's name reverberated around the huge auditorium. People were stamping their feet, clapping their hands in unison.

Flynn looked on from his position on the stage. He let the chants continue for a few minutes. Finally he bowed his head, raised his free hand slowly and waved it from side to side. The chanting subsided, the stamping died out, the clapping stopped. Gradually the theatre fell silent, the sense of anticipation greater than ever. Flynn lowered his hand and looked up. He scanned the room slowly, from left to right.

"Well, I don't know what to say right now."

"Say yes!" someone called out from near the front. There was nervous laughter, but the silence quickly re-established itself.

"I'm just a regular guy, who believes in doing the right thing. I came here this evening to help facilitate a democratic process. It seems that fate, in some very strange and twisted way, has seen to it that the people have been able to have their say. Not in the way any of us expected, and not in the way any of us would have wanted. But if the last three days have taught us anything, it is to expect the unexpected. If nobody else is willing to stand, and if this truly is the will of the people gathered here, then I must accept that the hand of destiny has touched me tonight. So it is my humble duty to accept your wishes. I will take the captain's chair, and I will do my best, with the advice of those who are willing to give it, and with the Lord's help, to lead us all to safety."

His last word hung in the air for a second. And then, explosive, rapturous applause. Anyone who was seated, stood. The chant started up once more.

"Captain Flynn! Captain Flynn! Captain Flynn!"

On the stage, Flynn smiled and waved his good arm, signalling for silence. It took a while, but the crowd slowly calmed down.

"Now, let's get these doors open. Someone get through that back window and unlock the doors from the outside. If there's a doctor or nurse present, I could really use some help with my shoulder here," he pulled his hand away and blood dripped from it onto the stage. "And you two heroes who stopped ex-Captain Noah, bring him to the bridge so we can decide his fate. I believe it is located on deck ten. The crew member who recognised him can show you the way."

FORTY-EIGHT

THE TWO MEN hustled Jake out of the room and towards a staircase. He felt immensely grateful that the other doors to the theatre were still locked, meaning there was no risk of being mobbed by an angry crowd. Martin had climbed through the window, and he exited the control room and took the lead without looking once at Jake.

"Martin, listen to me. I didn't do this, you have to believe me. Why would I? I willingly gave up the captain's seat. You were there! You saw me go, freely. It makes no sense for me to kill Melvin!"

"Shut it," one of the heavies grunted.

"I've been set up Martin! They've taken Lucya!"

At the mention of her name, Martin paused, looked round.

"Where is she? Where's Lucya?"

"I don't know, that's what I'm telling you. They took her. She left my cabin, someone took her, and then they came for me."

"I said shut it, or I will shut it for you."

Martin considered Jake's plea. "She was in your cabin? What was she doing there? Were you plotting this together?"

"No! We were…I mean, she came to see me and…They took her Martin, to set me up!"

The man restraining his left arm turned towards Jake.

"I said it twice, you must be a bit thick." He swung a huge fist into the side of Jake's face. The blow knocked him off balance and he tumbled to the floor.

The heavy bent down, grabbed his wrist, and pulled him back to his feet.

"You," he pointed at Martin. "You're done with the questions, now piss off back to wherever you come from."

"What about the bridge?" Martin looked affronted.

"We'll manage."

The two men set off up the stairs, leaving Martin somewhat confused at the bottom. Jake remained silent the whole way, he didn't want to feel the force of either man's firsts again.

They reached the bridge without getting lost or making any mistakes in direction, which Jake found odd. The route was not obvious, a deliberate design to discourage passengers from trotting up there and making a nuisance of themselves. One of the men knocked on the door. It swung open and the three of them went inside.

The captain's chair was empty, as were the other posts. There were people present, though. Four men. Jake recognised them. Two had been on the bridge with Flynn when Melvin had come to call for the election. Of the other two, one looked Chinese and the other was tall, blond, and, Jake thought, probably German. Jake was marched to a chair near the map table. One of the men holding Jake pulled out a couple of cable ties from his pocket and secured him to the chair in exactly the same way he had been back in the theatre. He was sitting in front of the weapons cabinet, which he could see was empty. The door was open, and covered in blood. In the middle was a dent, about the size and shape one would expect to see if a head had been slammed into it with great force. The key in the lock wasn't Jake's; it looked, from the keyring it was attached to, like it had been Max's.

• • •

It was nearly half an hour later when Flynn arrived on the bridge. In the intervening time the six other men present conversed infrequently, and always in voices too low for Jake to be able to make out what they were saying. When Flynn entered, letting himself in with his own key, the men fell silent instantly.

"Mr Noah, congratulations." Flynn spoke—and strode—with authority and none of the humility he had shown in the theatre. He had the air of a man very much in charge and in control. "You played your role better than I could have hoped. I was afraid you would have dropped the gun as soon as Gunter put it in your hands. But no! You stood there in the window, for hundreds of people to witness. And then you put up no fight when I sent Jonas and Aki here to restrain you, perfect!"

Jake's head was reeling, trying to process what Flynn had just said, the implications of his words.

"Gunter? He tried to shoot you...I don't understand. Why... how..." He couldn't articulate everything he was thinking.

"Gunter didn't try and shoot me, he actually shot me. Perfectly, I might add." He nodded an acknowledgement at the blond man, who smiled in response. "Not easy to hit a moving target in exactly the right spot, but Gunter is a bit of a sharp shooter. He avoided any major blood vessels, and the bone. Just took a nick out of my shoulder. Like I said, it all went better than I had hoped."

"You set this whole thing up?" Jake asked, still not sure he understood.

"Hey, boys? I think he's getting it! Yes Jakey, I set it up."

"But why? Melvin would have won that election hands down. He was a pain in the arse, but he meant well and he gave a reasonable speech. The other guy looked like a loser?"

"Of course Melvin would have won. That's why he had to die. And the other guy, well, obviously he had to go. And now you're out of the picture too."

"This was all about getting the captain's chair?"

"You're not very bright, are you, son? Yes, this was about getting the chair."

"Why didn't you just stand against Melvin?"

"Do I really have to lay it out for you?"

"Not really," Jake said, wondering if he would regret his next words. "I mean, you're going to kill me, aren't you? So you don't have to explain anything."

"Wow, son of a bitch, you really don't get it, do you? I can't kill you! You made me a hero. Take yourself out of your own tiny little head for just a second, and put yourself in the seat of one of those sorry ass passengers back in that theatre. I know this might be difficult for you, you being a bit dumb and all, but just try, okay?

So, sorry ass passenger sees some innocent old guy get shot. Then the shooter tries to get Melvin but misses. I dive in to try and save him, and take the bullet. Tragically, Melvin still dies. Loose end, see? Can't have loose ends. So now I'm a hero for taking the bullet. And then, to cap it off, I catch the gunman. That's you, dumbo. And to show I'm a caring human being, I don't execute you on the spot, even though you deserve it. Instead I will arrange a suitable punishment."

"Great, so you're a hero, you get elected captain, and two people are dead. I still don't understand why you didn't just stand for election. You could have won without killing anyone."

"Elected captain? I wasn't just elected captain. I've been given the biggest mandate to run this ship in any way I see fit. I was given a standing ovation. They chanted my name. I'm the people's hero! And the only two people who could have challenged me are out of the picture. One is dead, and the other is guilty of a double homicide. Now there is nobody to question the orders I give. Apart from these guys and a few more of my disciples. But they understand that I am on a God given mission. They are faithful to the cause."

"Where's Lucya?" Jake didn't want to listen to any more of this.

"Your girlfriend is safe. I won't be harming a hair on her pretty little head, don't you worry. I need her for the next phase."

"What phase? What are you going to do to her?" Jake began to struggle in his seat, tried to wriggle free. He couldn't move an inch.

"The next phase is the breeding," Flynn said, and walked away.

FORTY-NINE

LUCYA OPENED HER eyes. It made no difference, she couldn't see a thing. She could have been anywhere, could even have been dead. The pain throbbing in the side of her head made her think otherwise, though. She had no idea what had happened to her. One minute she was leaving Jake's cabin, the next, here she was.

She shook her head from side to side, as if doing so might shake out the fog of unconsciousness that lingered within, clouding her senses. Instead it just sent an explosion of pain through her skull. She screamed, but no sound came out. Something was holding her mouth closed. Duct tape? Whatever it was, it held fast. She breathed deeply through her nose and waited for the pain to subside a little. Collecting her thoughts, she tried to gauge her position. She was sitting, that much she could tell, but that was about all. Tentatively, she tried to move her hands. They were behind her back, and wouldn't budge. Something was digging into her wrists. The more she tried to pull free, the tighter it got. She tried to move her feet. Exactly the same thing happened. She attempted to stand, but discovered that her legs had been bound to whatever it was she was sitting on.

Realising that moving was not an option, Lucya changed tack. Any attempt at movement only served to tighten her bindings, cause pain, and waste energy. She had to use her head. Her first task was to try and figure out where she was on the ship. Remaining perfectly still and silent, she listened hard for anything that might give her a clue. There were no sounds from the immediate surroundings. There could have been other people around, but they would have to be breathing very quietly not to be heard. The only noise wasn't so much a noise, more a vibration. The throbbing of the engines idling at the bottom of the ship. Spending so long at sea, Lucya never normally noticed these vibrations or the noise as the ship cruised the world. It was always there in the background, like wallpaper. Too familiar to be remarkable. But that didn't mean she didn't hear or feel it. Unconsciously, those tiny pulsations were always being picked up by her senses, all the time. Everywhere she went, her brain was recording all sensory inputs. And so it was without any effort at all that Lucya instinctively knew from the intensity of the engine vibration that she was on deck nine. Deck nine comprised almost entirely of staterooms. Mostly the larger, more plush suites, for those with substantial financial means. Aside from these cabins there were a few cleaning stores, and some technical rooms for accessing systems such as plumbing and heating. She had seen inside the cleaning stores and they were tiny, packed full of linen and cleaning products, so she deduced that she had to be in a cabin. All of the cabins on this deck had balconies. Even the inside cabins had balconies, they overlooked Palm Plaza. Lucya smiled inwardly. Balconies were potential escape routes. There was hope.

FIFTY

FLYNN HAD TAKEN up residence in the captain's chair. He was looking out to sea.

"Get me someone who can drive this thing," he yelled.

Jonas and Aki, the two heavies who had escorted Jake to the bridge, headed for the door.

"And a navigator. We need a navigator," Flynn called after them before they were through it.

"You need a lookout, too," Jake said. "I mean, unless you're planning on crashing this ship."

"Bring him over here, I can't hear the son of a bitch from there." Flynn waved a hand at his remaining henchmen.

The German and the Chinese looking man came over to Jake's chair. Taking a side each, they lifted it up, with him still attached, crossed the bridge and dropped it down in front of the captain's seat. It landed with a thud, jarring every bone in Jake's body.

"What did you say to me, son?" Flynn was still looking out of the window.

"I said that if you intend to move this ship, and don't want to crash it, then you're going to need a lookout as well as a pilot and navigator."

"Is that so? Well I guess we'll have to hope the driver can do both jobs then huh? Ought not to be too hard. I wasn't watching the whole time we was out cruising, but I didn't notice a whole bunch of obstacles to hit out there on the ocean."

"What is the breeding?" Jake had to try and push for more. "What are you going to do with Lucya?"

"I told you not to worry about her. She's going to be well looked after. She's one of the lucky ones, pretty little girl like that."

The other men on the bridge chuckled. Jake felt a mixture of fear and rage welling inside him.

"And what about me, what will happen to me?"

"Like I said, justice will be done. You'll die, of course, but not at my hand. At least, not directly. Funny thing is, it wouldn't have made no difference if you hadn't been set up in my little plan there. Your days would still be numbered just the same. Just like nearly every other man on this ship."

"You mean every other person," Jake said defiantly. "Everyone is going to die, you included. This ship doesn't have the fuel to sustain you. I guess Melvin never told you, we're leaking fuel. You take this ship back the way we came and you're going to find yourself stranded in the middle of the Arctic Ocean with no heat, no electricity, no way to prepare or store food. If you sail away from here, you're killing everyone on board."

"No, not quite everyone." A smile spread across Flynn's face. "Oh most of them are going to die, of course they are. Nearly all the men. Most of the women too, at least, all those over the age of thirty. Great job on that census, by the way, it made my job of finding the younger women a whole lot easier. And yes, Melvin told me about the fuel. Another great job. Death will come even more quickly than I had hoped. With no fuel, people will die of the cold, of hunger, of dehydration. Oh I'll make a great show about how we're all doing what we can to help them. It'll provide them with some comfort in their final days and their final hours. They don't need to know about those of us living the high life on deck twelve. Those of us for whom the food will never run out, the heat will never go off, and the water will never run dry."

"You're completely insane!" Jake felt his stomach turn.

Flynn turned to look at him, grinning. "No, son, not insane. Denounce me and you denounce the Lord, for I am doing his work here."

"You're condemning thousands of people to death with your actions. That's not the work of any god, that's an act of pure evil."

"You're wrong. We have been the evil ones. Mankind. We have brought about the gradual destruction of his creation. He gave us a world, a beautiful world. An abundant world, filled with wonder. And how did we thank the Lord for his gift of life? With our factories and our bombs and our pollution and our consumption and our disregard for our fellow men, and fellow creatures. We plundered it. We ruined it. And for that, we deserve to die."

"You believe God sent an asteroid as punishment for what we've done to the planet? You're as crazy as Captain Ibsen. He wanted to kill us all, too."

"You're not listening to me, son. I told you, I'm not here to kill everyone. Most? Sure. But not all. See, the Lord spoke to me. He explained to me about the asteroid. Yes, it was punishment, in a way. But it was also sent to cleanse the world. To purge it of the scourge of humanity. Almost. But we were saved. He gave us a second chance. We get to start again. In time, the dust will go. The land will repair itself, become green again, safe again. It will be a new Eden, a new beginning."

"With you in charge?" Jake closed his eyes, shook his head.

"That's old world thinking. Nobody need be in charge. We'll make a better world. A world based on respect and love."

"Can you even hear yourself?" Jake fought to keep the anger within him. "A better world? Respect? Love? And how are you going to make this better world of yours? By killing thousands of innocent people!"

"Sacrifice is necessary. Billions have already died, what's a few thousand more?"

"So, why not you? Why don't you sacrifice yourself? Because you know what? You're right! In some sick, twisted way, you're right. The sacrifice of most of the people on this ship would allow the rest to survive. For a time, anyway. So why don't you do everyone a favour and sacrifice yourself, and your cronies here, right now, and leave the rest of us a tiny bit more resource?"

"Why not me? Because I am Adam!" Flynn's expression had changed to one of pride, mixed with a little confusion, as if he couldn't understand why Jake didn't see what he saw.

"You're what?"

"I am Adam. And these men," he gestured to the other two men on the bridge, "and ten others like them, are my disciples."

"Like Jesus? You think you're Jesus? You think you're the second coming? You're even crazier than I thought."

"The Lord spoke to me, after the asteroid. He told me my real name. That name is Adam. He told me that the world will be reborn. We will find our Garden of Eden. And with twelve others like me, we will start over. The men, and the women over the age of thirty, will be sacrificed. The younger women will join us in Eden, for the breeding. Together we will make a new world."

FIFTY-ONE

LUCYA WAS ROCKING from side to side. She was tied to a chair of some description, but she had soon worked out that the chair itself was not fixed to anything. She swung her weight from one side to the other. With each swing she felt two of the legs raise up from the floor, a little higher each time. As she swung in the opposite direction the legs thumped back down and those on the opposite side rose. The thud made by the chair legs hitting the ground was muffled. She was on a carpet, which meant she wasn't in a bathroom or cupboard.

The momentum was gradually building. Another swing and she knew the chair would tip. She put all her effort into it, straining her head and trying to shift the mass of her body to the left. The chair's right side lifted, tilted over. It teetered in perfect equilibrium for a second, two seconds. Lucya stretched her neck as far as she possibly could, trying to get every last ounce of weight to the left. Then the chair started to fall. It felt like it was going over in slow motion. A thought ran her head; what if there's something just to the left, something hard?

She hit the floor with another muffled thud. Her head bounced off the carpet. It may have been soft, but there was still a hard floor underneath and the impact sent bright flashes of light dancing before her eyes. The way that her hands had been tied behind the back of the chair meant that part of the back was now pinning her arm to the floor. With all her weight was on it, she could feel it already starting to go dead as the circulation was cut off.

She tried moving her legs. They remained stubbornly stuck together, but there was a tiny bit of give in the legs of the chair that they had been attached to. The swinging had weakened the structure of it. She tensed her thigh muscles and then her calves. She pulled them towards her bottom, then tried flexing them out away from her. The tiny movement grew a fraction larger. She continued to jerk her heels and thighs backwards and forwards, squeezing and flexing, crunching and stretching. Her muscles were burning, but she kept on pushing, glad of all those evenings spent in the gym. Then, finally, a cracking sound. The legs had started to become detached from the seat of the chair. Now there was lots of give. One more squeeze between thigh and calf, and there was another crunch and the sound of splintering wood. Three of the legs had come free, and one had snapped in two.

Her legs were still bound together, but she could at least now move them. She straightened them out, and then with her feet she pushed herself round on her side. She tried to grip the floor with her feet, to pull herself towards the broken legs. Another push to turn herself, and her outstretched fingers touched on a split chair leg. Carefully, with a combination of her bound feet and legs, her fingers, and her head pressed against the carpet, she was able to manoeuvre her hand around the sharp piece of wood. The tightness of her bindings made moving her hands difficult, but she found she was able to position the splinter between her hands and the plastic tie than held them together. Very slowly, she started to saw.

FIFTY-TWO

"UNTIE HIM, NOW," Flynn waved a hand dismissively as he spoke.

Gunter and his sidekick approached. The German's knife was pressed into service once more, severing the bonds that held Jake to the chair.

"Mr Jake Noah, for the murder of Melvin Sherwood, and another unnamed man, and the attempted murder of myself, I sentence you to exile from this ship. Take him away. Put him in that inflatable thing, the one he used before. Once we're out of the fjord, cut him free."

"You said you weren't going to kill me. That's a death sentence!"

"I said I wouldn't kill you directly. I'm giving you a chance. Maybe you'll find your own Eden, if you paddle long enough. If you survive long enough. Goodbye, Mr Noah. I'll be sure to give your regards to that lovely little Russian girl, when I see her for phase two."

The anger within Jake exploded. He drew in both his arms, pulling the two men restraining him in close, and then threw them outwards. It all happened in a split second, and the energy he put into the movement was enough to send both men staggering. He immediately drew back his hand, clenched his fingers into a fist, and rammed it into Flynn's abdomen. Jake had never hit anyone before and had no idea what to expect. Even so, the resistance in the tensed muscles his hand connected with took him by surprise. Flynn was no slouch, he kept himself in shape. If the punch caused him any pain, he didn't let it show. Before Jake could pull back for another shot, he felt his arms being restrained. He didn't put up a fight, he knew it was pointless.

"When you drop him in that raft, take out the oars," Flynn said. He turned and sat back down in the captain's chair. "And if you see the other two, tell them to hurry up with finding a driver. Let's burn some fuel."

Jake was marched off the bridge. The journey back down through the ship was not as quiet as that from the theatre an hour earlier. People were out and about. Word of events had got around, and even those who had not witnessed the shooting were aware of what had happened, even if their grasp of the facts was not entirely accurate. Most people simply stopped and stared at Jake as he was marched along by his escorts. Some jeered. A few shouted "murderer!" One spat. But at no time did Jake try and protest his innocence, he knew there was nothing to be gained by it. A thousand people believed that they had seen him shoot and kill. He hoped he might at least see Silvia, or Barry, or Grau. They might believe him. They knew him well enough to know he would never take a life, at least not in the way he had been framed. Ibsen had been a different matter, that was self-defence. The memory of the fight in his cabin, and how it had ended, turned his blood cold. He was a killer. He had taken another man's life. Was it so hard to think he would do it again? The realisation made his legs go weak. He stumbled and fell.

"Get up," the German grunted.

Jake couldn't get up. His head was spinning. Being framed, having people who didn't know him think that he was the gunman, that was something he could just about cope with. But having his close colleagues, his friends, believe that he was capable of this? That was too much. And Lucya? The thought of Flynn and his plans for her sent him over the edge. He began to shake uncontrollably, face down on the floor.

"I said get up!"

His convulsions were making it hard to breathe. He didn't care. He wanted to die, right there and then. He knew he should never have survived the asteroid. That he had survived but not stopped Ibsen before he'd killed Hollen just deepened his guilt. Hollen would have made a great captain, he would never have let all this happen. A confusion of thoughts coursed through his mind. A sharp blow to his ribcage sent a wave of pain through his body. He felt a rib crack. His breathing became even more laboured.

"Get up, or I will kick the life out of you," the German growled.

He was bent over Jake, speaking directly into his ear. Apparently unwilling to wait for him to comply, and with the help of his silent counterpart, he hauled Jake to his feet.

"Now, walk!"

The pain in his side overrode all other thoughts. A small crowd had gathered, they were jeering and calling out.

"Murderer!"

"You're pathetic, they should kill you right here!"

"Why did you do it?"

"Coward!"

Something snapped in his head, clicked everything into focus. He couldn't change these people's mind about what he had done, but he could go out with his head held high. Better to be remembered as defiant to the last, than as a coward. With considerable effort, and even more pain, he put one foot in front of the other and took as step. Then another, and another. He looked at the crowd of people. Tried to speak. The words came out in short bursts, between gasps for air.

"I didn't…kill anyone…I was framed…Believe what…ever you want…but I beg you…choose a new….a new captain…he's evil… Flynn is evil."

A punch to the kidneys made any further speech impossible. He was in too much pain to try and make words. Besides, it was clear that the few words he had managed had fallen on deaf ears; the blow he'd just taken was met with spontaneous applause and cheering.

The rest of the walk down through the decks felt to Jake like it took a lifetime. The lower in the ship they got, the fewer people they encountered. As they reached deck two, Jake felt the familiar vibrations of the engines spinning up to full operating speed.

Fifty-Three

With a snap, the tie binding Lucya's hands together gave way. She had lost all feeling in her left arm but, with her right arm in front of her, pushing against the floor, she brought herself back into a sitting position. Immediately she felt the blood rush back into the previously trapped limb. The numbness was replaced by a tingling which became so intense it was painful. She swung the arm backwards and forwards, trying to recover some sensation. With both hands now free she was able to grab another piece of smashed chair leg. It made short work of the tie holding her feet together. She tried to stand, but the cord that was bound around her legs and the seat of the chair restricted her movement too much. Trying to work it down her legs so that she could step out of it didn't help, it was tied too tightly. She picked up the sharp piece of broken chair again, and began sawing.

It took a good ten minutes to sever the cord, but finally she was free. She struggled to her feet and, with her hands held out in front of her, carefully and quietly she stepped forwards.

In the time she had taken to free herself, Lucya's eyes had grown more accustomed to the dark and she could just about make out silhouettes and outlines. She was fairly sure she was in a bedroom, given the large and flat shape in the middle. She headed for that first and reaching down to touch it, her fingers made contact with a thick puffy quilt. Rounding the bed and feeling her way as she went, she walked gingerly towards where she thought the door should be. Before her outstretched hands detected the extremity of the room, her knees came crashing into something low and hard. The noise of the impact sent her heart rate soaring. She froze, holding her breath for what seemed like an eternity, terrified that someone would come charging in to see what had happened. But nobody came to check on her, and the only sound was that of the blood pumping through her ears. She lowered her hands and discovered that her route had been blocked by a chest of drawers. Working her way sideways along the furniture for a few metres, she eventually found the unmistakable texture of the door.

With the tips of her fingers she lightly explored the surface until they alighted on the handle. She put her ear to the door and listened intently, trying to determine if there was someone on the other side. Once again, the only sound she could hear was that of her own heart thumping, firing adrenaline around her body, preparing her for a fight. Ever so slowly, she turned the handle, covering it with her free hand as if doing so might mask any noise. But there was no sound. The well maintained mechanism turned smoothly and silently. With the slightest of tugs the door came towards her. A vertical bar of light from outside streaked across her face. She glanced behind her saw that the window had been boarded up, explaining the lack of daylight in the bedroom.

Lucya turned back to the door, pulled it open a little more, and peered through the gap. Beyond it was a sitting room. Although much brighter than the bedroom, it wasn't well lit. Curtains had been drawn across the balcony double doors, letting through only a dim glow. A sofa and two chairs were arranged around a low table. Someone was sitting in one of the chairs, facing towards Lucya. She recognised who it was at once.

"Tania!" She exclaimed in a loud whisper.

Fifty-Four

For the second time that day, Jake stepped onto the extendible steps which led to the platform normally used for boarding the tender. This time though, there was no tender, only the inflatable life raft that he himself had ordered be tied up there.

"Down." The German prodded him in the back.

He looked around helplessly, half hoping to see someone, anyone, come charging out onto the steps to save him from his fate.

Nobody came.

"Do you want me to hit you again? I can hit you again."

He had a feeling the German enjoyed hitting people, and wondered what the guy did in life, before coming on this cruise. Before the world ended. He didn't think he worked as a henchman for a nutter who believed he was Adam reincarnate. He was probably a lawyer. Or a dentist. Or a computer programmer. Someone with a repetitive regular job that offered no excitement. And so what, he asked himself, would become of the others on the ship? How much did it take for normal, nice, ordinary people to turn mercenary? When the food started running out, things were going to turn nasty pretty fast. Entire wars had been fought for reasons less important than self-preservation. But Flynn must have known all that. He was probably counting on it. Find the women, make them all secure on one deck. Defend that deck at all costs, and then let everyone else fight amongst themselves. They would do the job for him, finishing themselves off.

"You are going to die in that boat, but I could just as easily kill you here. Flynn won't know any different."

The German was losing his temper. Jake shook his head, as if he might be able to shake the terrible thoughts and images out. He started down the steps towards the raft.

At the bottom, the Chinese man held onto him while Gunter reached into the inflatable and pulled out the oars. Behind Jake there was a sudden rush of water, an eruption of millions of bubbles. A strong current pushed the raft away from the ship, stretching the rope to its maximum extent. The bow thruster churned up the fjord, turning the blue green water white. The Spirit of Arcadia slowly started to ease away from the coast.

"Get in," the German commanded, pointing at the tiny vessel.

The sides of the raft were low, designed to make it easy to board from the sea. But that made it hazardous to enter by more conventional means. The pain in Jake's side caused by his broken rib, made it difficult to crouch. He was having trouble working out quite how to get in without tipping the thing over. Gunter saved him from having to think further with a hefty shove in the back. He was sent flailing into the raft, where he landed face down with a slap. With a bolt of excruciating pain shooting through his side, he blacked out.

Fifty-Five

Lucya pulled the door fully open and ran to the head of housekeeping. Tania looked up, smiling at her.

"Tania, we've been so worried about you!"

"There's no need, I've been fine. They've treated me very well."

"Why haven't they let you go? Melvin's in charge now, he's the head of the rebel passengers. They took you to force Jake's hand, so he had to let Melvin on the bridge. But now he's in charge, surely they don't need you?"

"It's not that simple, Lucya."

"Do you know why I'm here? Do you know how long I've been here? All I remember was walking to my cabin."

"I think they brought you in about an hour ago, maybe a bit longer."

"Okay. Did you see how many there are? Are they guarding the door? Are you hurt? Can you help me fight them?

Lucya looked at the woman seated in front of her. She seemed to be remarkably calm. Something didn't feel right. If she'd been here all along she must have heard the chair break, and the crash of the drawer unit. The door between the sitting room and the bedroom wasn't locked. Why hadn't she come and helped her?

"My dear Lucya, we're not going anywhere. We are going to stay right here. Why don't you sit down?"

"What? No! We need to get out of here. Jake could begin trouble!"

"I wouldn't worry about Jake anymore. I wouldn't worry about anyone else. Jake has been taken care of. Really, sit down for a bit. Flynn will be here soon, he'll explain everything for you."

"Flynn? Who the hell is Flynn? Are you working with Melvin?"

"Melvin is dead. At least, he should be by now. Flynn is the captain, if everything has gone to plan. He's going to save us, Lucya. We're the lucky ones, the chosen ones. We will be treated like queens. You'll see. Flynn will explain it all."

"Oh my God, they got inside your head, didn't they? They got you believing crazy stuff. Tania, I'm really sorry, if you can't help me then I'm going to have to go on my own. But we'll come back for you. When I find Jake, we'll get Max and come back for you, I promise."

Lucya started for the main cabin door. She heard Tania spring to her feet behind her.

"Stop!"

"Come with me, Tania!"

Lucya tried the door. It was locked. She heard a click, turned back to see what had made the sound. Tania was right behind her. Her hand flew up to Lucya's neck. She was clasping a knife.

"I said, stop. Now, walk very slowly with me. If you don't want to sit here with me in comfort that's fine. But you're going back in your cage until Flynn comes."

Lucya tried to resist, but the blade pressed harder against her throat, stretching the skin dangerously close to breaking point. She had no choice but to obey. A wrong move and the sharp knife would slip through her flesh, opening her windpipe and severing arteries. Very carefully, the two women shuffled back to the bedroom. Once inside, Tania turned them both around so that she had her back to the door, then pulled away the blade and stepped back, pulling the door shut behind her. Lucya heard a sound like a bolt sliding. She immediately tied opening the door, pulled it hard several times, but it was no good. Someone had fitted a fastening to the outside. She was locked in.

Fifty-Six

Jake wasn't allowed to remain unconscious for long. Icy cold water splashing onto the back of his head brought him round quickly. With a groan he tried to roll over onto his back. Another splash of water soaked his legs. He heard laughing behind him. With difficulty he managed to pull his knees up and get onto all fours, and turned on the spot so that he was facing the landing platform. The Chinese man was batting one of the oars into the sea, sending arcs of water into the raft. Gunter apparently found this hilarious.

"Okay," Jake cried out, "you got my attention, you can stop."

This only made Gunter laugh even more. He picked up the other oar and joined his colleague. Between the two of them they were able to shift a surprising amount of sea water. There was already a couple of centimetres accumulated in the bottom of the raft and Jake's hands were submerged. He tried uselessly to evacuate it with a cupped hand, but it was useless. Quickly out of breath, he turned and collapsed onto his back, lying in the freezing water, staring at the sky.

Now that they weren't getting a reaction, the two men stopped thrashing around with the paddles. The German sat down on the bottom step, propped his oar against the railing, and pulled his thick coat closer around himself. The other man remained where he was, watching over the raft. He dropped his oar at his feet.

An idea occurred to Jake. Still looking at the sky, he spoke to the men.

"You realise he's going to kill you too, don't you?"

Gunter laughed. "You don't know what you're talking about."

"Really? And I suppose you think you know him? I mean, how long have you actually known him? Three days?"

"You can learn a lot about someone in three days. We have the same ideals, we see the same future."

"I expect Melvin thought that as well."

"Melvin was a puppet. A means to an end. He was always going to be disposed of."

"Which is my point," Jake said, sitting up now. The damage to his ribcage made it painful, but he closed his mind to it, determined to get his point over. "He was always going to die, yet he trusted Flynn. Just like you trust him."

"That's different."

"Why exactly?"

"Because we were in on it from the start. We knew Melvin would die."

"And who's to say he's not in on it more than you?" Jake pointed to the Chinese man. "Maybe you're the next Melvin. Maybe he knows you're next to die."

A look of uncertainty flashed across Gunter's face. The other man's expression remained inscrutable.

"Think about it," Jake sensed he might have struck a seam of doubt. He intended to mine it as far as he could. "Flynn is planning on killing thousands. Why save twelve? Why save anyone other than the women?"

"He needs us, for the breeding." Gunter got to his feet. "He explained it to us. One man isn't enough, he needs a wider gene pool to build Eden."

"But why your genes? What's so special about you? I mean, I suppose you're strong, but you're not exactly the smartest man on this ship are you? I'm pretty sure that he could find more intelligent men to breed from, fitter physical specimens. Why would he pick Laurel and Hardy when he could find some intelligent, funny and, dare I say it, attractive men to father his next generation?"

"That's it, I'm going to kill him now," Gunter said.

He picked up his discarded oar and lifting it above his head, strode towards the raft. The Chinese man put out an arm to stop him, shook his head once, silently.

"Taking orders from him now are you?" Jake smiled. "I guess not all disciples are created equal? Or are you not a real disciple? Maybe he's a true follower and you're just a foot soldier. A pawn to be sacrificed, when it suits, or jettisoned when you're no longer of any use."

"Let me past, Zhang," Gunter looked at the smaller man.

Zhang shook his head once more.

"Well I think it's clear who's the boss around here, isn't it?" Jake said. A tiny flame of hope ignited in his gut.

"Flynn is in charge. You don't order me around Zhang. Now let me past, or do I have to force you?"

Zhang stood his ground, staring at Gunter.

"Fuck, Zhang!" Gunter was losing his temper fast. "It's true what he said, isn't it? Are you using me? I swear, if you are using me, I will kill you."

Still Zhang said nothing. His arm remained outstretched, a barrier between the German and the raft.

Gunter's face exploded into a ball of rage. He swung back the oar with both hands, like a golf club, then heaved it forwards with all his strength. The height difference between the two men meant that the paddle of the oar was on a trajectory to meet directly with Zhang's neck. Jake watched as it twisted in the air, turned sideways on. The force with which it was swung, the speed with which it travelled through the air, it was sure to decapitate the diminutive disciple.

Except that he ducked. At the critical moment, Zhang's legs folded beneath him and he lost half a metre in height in a matter of milliseconds. With nothing to arrest its momentum, the oar kept on swinging, taking Gunter's hands with it. As soon as it cleared the airspace above Zhang, he bounced back to his feet. In his hands was his own previously discarded oar. He held it in front of him, between the legs of the German, and it rose with him until it met resistance. It connected with Gunter's crotch with such force that it broke cleanly in two. The paddle fell clattering to the platform.

Now it was Gunter's turn to drop. His hands flew open, releasing the oar which flew into the fjord. He fell to his knees, clutching his groin and bellowing something in German. By the time the blond man's knees hit the deck, Zhang had brought the half of the oar still in his hands back, ready for another strike. He swung it forwards like a baseball bat. Jake heard a terrible crack as the shaft connected with Gunter's throat. It crushed his windpipe and sent him flying backwards, where his head smashed against the lowest of the metal steps. Spots of blood erupted from his skull, spraying the other steps with tiny red polka dots. Zhang stepped over the broken paddle of the oar and with one foot rolled the limp and broken body of the German off the platform and into the fjord. The bow thruster was still turning at full pelt, and the churning water spun the corpse around several times before sending it off towards the shoreline.

Jake sank back into the raft, dumbstruck. Any hope of trying to overpower the man, or to reason with him, was dashed. He watched Zhang calmly untie the rope that held the little raft captive, throw it into the inflatable, and with the same foot he had used to dispatch his former colleague, push it away from the ship.

Fifty-Seven

Lucya felt her way back to the boarded up window. Having seen the room illuminated by the light from the next room, she had a much better idea of the layout. This time there was no crashing into furniture and she located her target with ease. She ran her fingers around the frame, looking for a break in the tape that held in place whatever had been use to board it up. Once she touched upon a serrated edge and began to peel it back. The tape was well stuck down. It felt like a super sticky plumber's tape, capable of sealing leaks in high pressure pipes. Using her long and well manicured nails, she scraped back the edge, millimetre by millimetre. Once she had successfully removed enough to get a decent grip, things moved much faster. She was able to pull of strips of the tape with relative ease. She expected to see light flood in through the gap between the boarding at the window, but there was none. Instead, there was just more tape. Layer upon layer of tape.

It took nearly a quarter of an hour and four broken nails to finally reach the last layer. This time, when she pulled at the end, the scratching noise of the sticky material coming away from the frame was accompanied by a crack of daylight appearing. Spurred on by her success, she finished un-peeling all four sides. To her amazement, the boarding wasn't screwed to the window or fixed by any other means than the tape itself. As the last stretch of it came away, so did the window covering. Light flooded into the room, temporarily blinding her.

When her eyes recovered she found that the board she had removed was in fact a piece of wood, roughly cut from a wardrobe door. She turned her attention to the window itself. It was small, but not so much that it wouldn't be possible to climb through it.

The only problem with that idea was that the window didn't open, it was the kind that was fixed into a riveted frame. It was also double glazed, making it very strong. The block of wood that was previously covering it would perhaps make a useful tool for breaking through, but Lucya could see that it would require repeated strikes to fracture the glass. Every strike would be a risk, the noise would be sure to draw the attention of Tania and anyone else who might now be in the next room.

A new idea occurred to her. She picked up the piece of the wardrobe door and gauged its weight, balancing it in her hands, turning it from end to end, evaluating its strength. Once confident it could withstand a reasonable amount of punishment, she set it down on the bed and took a proper look around the cabin for the first time. It was a standard bedroom. A small double bed opposite the window, modern cabinets to each side, wardrobes along one side wall, a couple of chests of drawers on the other side, by the door to the sitting room. Between the wardrobes was a narrow door that provided access to a tiny shower room. Peering inside she found a small plastic shower cubicle, toilet, and a sink with a mirrored cabinet above.

"Perfect," she said to herself.

She closed the shower room door behind her, hoping it would block out any noise, then opened the cabinet door. It was held in place with two flimsy hinges. She knew they would break without much effort because her own cabin had exactly the same unit, and the door was forever falling off. Gripping it with both hands, she pulled sharply downwards, twisting as she did so. The door came away easily, with just a light pinging sound as the short screws holding the hinges in place popped out.

Slipping back out of the en suite, she carried the mirrored door across the bedroom and placed it on the drawer unit by the door to the sitting room. Then she pulled the duvet from the bed, doubled it over, and arranged it on the floor in front of the the same door. She paused for a moment, thinking, then added the pillows from the bed to the duvet. Finally she picked up the solid board that had covered the window, and positioned herself near the door and next to the chest of drawers. After carrying out a few practice swings, she was happy that everything was ready. She brought the board up over her head, and then brought it crashing down onto the mirror with all her might. The glass shattered, sending shards and splinters flying in all directions. Most importantly though, it made an incredible noise. Anyone in the sitting room could not have failed to have heard it. It sounded for all the world like a window being broken.

Within a second of the glass shattering, she sprinted forwards, getting herself in place behind the door. She arrived just in time. The sound of the fixing being unbolted coincided with her taking up position. The door flew open, Tania came running in. She almost tripped on the folded duvet, but caught herself in time, stumbling forwards. Lucya stepped out from her hiding place, the board once again raised high above her. She hesitated, but only for a split second. The heavy chunk of wood came swooping back down, meeting the back of Tania Bloom's head with immense force and sending the woman crashing to the ground. She landed right in the middle of the duvet and the pillows. Lucya dropped the board and fell to her knees, checked the back of the other woman's head trying to assess the damage.

"I'm so sorry, Tania," she said. "But what you're doing, it is wrong."

Tania was out cold, but there was no blood spilt. Lucya arranged her in the recovery position. She was already immobilised, there was no need to cause her any more damage or risk anything else happening. When she was satisfied with how the woman was arranged, she collected up some of the discarded tape and used it to bind her captor's hands behind her back. Happy she had done what she could, she backed into the sitting room, closing and bolting the door behind her.

She skipped across the room to the main door, put her ear to it and tried to listen out for the sounds of anyone else who might be standing guard. Silence. She curled her fingers around the handle, quietly pushed it down, and pulled it towards her. No sooner was it opened a few centimetres than her eyes peered out through the crack. She could only see in one direction without opening the door wider, but it was clear, the passageway was empty. She pulled the door open and slipped outside, looked left, the side that was previously blind, and let out the breath she had been holding in. It was all clear, there was nobody to be seen.

There were three main staircases that ran between all the accommodation decks. One fore, one aft, and one in the middle. Lucya checked the cabin number. She was nearest the aft, which suited her fine, as her first thought of a destination was the engine room, which was located at the rear of the ship. It meant descending a long way, which increased the risk of getting caught, but there really wasn't anywhere else to go. The bridge was off limits, and she had no idea where any of the rest of the crew might be. At least in the engine room there was a good chance of finding Martin, and refuge. She turned left, and stopped in her tracks. The door of the opposite cabin had just opened.

"Well hello there young lady. I must admit I didn't expect to see you out here."

Lucya's heart almost exploded in her ears. She tried desperately to keep calm. There was no need to panic, she told herself. Just a passenger making conversation.

The man in the doorway clicked his fingers. Immediately two other men appeared behind him. The three stepped out of the cabin. The first man was well built, strong looking. The other two were even heftier.

"I was just on my way to come and introduce myself," the first man said. "My name is Flynn, I am the captain now. I've just been talking to your boyfriend, Lucya, the ex captain."

"Jake? Where is Jake? What have you done with him?"

"Well, you know, he killed a few people, so we had to get rid of him."

"You're lying! Jake would never kill anyone or harm anyone. Where is he?"

"I told you, he killed two men. I was lenient, probably too much so. He has left the premises."

Lucya tried to charge forwards, to do physical harm to Flynn.

But his men had anticipated the move and grabbed her before she got too close. They held her in a vice-like grip.

"But I don't want to talk about him, let's talk about you," Flynn continued. "You've proved yourself to be quite remarkable. I assume you have somehow overcome Ms. Bloom in there?" He looked at the door to the cabin where Lucia had been held captive. "I don't think she let you out willingly. She has made a surprisingly good convert to the cause. She doesn't have your spirit or, dare I say it, inventiveness, though. Getting out of there, that takes talent. I think you'll be one of our top specimens. It seems to me you've compromised Tania's cabin. Let's take you somewhere else, somewhere more suitable. It seems a shame to lock up such a pretty one as yourself," he caressed the side of her face with rough dry fingers, "but this is as much for your own safety. We have a more secure cabin my boys here have been working on. The good news is that some of your old crew mates are already there. You can talk about how great things were before! Silvia will be delighted to see you, as will Doctor Lister. Taker her," he said, clicking his fingers once again.

Lucya struggled, kicked, lashed out, tried to scratch, to scream, but either man on his own was more than capable of overpowering her. Together, she stood no chance. One of the men was behind her, he encircled her with his arms, squeezing her arms against her and rendering them inoperative. The other lifted her feet. The carried her off down the corridor like they might have carried a corpse. This body was a lot noisier, though.

FIFTY-EIGHT

JAKE WAITED UNTIL Zhang had mounted the steps and returned inside the boat before he moved. He could see Gunter's discarded oar still floating, some way away. He was being pushed towards the shore, and so was the oar, but the oar had a considerable head start. He crawled to the front corner of the raft, and leaning over the side he started to paddle. His movement was severely restricted by the pain in his side. He felt pathetic, splashing his hand in the water ineffectively. Every stroke was agony, and not only did it not seem to bring him any closer to his immediate goal of the oar, it also took him further away from the ship in terms of time. He knew the longer he took to reach the paddle, the less chance he had of ever catching the Spirit of Arcadia. So he kept on paddling like a puppy at sea.

When fatigue almost overcame him, and he was forced to his knees to relieve the pressure on his ribs, something remarkable happened. The oar appeared to stop dead in the water. It was no longer advancing, he was actually gaining on it, and without any effort on his own part. The wake of the bow thruster alone was propelling him forwards, but not the oar. Within a minute he was almost on top of it. He could see the reason it wasn't moving. It was caught against one of the submerged pieces of pier. A jagged triangle of concrete and steel poking through the surface of the fjord like a spring shoot. Jagged, and very sharp. Easily capable, Jake realised with horror, of puncturing an inflatable life raft.

He hurled himself forwards, bouncing on the front inflated section sending a surge of pain through his side. With arms outstretched, he tried to grab the oar with one hand while simultaneously pushing off from the fragment of pier. His left hand closed around the shaft of the oar and he pulled it out of the water, threw it over his head and heard it land on the rubber bottom of the raft behind him. At the same time, a spur of reinforcing steel jutting from the smashed concrete caught him in the middle of his right hand, reopening the wound there, created during his battle with Ibsen. Blood gushed from the tear in his skin, but he couldn't let the pain distract him from his task. With both hands, he pushed off from the pier with all the force he could muster. The raft floated away from the obstacle. Jake scrambled to the other end, clambering over inflated air chambers that were designed to add buoyancy and redundancy and also to provide somewhere to sit. He collected the oar on his way. Reaching the end, he started paddling furiously. The ship was now a considerable distance away and was executing a turn. The raft began to move, but by paddling only on one side it was not only advancing but also turning to the left. He shuffled on his knees to the right hand side, lowered the oar into the water and began paddling again, bringing the craft back straight, and then round to the right. Shuffling back to the left hand side he repeated the operation. But it was no good. One man alone could not paddle fast enough. And a man with at least one broken rib, who was losing blood through the gash in his hand, stood no chance. Jake fell back onto his back, splashing down into the water that was still swilling around in the bottom of the raft, and roared.

"Nooo! Lucya!"

His cries and screams carried across the water, bounced off the sloping remains of Longyearbyen, and echoed back out over the fjord. Jake was beaten.

In the distance, the Spirit of Arcadia had turned one hundred and eighty degrees, and was sailing towards the mouth of the fjord, and the open sea.

FIFTY-NINE

23 HOURS LATER

JAKE OPENED HIS eyes, frightened. Something had made a sound. This was odd, because since he had seen the ship sail out of the fjord and head south, there hadn't been any sign of life, at all. No birds. No butterflies, or moths. No sea lions, or polar bears. Not even any fish. And certainly no people. The world was dead, and he had accepted that he was going to die here too. The wake from the ship and the current in the fjord had carried him further east, away from the open sea. There was no broken pier here, and no pulverised town. Just steep sloping hills on either side. Grey hills, thick with toxic ash. Nowhere to go on land, nowhere to go at sea. Jake was beaten and he knew it.

He had tried to make himself as comfortable as he could, given the circumstances. He had succeeded in removing most of the water between two of the parallel inflatable sausage benches, making a third of the raft more or less dry. The wind had changed direction and was now blowing up the fjord, the mountains to either side offered no protection. So he had unrolled the bright orange hood and erected that, giving him some degree of shelter. A bright pink buoy had fallen out of the folds of the hood as he had unfurled it. It looked like it had been punctured and hastily repaired with silicone. He'd wedged it into the corner between the outer air chamber and an inflatable bench, and used it as a head rest. Staying down low, curled up, he was able to conserve a little body heat, despite his wet clothes and the icy conditions. He'd even managed to go to sleep for a while.

But then there had been the noise, loud enough to rouse him

from his slumber. He pushed the orange cover back down into the raft, got to his knees, and scanned the landscape in every direction. Nothing moved except the water, rippling in the wind. Had he dreamt the sound, he wondered? Maybe it was the dehydration, causing his mind to play tricks on him. When had he last eaten, had anything to drink? He had no idea. He'd been adrift for hours, perhaps days? And before that he had hardly eaten on board. His mind wandered. How would he die here, what would kill him first? The cold? Or the hunger? Maybe a combination of both. Perhaps he should try and get to the land. Choose his own demise, rather than letting fate decide. He had options. The toxic ash could finish him off. The memory of Stacey, writhing in agony, flashed before his eyes. Too painful. He could deliberately drown himself, that would seem fitting for a sailor. But he knew he'd never have the courage to go through with it. The survival instinct was too strong.

There it was again, the noise. Jake snapped his head around in the direction he thought it had come from. He hadn't imagined it, he had definitely heard something that time. A splash. Something in the water. Not loud, but its effect was amplified a thousand times by a total absence of any other sound.

Jake strained his eyes, stared at the water where he thought the sound had emanated from. Was it a fish? No, he didn't think so. But there was something there. Something black, protruding from the surface. It was about a hundred metres away, small, difficult to see. He considered the possibilities; a fin of some kind? But it didn't seem to be moving. Perhaps another piece of the pier, or other wreckage? But he had drifted a long way from Longyearbyen, he couldn't image there would be any wreckage this far out. Whatever it was, Jake had a strange feeling that it was watching him. His curiosity was intense. If there was something alive over there, he had to find out what. He positioned himself in the tapered front of the raft, picked up his only oar, and began paddling towards the mystery excrescence. It was slow going. Two strokes. Pull the paddle out of the water. Shuffle to the right. Put the paddle in the water. Two strokes. Pull the paddle out. Shuffle to the left. All the time he had his eyes fixed on the mystery object. Inexplicably, it appeared to be growing. Rising out of the water. Where previously it had looked like it was maybe thirty or forty centimetres, now it was over a metre. It looked suspiciously like a head on a stick. Were those eyes? They certainly looked like eyes, but they weren't aligned properly, weren't symmetrical.

It was then that he noticed the bubbles. A million tiny bubbles breaking on the surface. He was now about fifty metres from the stalk that was sticking out of the water. The bubbles looked like they were radiating from it. They covered a huge surface area. While he looked on they grew in size and in intensity. The water around the object was no longer blue green, it was turning white, churning, fizzing like a gigantic jacuzzi. As the bubbles reached the raft and broke against its side, their inertia pushed it backwards. Jake stopped paddling. Whatever was happening, he didn't want to get any closer.

The object in the middle of this aquatic chaos was rising again. Another protrusion joined it. Thinner, without a bulge on the end. A simple stick rising out of the water. And then a third, shorter and fatter. And then the white water turned black, as a gigantic fin appeared to rise out of the fjord. As it broke the surface, sheets of water cascaded off of it. Spray flew into the air and rained down on Jake and the raft. But it wasn't over. Because the fin was attached to a body. An immense, dark, hulk of a body. It too broke the surface with an almighty roar, torrents of sea water tumbling from its back. It must have been almost a hundred metres long Jake estimated. It dwarfed his little raft. The central fin itself was the size of a house.

And then, silence returned. The last of the water trickled down the side of the massive black beast. It was magnificent. It was unreal. It was, Jake knew, his saviour. He sank to back into the raft and stared up in awe, at the sight of the submarine in front of him.

Sixty

Nothing happened for a few minutes. The periscope array that had foretold the vessel's arrival still seemed to be watching Jake, now from on high. Once over the initial shock, he got back onto his knees and started paddling slowly towards the monster. As he got closer he could see that the surface was not as smooth as it looked from a distance. It was covered in thousands of square tiles, each one a slightly difference shade of matt black. It seemed to absorb light and sound, a hole in his field of vision. Rivets the size of dinner plates marked out sections. At one edge of the towering fin, a door opened up, and two uniformed men stepped out. Jake couldn't help but be dismayed to see they were carrying guns. He had seen enough guns in the last few days. A third man stepped out, older than the others. Mid fifties, Jake guessed. Shorter than himself, and with a neat moustache.

"Hello there!"

The cheery way the man flanked by two armed ratings spoke, taking Jake by surprise.

"Well don't just sit there staring, come aboard, come aboard! Throw that man a line, help him on, will you?"

The younger men put their weapons down on the deck and set about getting a rope from inside the tower, attaching it to the sub, and throwing it to Jake. His condition meant he wasn't fast enough to catch it, but it landed inside the raft and he was able to pull himself in.

"Just you then?" the older man called out as he waited for Jake to close the gap. "Nobody with you?"

"Just me," Jake called back. His voice was hoarse, his throat dry.

"Good, good. Well I'm sure you have a story to tell. But it looks like you've been out here a while. I expect you could do with something to eat and drink? We'll get you sorted out, my friend. You'll find it a jolly sight warmer inside, too!"

The front of the raft nudged the black hull. The junior sailors reached out and grabbed a hand each, heaving Jake aboard. He couldn't help but cry out in pain as they did so.

"Gosh, are you injured?" the senior man asked. "Well I think we should get you down to the medical berth as quick as. I'm Coote, by the way, Captain Coote. You're not Navy, are you?"

Jake shook his head.

"So you can call me Coote. Or Captain. Whatever you prefer. We're quite informal, here. Life on a submarine works better that way. Mutual respect and friendship, that's the ticket. These men will take care of you. This is Able Seaman Ewan Sledge, and Able Seaman Eric O'Brien. They will take you down to the medical berth, get you patched up, then we can have something to eat and you can fill me in on what has happened to the Spirit of Arcadia."

Jake looked at the captain with surprise. Not only had he miraculously found him in the middle of a remote fjord, he somehow knew where he had come from.

The two seamen helped Jake in through the door before he could introduce himself properly. They had to climb down a ladder to the main deck, something Jake had trouble with. He was led through a room packed from floor to ceiling with beige computers, screens, and flashing lights. A number of officers, who were manning the equipment, watched him pass through. They wore expressions of curiosity, but there was something else there, too. Jake realised it was hope. These men saw him as a reason to hope that not all was lost.

"The medical berth is down on the next deck," O'Brien said

He took Jake down a narrow metal stairway, through more densely packed rooms and thick bulkheads, eventually arriving at a tiny cabin, dominated by a single bed covered with a deep red blanket. Sledge had carried on deeper into the submarine.

"Sit yourself down there, sir," O'Brien said. "Ewan's gone to find Surgeon Lieutenant Vardy."

"Please, call me Jake."

"And you can call me Eric. Like Coote said, we're like a big family on this sub. A brotherhood. Have to be, you couldn't survive it otherwise. Ninety eight people living in a tin can for months on end, it's the only way to be."

Ewan appeared at the door with another man, tall, blond, he looked a lot like Gunter, the recently deceased German. Jake got the impression the man had just been woken up, his eyes were red and puffy.

"Right, what have we here? A survivor! There's hope for us all. I'm Vardy, medical officer." He stuck out a hand, Jake shook it with his left, hand, at the same time holding out his right to show the deep cut.

"Jake Noah," he croaked simply.

"Well then, Jake, looks like we need to start with that hand. And you look like you need some fluids in you, too. That makes two of us. Eric, get me some coffee would you? And some water for our friend here, lots of water."

Eric nodded and disappeared off back the way they had come with Ewan in tow. Vardy opened a cabinet above the bed, took out antiseptic and sterile gauze pads, and with a delicate touch he began to clean the wound.

"Anything else I need to look at, Jake? Or just the cut?"

"I think I have a broken rib, maybe more than one."

He rubbed his side with his free hand.

"Okay, I'll take a look at that. We have some strong pain killers, but I don't want to dose you up too heavily. I expect Coote will want to talk to you. That will be easier if you're conscious."

• • •

Vardy spent twenty minutes with Jake. He stitched the cut in his hand and bandaged it. He checked for broken bones and concluded that he had almost certainly cracked a rib, but it wasn't broken. Most of the pain came from the bruising, the whole of his side was very tender. There wasn't much to be done, he mainly needed rest. The painkillers took the edge off. Eric had come back with water, and Jake downed more than a litre. He would have kept going but Vardy told him to take it easy, he needed to get some solids into him before he flooded his gut. When the medical officer was happy, he escorted him back through the submarine to the officer's mess, where they found Coote, alone. The captain stood as soon as the men entered, beaming at Jake.

"Ah, here you are! Sit down, sit down. Take the weight off. Now then, we didn't have time to be properly introduced before. You are?"

"Jake Noah. First officer aboard the Spirit of Arcadia, and until recently, I was acting captain of that same ship."

He extended his newly bandaged hand, the captain shook it heartily, causing Jake to wince with pain. All three men sat at a long table.

"Welcome aboard HMS Ambush, Captain Noah. Dreadful name if you ask me. A nuclear submarine fleet is an excellent deterrent against acts of war, but they gave us such an aggressive name. That's the admiralty for you. But, I digress. We followed your message in the buoy. I must say we were rather hoping we might find an entire passenger ship, not just a single raft. Not that we're not pleased to have you aboard you understand! Delighted, yes, delighted to have you here."

"The buoy?"

"Yes, the buoy. Very clever, by the way, putting an emergency transmitter in a buoy like that. Who knows if we would have found you otherwise?"

"I'm sorry, I'm not sure I follow. What buoy are you talking about?"

"Russell, would you find Eric and get him to bring us the buoy? Good chap, thank you. Ah, excellent doctor, our Mr Vardy, very experienced. Splendid bedside manner. Poor chap doesn't get to practice much medicine here, of course. A few cuts and bruises, minor things. Quite a lot of burns. Not from the engine room, as you might expect. It's our chef. Awfully accident prone. He does make a particularly good curry on Wednesdays though, so we can forgive him for the odd saucepan of soup ending up on the floor!"

Coote roared with laughter. Jake smiled politely.

"Captain Coote, my ship, Spirit of Arcadia, it's in real danger. This is going to sound crazy, but it's been taken over by a madman. He's a religious nut case. Sorry, I don't mean to suggest all religious people are mad…" Jake flushed red, worried he had just insulted the man opposite him.

"No no, of course not. Don't worry, Jake, you can speak freely here. All views are tolerated. We have had many a debate about such matters. Passes the time when we are stuck at the bottom of the ocean! Carry on."

"This man, Flynn, he's called. He framed me for murder, became captain, and is now sailing the ship off to goodness knows where. He plans to starve most of the passengers to death. All except the women, and a few of his friends. He says he's doing God's work. Starting again. Building a new Eden, he says."

"I see. Yes, I can understand your choice of words in describing him as a madman. Ah, here's the buoy!"

The doctor had returned. He handed a bright pink buoy to Coote. He had also brought a tray on which was a bowl of soup and a couple of bread rolls.

"Here we are. And something for you to eat too, excellent. Now, let's see. Yes, very clever. An emergency radio transmitter inside, and a note."

As Jake tucked into the soup, Coote pulled open the flap that had been cut in the side of the buoy, pulled out the piece of paper and read from it.

"Spirit of Arcadia. Cruise liner. Approximately three thousand survivors. Departed from this location for Longyearbyen, second of May 2014. Then some coordinates for Longyearbyen. So you say this wasn't you?"

"No. But I think I can guess who. May I?"

Coote handed the paper to Jake.

"Lucya. It's the handwriting of Lucya Levin, our chief radio officer. She never told me. She must have dropped this when we left the pole. That explains how you found me. There's one of these in the life raft. She must have stuck it in there before he took her. I had no idea there was a transmitter inside."

"We picked it up this morning," Coote said. "We were heading back to our base in Scotland. See if there were any survivors."

"How much do you know about what happened?" Jake asked. "I mean, if you were submerged, do you get to see the news? I have no idea how these things work."

"Just as well!" Coote laughed heartily. "We can't have every Tom Dick and Harry knowing military secrets, now! No offence, no offence. Well, you'd be surprised. Provided we don't dive too deeply, we can pick up a lot of communication traffic. That is a lot of what we do, intercepting communications. As soon as we started hearing reports of that damned asteroid, well we surfaced so that we could get a better picture of what was happening. We saw the television images. I expect you did, too. Terrible business. Terrible. We dived again before it reached our location. Went deep, took cover, you might say. Stayed down for twenty four hours, then came up very slowly. At first we thought our communications equipment was damaged, we couldn't hear anything. So we surfaced and found that there was nothing to hear. Now we have to go to Scotland. But it sounds like your ship is in danger?"

"Captain Coote, there won't be any survivors in Scotland. Or anywhere else. Everything is gone. We landed at Longyearbyen. Well, where Longyearbyen used to be. It's turned to dust. But it's worse than that. The asteroid scattered ash, thick ash. It's toxic, dangerous. Acidic or something, I don't know. I lost two people to that ash, it melted their skin. Trust me, there's nothing in Scotland for you. But we can save three thousand people on that ship."

"Tell me," Coote said. "How did you end up in the raft?"

"I'd better tell you the whole story," Jake said.

He recounted the events from the time the asteroid flew overhead. He explained about Melvin, Flynn, the landing party, as well as how he had been framed for murder. He told the captain about being thrown into the raft, being cast adrift.

Coote remained silent for a long time. He looked at Jake, studied him.

"It's a heck of a story. Now, don't get me wrong old chap, but how do I know you're not the madman and you want our help to take control of a perfectly well run ship?"

"You don't believe me?"

"I didn't say that. But you have to look at this from my point of view. I find you battered and bruised, in a life raft. Perhaps you were thrown overboard for good reason? Perhaps you are hoping to use the force of Her Majesty's Navy to exact revenge? What I am asking is this. If we find your ship, will we also find others who can corroborate your version of events?"

"We can do better than that," Jake said, a smile spreading across his face. "If we find the ship, then I can give you absolute proof that what I have said is the truth."

"Do you know where your mutineer plans on taking your ship?"

"No. Flynn just said he wanted to burn off the fuel. It won't take them long. We ruptured a fuel line, there's very little fuel left. But Lucya had been scanning the radio frequencies, and I'm certain she would have activated the emergency beacon on board. If he hasn't found it then surely you could locate them with that?"

"Aside from your buoys, we haven't picked up anything else, I'm afraid. Did you see the ship sail out of the fjord? Did you see in which direction they went after that?"

"South. They definitely went south."

"Then, Captain Noah, we shall do the same."

SIXTY-ONE

ONCE JAKE HAD finished the soup and bread, Captain Coote took him upstairs to the main deck, through the control rooms, and into his cabin. He explained that although the lower deck had bunks for every crew member, they were tightly packed and not comfortable. Jake would be able to get some decent sleep in the captain's quarters. The cabin opened directly into a communications control room, manned by six crew members, but they didn't make much noise. Besides, Jake was exhausted, and the painkillers were kicking in, too. He knew he wouldn't have much trouble sleeping. And indeed, as soon as his head hit the pillow, he was gone.

While he slept, Captain Coote gathered all his crew who weren't taking their sleep shift into the junior rating's mess. He relayed the information that Jake had provided earlier, telling them about the toxic ash, the fate of Longyearbyen, and the survivors on the Spirit of Arcadia. The news was difficult to deliver, and to receive. The men were used to not seeing their families for long periods of time, but that did nothing to soften the blow of having it all but confirmed that they were almost certainly dead. Coote knew that keeping up morale was key to their own survival, and he put a great deal of emphasis on the mission ahead. They were to track down the cruise ship. The passengers were threatened. Weapons were involved. This was the kind of situation they were trained to deal with in the navy. Seamen rarely saw this sort of action once they left behind the surface skimmers for life below the waves, so the plan was met with enthusiasm. It was a welcome distraction from thoughts of the fate of those back home. There was work to be done, and everyone knew their place and their role. Coote's sub ran like a well-oiled machine.

• • •

Jake was woken by a knock at the door. He pulled himself upright and twisted round to a sitting position, with his legs over the side of the bunk. His hand felt much improved, but his side was still very painful. He got to his feet and opened the door.

"Hi, Jake, I brought you some breakfast," Ewan said.

He walked in with a tray, set it down on a tiny table. It was loaded up with buttered toast, jam, fruit, cereal, and black coffee. There were also some more painkillers. Jake picked them up straight away, knocked them back and washed them down with a couple of gulps of coffee. It was obviously instant, but he wasn't complaining.

"Thank you," Jake managed at last.

"You're welcome. We don't get many visitors. Nice to see a new face around here. It sounds like we might get to see a lot of new faces soon?"

"Where are we? How long was I asleep?"

"You've been out for about ten hours. As to where we are, somewhere in the Norwegian Sea, I'm not sure precisely where. They think they've picked up a signal from your ship."

"But they're not sure? Could it be other survivors? Another submarine, perhaps?"

"Unlikely. Even after the end of the world, protocol would prevent most submarines from broadcasting a distress signal unless they were genuinely in trouble. We're detecting a search and rescue radar transponder, approximately thirty nautical miles ahead. No GPS location, we believe the satellites were taken out by the asteroid. We should have visual confirmation within the hour."

"If you're picking up the SART, then I guess we're not underwater?"

"No, we didn't dive. The antenna array works better out of the water."

"Will they see us coming?"

"Not from this distance."

"We'll need to get close, though. Without being seen."

"Not being seen is something we're very good at." Ewan hesitated, seemed to be debating with himself whether to speak further. He made up his mind. "If I may ask, was it really that bad? At Longyearbyen? Was everything destroyed?"

"I'm sorry," Jake said. He stopped eating, looking at the young sailor. He could imagine what he was thinking. "Yes, it was bad. But it must have been over quickly. Like being in the blast radius of one of your nuclear warheads. The town was vaporised. The people, they wouldn't have felt anything. It would have been over very quickly, for them."

Ewan nodded slowly. "It's strange. We carry these weapons. We all know what they're capable of, the damage they can do. And we all hope we never ever have to use one in anger. My father served in the navy all his working life. I was too young to really understand, but I knew he was afraid of all out nuclear war. He never said it, of course. But I knew. When I joined up the cold war was already over. Some of the older sailors, they talk about the old days. We talk a lot on here, there's not much else to do. They tell me the same thing, about the fear they had that one day, one day they would have to launch these things, and that when the submarine surfaced, months later, everything would be gone. Us younger ones, we never had that fear. We're told that the nukes, they're a deterrent, to make sure the end of the world never happens. And despite all that, for all the money, the technology, the arms race, the standoffs, the world still ended. We couldn't stop it."

"Ewan, the world didn't end. Not for everyone. You're still here. I'm here. There are three thousand people on the Spirit of Arcadia. And who knows how many others? Other submarines. Maybe other boats. Perhaps some corner of the world got spared, just like we did?"

Coote stuck his head round the door.

"Ah, awake! Excellent. Very good. Ewan told you that we've picked up a signal? We're tracking it on the radar, it looks like it's your ship. That or a bloody big whale with a radio transponder!

When you've finished your breakfast, Ewan will bring you through to the communications suite. You need to meet Ralf. He's something of an ace hacker, but I expect you can find us a quicker way in."

Jake nodded. "I'll be right out."

He wolfed down the rest of the food on the tray. The previous night's soup had settled his stomach, but he still felt like he hadn't eaten in a week. By the time he was done the painkillers were taking effect, and he was starting to feel human again.

• • •

The communications suite was one of the rooms he had passed through when he arrived. Men sat at floor to ceiling workstations that Jake thought looked surprisingly old fashioned, for such a recent vessel. It was something about the solidity of the equipment. He had no doubt it was state of the art, but it wouldn't have looked out of place on Ewan's father's cold war ships.

Coote beckoned them over to the end station. A young man with a shaved head and tattoos up both arms was sitting in a swivel chair. He was the only crew member in the room not to be wearing a headset.

"This is Lieutenant Ralf Cormack, he's one of our senior communications officers. Ralf can do things with a computer that even the makers wouldn't think possible."

Ralf held out a hand. Jake shook it, all the time thinking that the Lieutenant looked like anything but a hacker.

"We're closing in on your ship. Coote tells me that you have the latest anti-piracy measures on board?"

"That's correct," Jake said. "I just hope Flynn doesn't know that and hasn't disabled them."

"That's what I'm here to find out, sir."

"Jake, please. Call me Jake."

"No problem. Does the system have a live feed, or record only, Jake?"

"Both, live and record. There's also a facility for remote playback. It can be triggered externally. There's a web page interface, you just need a username and password. We can try mine, but I think it only works from an on-board terminal. The navy are supposed to have some kind of access, though."

"We wouldn't be issued with that. Fighting civilian piracy is a skimmer's job, not something that us dolphins deal with."

Jake looked enquiringly at Coote.

"Dolphins are submariners. Skimmers are surface ships," he said. "You'll have to excuse us, we have our own dialect, down here."

Jake was starting to sense how the crew really was like one family. Shared language, like code. Mutual respect, despite the banter he had heard around the place. He wondered if it had been like that for Lucya, when she was in the Russian navy, and whether she missed that camaraderie on the Spirit of Arcadia.

He brought his attention back to the task in hand, and reeled off some technical details to the communications officer, information about how to connect to the ship's anti-piracy system remotely. Ralf bashed away on his keyboard at an impressive rate. The screen in front of him seemed even more incomprehensible to Jake than the submariner's lingo. Tiny green text against a black background. But when Ralf hit "Enter" and sat back, the text was replaced by an image. It looked like a website was loading, but very, very slowly.

"We're too far away to get decent bandwidth…good connection speed. It will improve as we close in," Ralf explained.

"I think it's about time we made ourselves less visible," Coote said.

He picked up what looked like a phone handset from the console, punched a button and relayed orders. Before he'd even replaced the handset, red lights began to flash, a speaker crackled into life and a voice called "Dive, dive!"

A klaxon sounded throughout the submarine, resonating around the confined space, blaring out its deafening message for ten full seconds, before stopping as abruptly as it had started.

"You might want to hold onto something Jake," Coote said, smiling. "We're about to dive."

Jake grabbed onto the back of a chair. Ralf and Coote both burst out laughing.

"Sorry, old chap," Coote said, grinning. "Couldn't resist! We don't see many newbies. At ease sailor. This sub is as smooth as they come."

Jake felt the submarine tilt very slightly towards the front as it pushed itself below the surface. A minute later, the ride changed entirely. Since he had spent months at sea it was quite an unusual sensation to no longer be rolling. The submarine slid through the water with such stability and precision it was as if they weren't moving at all. To Jake, it felt for all the world as if he had stepped off onto dry land.

Someone called across from another console on the other side of the room.

"Sir, I believe we have established visual contact."

"Come with me," Coote said to Jake.

The two men crossed the confined space of the suite to find another officer operating a colour screen. There was a clear image in the middle. It was distant, magnified and pixellated. But it was without question the Spirit of Arcadia.

"That's her," Jake said. "That's my ship."

Coote picked up another handset, pressed a button and relayed more orders to an unseen helmsman.

"Maintain periscope depth and heading, reduce speed to 15 knots. We're closing in on them."

He hung up and turned back to Jake.

"We're not deep, but they won't see us coming. Staying at this depth means we can keep the photonics mast up and get a good visual approach. I daresay we'll get a better signal for accessing the computers too."

Jake nodded.

"About another thirty minutes and we should be close enough to have a look at getting into that system. In the meantime, maybe you'd like to get cleaned up a little? No offence, but you do look like you've been through the wars, somewhat. Ewan can show you where the bathrooms are. We have some spare uniforms, I'm sure there's something in your size."

"That would be great, thank you." Jake was glad of the diversion from the mix of emotions he'd felt upon seeing his ship again.

Sixty-Two

Jake spent too long in the shower, but he didn't care. The hot water was bliss. When he was done, he found a clean pair of navy trousers, a shirt, and a navy jersey, all laid out for him. They fitted almost perfectly.

Ewan was waiting for him outside the bathroom, and escorted him back through the submarine. Jake couldn't imagine spending weeks or months cooped up in such a confined space. The ceilings were low and, although the fixtures and fittings were modern and clean, the complete lack of any natural light was oppressive. The crew had tried to make the place homely. Photos adorned many surfaces, drawings sent by children were common, too.

Every room they passed through looked to have more than one use. Food was stored everywhere, even under bunks. The efficient use of every tiny nook and cranny reminded Jake of caravanning holidays, and of his first trips on small pleasure boats back home.

All the submariners he encountered were polite. Many were keen to talk to him, to hear first-hand what he had seen outside, on the surface. Ewan did a good job of fielding these requests, hurrying his charge through bulkheads to the next room each time they were slowed down by inquisitive sailors. Jake didn't mind answering their questions, but they didn't really have the time for it.

He was struck by the ways the crew kept themselves occupied. There appeared to be at least two separate poker tournaments going on. Ewan explained that these could last for weeks. When they went through the junior ratings' mess, he saw a group of young men huddled together, studying materials for a test that could see them promoted. They must have known that the exams would never happen now, but he could totally understand the desire to carry on as normal. Indeed, down here, under the water, cut off from the rest of the world, it was easier to just keep pretending everything was normal.

They called in on the medical berth, and Vardy changed the dressing on Jake's hand. The rest had done it some good and it was starting to heal nicely.

When they eventually got back to the communications control room, Ralf called them straight over.

"We're right behind them, less than a nautical mile between us. We've got excellent visual contact, and a high bandwidth connection to the computer system. I've had a go at cracking the security. It's not bad, not great. With time, I can get in. But it would be worth trying your own password first."

He moved to one side, making his keyboard accessible. Jake leaned over and typed in his username, and then a password below. It was masked by dots as he entered it. He hit "Enter", and the page refreshed in the web browser. A message written in red informed them that his account was not valid for remote access.

"Sorry," Jake said. "I didn't think it would work."

"That's okay. Actually, what I really needed was your username. I can get into the authentication database. It's one way encrypted, hashed and salted, difficult to break without a lot of computational horsepower and time. We've got the power, but my understanding of the situation is that time may not be on our side."

"I have no idea what any of that means," Jake said, feeling dumb.

Ralf laughed. "No probs. It just means I can't crack your password quickly. But I don't need to, I just need to change your access level. I already hacked into the database, and now I know your username, I only have to do this."

He tapped a button and his screen switched from the web page back to the green text on black. He bashed away furiously at the keyboard sending lines of text scrolling up the screen, then sat back, tapped "Enter", and the screen flicked back to the web page.

"Try again," he said.

Jake leaned over once more, and re-entered his username then his password. He hit "Enter" and this time, the page refreshed, and a message read "Processing…" A few seconds later the screen changed and a complex page came up. It was headed Spirit of Arcadia Anti-Piracy Security System Console.

"Shit!" Jake said. "It worked!"

"Of course. That's what we do here. Okay, let's see. We should probably get Coote back, before we do anything else."

"I'm on it," Ewan said, and sprinted off out of the console room.

"Do you have any idea of the date and time we need to access?" Ralf asked.

"The date was May third. The time, I'm not sure. Let's see… the election meeting was called for twenty one hundred hours. It would have been maybe half an hour later that they marched me up to the bridge. Flynn didn't come up straight away, he had to get his shoulder patched up where he took a bullet. I would estimate twenty two hundred hours, that would be a good starting point."

"Okey dokey. Let's see here."

Ralf navigated his way through various menus relating to archived security information. He found a page labelled "Bridge Feed". There were a list of dates. He selected one. The page reloaded, and in the middle was a large video player. He looked up at Jake and grinned.

Coote stepped through the bulkhead door.

"Righto lads, what have we got?"

"We're about to find out. Ready when you are," Ralf replied.

Coote took up position behind him. Ralf moved the playhead on the video window to 22:00 and hit the play button.

A circle of dots animated in the middle of the black video window, indicating that the file was buffering. Suddenly it filled with a colour image. The video couldn't capture the whole of the bridge, but it showed enough. The camera must have been hidden somewhere above and in front of the captain's seat, looking back over the room. Visible in the background was a chair, and Jake was tied to it. Flynn's henchmen milled around close by. The sound quality wasn't great, and they were talking in hushed voices. It was impossible to make out what they were saying.

"He'll appear any minute," Jake said without taking his eyes from the screen. "The guys guarding me were altogether in a group like that just before he arrived."

The three men continued to watch the footage. Sure enough, three minutes later they saw the door open and Flynn stride in.

"Mr Noah, congratulations." His voice could clearly be heard from the console's little speaker.

"That him?" Coote enquired.

"That's him," Jake confirmed.

They watched for ten minutes as the video confirmed everything that Jake had told Coote about Flynn and his plan.

Sixty-Three

Half an hour later, Jake, Coote, Ralf, and two dozen submariners including Eric and Ewan were assembled in the junior ratings' mess. The video of Flynn and Jake on the bridge had just been screened to all the men present. Ralf tapped at the touchscreen of a small tablet he was holding, and the big screen on the wall flickered, then settled.

"This is the live feed from the bridge," he said.

"Jake, can you give us a quick who's who? For the benefit of these men?" Coote looked around the room.

Jake stood up, walked to the screen.

"This man sitting in the captain's chair is Flynn, as you just saw. He's in charge, no doubt about that. He took a bullet to his shoulder, but I don't think it affected his mobility in any way. This man here on the helm, that's Pedro. The man watching him, the one with the gun, is called Zhang. He's dangerous. I watched him kill a man, one of their own. It certainly looks like Pedro is acting under duress. He's a good man, I don't think he's working with them by choice. These other men, I don't know their names but they are all working with Flynn. They're some of the disciples you heard him talk about."

"He said there were twelve disciples in all," Eric said. "With Zhang, I see five on the bridge. Where do you think the others are?"

"No idea. I am guessing they're keeping some of the bridge crew captive somewhere. Hoping, anyway. We know that he took Lucya, the chief radio officer. And before that they took another hostage, the head of housekeeping. They may have other hostages, and they must be holding these women somewhere. Some of the disciples will be guarding them."

"Any thoughts on where he would be holding them?" Coote asked.

"None. There's no brig or secure cell on the ship. We looked for Tania and didn't find her, even when we surveyed every cabin. I guess they moved her around. They could be anywhere. Maybe more than one location."

"So we have no way of identifying these guys," Ralf said.

"Not all of them. But anyone carrying a gun you can probably assume is one of them. Apart, maybe, from Max, our head of security. He had access to the gun locker, but I believe they took his key, violently. I might be wrong, and he could be armed and active, but I think it's more likely he's a hostage, or dead."

"Thank you, Jake. Ralf, the plans if you could?" Coote looked over to the tattooed man.

Ralf tapped away on his tablet. The screen flickered, then the image was replaced with deck plans.

"Our entry on board is here, the landing platform for the tender. We have visual confirmation that they haven't closed it up. It provides access to deck two. The bridge is located on deck ten. This is the most direct route."

As Coote spoke, Ralf zoomed in on the relevant sections of the blueprints. The plan was discussed in detail for two hours, with Jake providing as much information as he could.

They were to board the Spirit of Arcadia at twelve thirty hours. There had been discussion about waiting until night, when most passengers would be asleep and out of danger. The consensus was there was too great a risk that Flynn could already be harming or even killing people, that they should not waste any time. At the hour they had chosen, passengers were likely to be in the restaurants for lunch rations, so the risk was somewhat reduced.

They filed out of the mess to take up positions for the mission. Coote turned to Jake.

"Maybe this sub isn't so poorly named after all eh? The Ambush is about to engage in an actual ambush!"

• • •

Jake was to remain aboard the submarine until the men had secured the bridge of the cruise ship. They were trained in combat and he wasn't. He would only get in the way and risk the mission. Instead, he was stationed next to Ralf. They were to provide radio support. The live feed from the bridge would provide crucial information.From a station next to Ralf's, another officer was monitoring the video feed from the periscope array.

The most delicate part of the operation, Coote had explained, was surfacing at exactly the right spot. They wanted to remain hidden for as long as possible. The captain was now in the main control room, overseeing the helmsman. An open audio feed between the two control rooms meant Jake had a good idea of what was going on. They had pulled alongside Spirit of Arcadia and matched her speed exactly. Using a fancy sonar trick, they had been able to engage some sort of autopilot that would keep them in position, provided the cruiser stayed on relatively straight course and didn't execute any tight turns. They were now in the process of surfacing. Instead of just rearing up out of the water as they had done in front of the life raft, they were attempting to partially surface. Clipped orders were called out, status updates called back. Jake got the impression from the tense atmosphere that this was not something they practised regularly.

"Steady!"

"A little more out of the aft tank please, Budden."

"Aye, sir."

"Tower has broken the surface!"

"Keep it steady, Budden. Another three metres."

"Two…one…"

"Hold her here!"

"Holding."

"How do we look from outside?"

The officer to Jake's left replied into his headset: "Looks like we're creating a slight bow wave, nothing too conspicuous."

"Any sign they've spotted us?"

"Negative," Ralf responded. "All quiet on the bridge. Primary target looks to be sleeping."

"Red team, proceed with caution. I repeat, proceed with caution."

Jake watched the periscope monitor intently. It had a wide field of view, and he was able to see a hatch on the top of the fin pop open. He counted a dozen armed submariners as they crawled out of the small round hole, then leapt from the tower onto the landing platform from which he himself had been dispatched so recently. They mounted the steps in formation. The lead man entered the ship. Thirty seconds later the others followed.

"Red team aboard."

"Roger. Blue team, stand by."

"Standing by."

There was radio silence for a few very tense minutes.

"Red team approaching engine room."

"Roger. Blue team—go, go, go."

Jake listened attentively. Ralf's screen showed no movement on the bridge. On the other screen he saw twelve more men leave by the hatch. The followed the same formation, and within two minutes all had disappeared from view.

"Blue team aboard."

"Red team, we have secured the engine room. I repeat, we have secured the engine room."

"How many disciples?"

"Two gunmen. I don't think they were expecting us."

"Casualties?"

"None. No shots fired. These boys gave themselves up easily."

Jake breathed a small sigh of relief. They knew that until a few days ago these so-called disciples were just regular passengers, not soldiers. They hadn't expected too much of a fight. Even so, Coote had insisted that frightened men with guns could be unpredictable. Nothing was to be taken for granted.

"Blue team, we are on deck ten. Approaching bridge."

"Roger. Keep this channel open."

Jake's heart was beating fast again. This was the most dangerous part of the operation. There was a good chance that Flynn had stationed men outside the bridge door. The speakers hissed quietly as the radio transmitted the breathing of the lead man. Then everything happened very fast. Shouting erupted from the speaker.

"Armed forces, drop your weapons! Get down on the ground, now!"

Incoherent noise, more shouting. Two shots fired. Then another.

"Down, now!"

On the monitor, Jake watched as Flynn's men ran to cover the door. They took up position behind consoles, two each side. Flynn ran.

"Primary target appears to be going for the escape hatch," Ralf said into his headset. He turned to Jake. "Looks like you were right about him trying to escape."

"Blue four, confirm your position?"

"Blue four in position above bridge hatch."

"Standby, primary target headed your way. Blue one, report."

"Blue one, one man down, dead. Another immobilised. No casualties on our side. About to blow the door."

Flynn was halfway up the ladder, but stopped. He paused for an instant, then jumped back to the ground, landing in a crouching position. He sprang to his feet and sprinted to the rear of the bridge, and out of view of the camera.

"Primary target has changed direction, no longer headed for the hatch," Ralf reported. "You've got two targets either side of the door. Repeat, two either side, behind consoles. Further target at five metres from door. Shit, what the hell is he doing?"

At the same instant, the screen flared bright white. The camera came back into focus. Dust was blowing across the room. More shouting issued from the speaker.

"Armed forces, drop your weapons and give yourselves up. You are outnumbered!"

Gunshots rang out.

Jake looked on in horror as he saw Pedro being walked up the middle of the bridge towards the door. Zhang was behind him, a gun held to the pilot's neck.

One of the men behind the console popped his head over, fired off a shot. More shots were being fired from the door by the unseen navy men.

"He's using Pedro as a shield," Jake said. "He thinks he's going to get out of there."

Ralf relayed this to Blue team, but it was too late. As he spoke, Pedro and Zhang both dropped to the floor. The gunshots rang out through the speaker.

"I can't watch this anymore," Jake said. "I'm going in. Flynn's getting away. They could be held up there forever, it's a standoff."

"Coote wants you here until the bridge is secured," Ralf said.

"That's my ship. I'm responsible for those people. I've let them down once, I'm not doing it again."

"I can't stop you, Jake, you're a civilian. But I'd advise you to let us take care of this."

"Your advice is noted, thank you."

Jake smiled, then turned and left the communications room.

Sixty-Four

Jake noah ran through corridors and up several flights of stairs. It seemed strange, being back on board the Spirit of Arcadia after seeing her sail off, assuming he would die. He passed a few passengers; fortunately none seemed to recognise him. Had he not been running they probably wouldn't even have given him a second glance. As he reached deck ten, he heard gunfire from the direction of the bridge. The blue team were evidently still trying to take it. He spoke into the radio Ralf had insisted on giving him before he left.

"Ralf? Jake. Any sign of Flynn on the bridge?"

"Negative. Blue team are being held at the door. Two more disciples down, two still firing."

Jake had an idea how Flynn had got away. He climbed another flight of stairs. On deck eleven he found an exterior door, went out on deck, and sprinted towards the bow of the ship until he was above and slightly behind the bridge. Its floor to ceiling windows extended out over the sea giving almost full three-sixty degree visibility. The rear facing windows that had been blown out by the ash cloud had since been covered in plastic, keeping the cold air out. Jake looked down, his suspicion was quickly confirmed. The plastic sheet covering the innermost window was shredded. Flynn must have climbed out. If he hadn't fallen into the sea, he must have either jumped and landed on one of the balconies below, or climbed up and onto the bridge roof, where he could then get onto the deck eleven promenade. It was a sizeable drop to the balconies, and they were a small target to hit. Climbing seemed like the most obvious choice. Even so, he'd had time to get a good distance away. He could be almost anywhere, by now.

Jake turned and ran back the way he had come, searching around desperately, but there was nothing to give any clue as to which way the mutineer had gone.

The radio in his hand burst into life.

"Jake? Ralf. I've hacked into the security cameras. Four of us are sweeping the ship now."

"Understood," Jake replied. Then he had an idea. "Ralf, the cameras store the last twelve hours footage. If you can, check anything on the starboard side, deck eleven. Flynn climbed out of the bridge window. You might be able to track him."

"Roger that, we're on it."

Jake attached the radio to his belt. He had no idea what to do next. In desperation he set off around the exterior promenade of the deck. If Flynn knew the game was up, he figured he would probably try and keep a low profile, avoid going inside where he might come face to face with the Royal Navy.

He walked fast, checking anywhere he thought the fugitive might hide. Behind stairways, inside deck-chair stowage units. There were a thousand places to hide, just on the sun deck alone.

The radio crackled again. He whipped it off his belt just in time to hear Ralf's voice.

"Jake, we see him! You were right, he climbed out over deck eleven. We tracked him down to deck seven, he's in some kind of park. I've sent some of the red team up there. You should stay put, out of harm's way."

Jake stood where he was, rooted to the spot. He knew that he should let the professionals handle it. On the other hand, he knew the ship better than they did. He could get there faster. His mind made up, he ran inside.

• • •

He flew through the ship and down the stairs, taking them two at a time, arriving at deck seven out of breath but no less determined. The nearest entrance to Palm Plaza was just metres away.

Also between himself and that door, was the door to one of the larger cafes. It was full, they had evidently been using it for the lunchtime ration service in addition to the three restaurants. The service was coming to an end, and the first diners were starting to leave. A group of a dozen or so people were pouring through the doors. One of them spotted Jake.

"Hey! Look, that's that guy! The captain. The murderer!"

"Jesus, it really is him!"

Somebody screamed.

"What the fuck is he doing, walking about freely?"

Jake raised his hands slightly showing he wasn't armed.

"Now, now, take it easy folks. I didn't kill anyone, okay? I was framed."

"Framed? You hear that, Jimmy? Says he was framed?" The man spoke with a thick northern Irish accent.

"Aye, I heard what he said Paul, but I know what I saw, and I saw that man with a gun."

"So what are we gonna do with him then? The murdering bastard?"

The two men advanced on him menacingly, the rest of the crowd huddled behind them. Jake backed up slowly, keeping his hands in the air.

"You're making a big mistake!" he said.

"We're making a mistake? I'd say you made a big fucking mistake when you shot three people. And if the new captain isn't going to take care of you, then we are!"

The leading men broke into a run. Jake turned and ran back up the stairs. His legs were burning from the effort of his sprint down, but the adrenaline pumping through him pushed him on, regardless. He mounted one flight and charged out of the stairwell into the deck eight main passageway, bounced off a wall, righted himself, and ran as fast as he could. A glance over his shoulder and he could see the four men just metres behind.

"Come back here, you coward. Time to face real justice!"

The effort of pumping so much air into his lungs was making Jake's side explode with pain. Vardy's pills taken with breakfast were no match for the physical exertion he was subjecting his body to.

He reached the next staircase, threw open the door and ran down the steps, missing the last five entirely. He landed heavily, tripped, stumbled. The men were gaining on him, he forced himself upright, ran again, limping slightly. His ankle had twisted. They were almost upon him now, but they hadn't got him yet. With monumental effort he have pushed half fell through a door into Palm Plaza.

Only a rudimentary effort had been made to clear the park area since the asteroid. There was still a lot of ash around, although somebody had swept around the perimeter, keeping it out of the cafes and bars. The palms themselves looked dead, broken. It was a grey, desolate place.

In the middle, on his knees, was Flynn.

• • •

Jake limped forwards, the men chasing him bundled through the doors. They stopped dead when they saw Flynn. He was facing them, getting to his feet. He had a gun in his hands.

"Hello, Jake," he said. "So you came back then?"

"I brought some friends with me."

The men behind him looked at each other, confused.

"Hey, Captain Flynn, we're no friends of this murderer. Are you going to finish him off properly, or do we have to do it ourselves?" Jimmy said. There was a murmur of others agreeing behind him.

"No, these aren't my friends," Jake said. "Mine are from the Royal Navy. They're on their way here, right now."

"Jake, Jake. Your terrorist friends are stuck fighting on the bridge. My men are well armed. There's only one door. They can hold out indefinitely. As for my friends? I have many. Thousands. You cannot possibly over-power me." Flynn laughed.

Then he stopped, raised his gun, pointed it at Jake.

Jake raised his hands in the air, and stole a glance over his shoulder. The men behind him came around to his side, out of the way of any bullets that might go astray.

"Flynn, the game's up. You know it, I know it. We're going to show these people the truth. We're going to show them how you framed me, and how you plan on killing them all."

Jake looked around nervously. He could see the tiniest shadow of doubt play across the faces of the men who had led the chase. Flynn must have noticed too.

"You're a desperate man, spouting desperate rubbish. I shouldn't never have given you the chance to survive. Setting you free was a mistake. But mistakes can be corrected, and I intend to fix that one. I'm changing my sentence. For the murder of two men, you are now sentenced to death."

There was a click as Flynn released the safety catch.

Jake cried out and tried to move, but his feet remained rooted to the spot.

A gunshot echoed throughout Palm Plaza.

SIXTY-FIVE

THE EXPRESSION ON Flynn's face was something Jake would never forget. It morphed, slowly, from an evil snarling grin, to a look of incomprehension. He stared down at his chest. Blood was pumping out of a hole in his heart, spurting over the floor, turning the grey ash red. He looked up and saw something above Jake's head. His eyes opened wide, disbelieving. The gun clattered to the floor, sending a little mushroom cloud of dust and ash into the air. His legs buckled, and Flynn fell to his knees.

Another gunshot rang out. The sound bounced back and forth between the walls of the six decks that overlooked the Plaza. A second hole appeared in Flynn's chest. He opened his mouth, tried to speak. No words came out, only a dribble of blood. He keeled over and landed, face first, in the ash.

Then, silence.

Jake looked at the dead man in front of him.

The men either side of Jake looked at the dead man.

Then everyone turned and looked up, behind Jake, to where Flynn had cast his gaze. Standing on a cafe balcony, one deck above, trembling, was Martin. His arms were outstretched, a pistol held tightly between both hands.

"What the...? You killed him!" Jimmy yelled. "You killed the fucking captain!"

The doors burst open. Five submariners, brandishing automatic weapons, charged out.

"Everyone down on the floor, now! I said now!"

Jimmy and Paul looked around bewildered. They sank slowly to their hands and knees, then lowered themselves onto the dusty ground. The others in the mob did as they were instructed. Jake also made to lie on the floor.

"Jake? Come here, get behind us!"

"Ewan! It's okay, he's dead. Flynn is dead."

He stepped aside so the navy man could clearly see the body. Three others surged forwards, guns raised, alert and searching for any threat. They soon spotted Martin, who remained frozen to the spot.

"You! Put your weapon down and your hands on your head! Do it! Do it now!"

Three guns were quickly trained on the engineer.

"No!" Jake yelled. "Don't shoot him! That's Martin, our chief engineer. He shot Flynn. He saved my life."

Martin seemed to snap out of his daze. He lifted his hands above his head, the pistol still in his right hand. Slowly and carefully he brought his right arm down by his side, lowering the gun onto a table, then quickly raised his arm again.

"Eddy, get up there and check he's alone," Ewan said.

"Jake, I'm sorry. I should have believed you from the start," Martin called out.

"It's okay, Martin. I can't blame you for what Flynn did. How did you know I was here?"

"I've been monitoring them on the security cameras. When you said you'd been framed, I wanted to believe you. I went back and found the bridge videos. Saw everything Flynn said. Then I hid out, down below, keeping an eye on the cameras. I saw what was happening. Jake, I know where they're holding the others."

Eddy appeared on the balcony. He patted Martin down, turned and nodded to Ewan.

"Show us," Ewan said. "Show us where they are. You two stay here, keep this lot under control. You, with me," he signalled to the third man who had entered with him. "Jake, I suppose I can't convince you to wait here?"

"You suppose correctly," Jake said, heading for the door.

Sixty-Six

"How is he holding up, Grau?"

"There is nothing more I can do for him, Lucya, I am sorry. I have made him comfortable, but further than that, I have nothing here to work with."

Lucya bent over the man laid out on the floor between herself and the doctor.

"It's okay, Max," she said, "we'll get you out of here. Somehow."

"It's a good job he can't hear you," Barry said. "Because we're not getting out of here, are we? He's going to leave us to die down here."

"No, I told you. He needs me. They have to come back for me, sooner or later. When they do, we'll storm the door. It's our only chance."

"Right," Silvia said. "She's right. And I'm with her."

The conversation was interrupted by the sound of shouting. It was coming from the other side of the thick steel door, impossible to tell what was being said.

Lucya ran over, put her ear to the metal.

"What is it? What's going on out there?" Silvia asked.

"I don't know. I can't hear -"

She was cut off by what sounded like gunshots.

"Get down!" she screamed. "Everyone, down! Barry, get over here. If that door opens, this is our chance."

Reluctantly, he did as she asked and took up position next to the door, his back to the wall.

More gunshots. The sounds of a bolt being slid back. The door opened just a crack.

Lucya looked at Barry. Mouthed to him, "Ready?"

He nodded quickly.

The door opened further, the barrel of a rifle poked through the gap. Lucya grabbed it and tugged as hard as she good. The man holding the gun came tumbling through the door and crashed to the ground. Lucya pulled the gun from his hands, swung it round and pointed it at him.

Another man stepped into the small dark room. Barry leapt out from the wall and onto the man's back with a primal scream. The man turned on the spot, trying to shake him off.

"Stop!" a voice cried out. "Everyone stop!"

Lucya swung around.

"Jake? Is that you? Jake!"

She saw him staring there, framed in the doorway. She threw the gun to the floor and ran to him, threw both arms around him, hugging him tight to her.

"Argh, ouch! No!"

She fell back, he grasped at his side.

"You're hurt? What happened?"

"Save it!" Ewan yelled. "He pushed the two of them aside as he entered the room, weapon raised. He swept quickly left to right, back to the left."

"It's only us," Lucya said. "There are no guards here, only us."

Ewan lowered the gun, grinning at the girl.

"You must be Lucya," he said. "I've heard about you." He looked down at his colleague, cowering on the floor. "Looks like it's true, what Jake said!"

Jake grinned. He picked up his radio and found the transmit button.

"Ralf? Jake. Are you receiving?"

"Jake, got you loud and clear."

"What's happening on the bridge?"

"Blue team have taken it. They've confirmed four disciples dead."

"We've taken out two, and there are two under guard in the engine room. The hostages are safe. You can go ahead and play the tape."

"Understood," Ralf said. The radio went dead.

A few seconds later, a voice began to speak. It could be heard throughout the ship through the public address system.

"Mr Noah, congratulations. You played your role better than I could have hoped. I was afraid you would have dropped the gun as soon as Gunter put it in your hands..."

For the next ten minutes, everyone on board the Spirit of Arcadia listened in silence to the recording, and learnt how very close they had come to death.

Sixty-Seven

Jake, Lucya and Martin sat at the table in the cafe. Claude had brought them all extra rations.

"I meant to ask you," Jake said. "Where did you get the gun?"

"I found it." Martin said. "On deck three, near your cabin. It was just lying there. I picked it up, meant to bring it up to the weapons cabinet, but then everything went mad."

"So that's where it went," Jake said nodding.

"You know, there are still three guns unaccounted for," Lucya said. "And there are at least two disciples out there and we have no idea who they were."

"At least?" Martin asked.

"It could be three. We don't know if he replaced Gunter, after Zhang killed him."

"Well, whatever happened to them, I feel a lot safer now with your new friends around," Martin said, nodding towards the next table at which half a dozen submariners were sat eating. "And I have to say, great choice in friends. They come with their own nuclear power station. You've not only saved the ship from Flynn, you've solved our little energy crisis."

"You think that could really work?" Jake asked. "Can we really power the Spirit of Arcadia from the sub's reactor?"

"Well, it's not quite as simple as plugging it in like a television. But yeah, technically there's no reason why not. For electricity at least, if not propulsion. That thing could provide power for this ship for at least twenty five years."

"It's not just about power though is it Martin?" Lucya said. "We'll run out of food before twenty five years."

"Well, I had some thoughts about that too," Martin grinned at

Jake. "It starts with planting up Palm Plaza with fruit and vegetables."

"As long as it doesn't include culling the population, I'm all for giving it a try," Jake said.

"Then you'd better start reassigning roles, Captain Noah."

"Wait, what? You're going to take over as captain again?" Lucya's face lit up. "Really?"

"There are some fine details to work out with Coote. His ship is still his ship, even if we're going to be tied together from now on, sharing resources. But yes, I'm ready to take it on. There's hope now, real hope. There must be more submarines out there, and maybe other survivors. And it's like you said, we have all the skills on board to create a real society. It will be hard, but life is worth fighting for. I'm ready to lead that fight. We're the survivors, let's keep on surviving."

Also By The Author

Parallel One (DreamShifters Series)

Discover a world where dreams are real...and so are nightmares.
Discover the world of the Dreamshifters.

Jessica Kayne's life is in danger, not that she knows it. She's busy trying to work out how it can be that a man she's been dreaming of, just turned out to be real. Real, and recently murdered.

Then there's the mysterious Selena, who keeps turning up in a recurring dream. She's trying desperately to tell Jessica something, and it seems important. But a dream can't be important, can it?

As Jessica investigates the murder of the man from her dreams, she begins to discover her incredible power. A power to cross between worlds. A power that is desired by another. Someone who thinks nothing of killing to get what they want.

www.HarryDayle.com
harry@harrydayle.com

4471655R00153

Printed in Great Britain
by Amazon.co.uk, Ltd.,
Marston Gate.